I0817738

the library of fates

Also by Margot Harrison

The Midnight Club

For additional books by Margot Harrison,
visit her website, margotharrison.com.

the library of fates

margot harrison

GRAYDON HOUSE

Recycling programs for this product may not exist in your area.

ISBN-13: 978-1-525-80431-1

The Library of Fates

Graydon House
22 Adelaide St. West, 41st Floor
Toronto, Ontario M5H 4E3, Canada
www.GraydonHouseBooks.com

HarperCollins Publishers
Macken House, 39/40 Mayor Street Upper,
Dublin 1, D01 C9W8, Ireland
www.HarperCollins.com

Printed in U.S.A.

For all the librarians who work tirelessly to keep books accessible—you do magic every day.

the library of fates

When you weary of trying to write your own life,
allow yourself to be written by a well-curated library.

—Julien Theuthet, *Aphorisms of Textual Potential*

Now

September 26, 2019, 1:15 p.m.

The Library of Fates lived tucked under the mansarded roof of a tall, charcoal-gray building in Harvard Yard. To a casual visitor, it was like any other library, lined with shelves for hours of pleasantly aimless browsing. But every student knew that if you came to the Library of Fates and asked for a book to guide you safely through turbulent times, the librarian would go straight to the shelf and put a book in your hands. And that book would change your life.

Eleanor Dennet was that librarian now, but the knowledge felt hollow. Her predecessor, Odile Vernet—her mentor, her guiding star, her best friend—had died suddenly three days ago, and she could barely process it.

Her throat still raw from crying, her brain still woozy from too much vodka, she stepped over the threshold of the library that had been her refuge for most of the past twenty-four years. On the surface, everything seemed the same: the dark oak paneling and moss-green area rugs and accents; the pearly glow that came through the recessed skylight; the sweet, faintly musty smell. The custodian had opened the curtains and blinds of the nine bay windows on each long side of the room. Sunlight bathed the books in a greenish haze and washed over the varnished seminar table and armchairs. The mural on the ceiling evoked the magic of stories.

But something felt different here. Something was wrong.

Then Eleanor saw him.

From his seat in a green brocade armchair angled toward the window, he didn't seem to have noticed her entrance. Barely daring to breathe, she took in black hair sprinkled with gray on the headrest and long lashes outlined on his cheek as he gazed down at a sheaf of papers in his hand.

Daniel Vernet, Odile's son.

The last time they'd seen each other, in 1995, they'd been standing here in the library. Eleanor's view of Daniel had been clouded by tears, but she would never forget his dark eyes gazing back as if she were a stranger. The bland way he'd smiled, as if she meant nothing to him after everything they'd been through.

And here were more damned tears, rising and choking her. She would have to face Daniel eventually, to give condolences and make arrangements for his mother's memorial. But not yet. She wasn't ready for that. She darted to the window bay farthest from his chair, silent on the thick carpet, and slipped behind the floor-length curtain.

Daniel sighed heavily. The papers crackled. Frozen in place, Eleanor watched through a gap as he stood up. He didn't look his age, the lines of his chin and cheekbones still firm.

A sharp click-clack of heels sounded on the stairs behind them. "Ready, Daniel?" asked a slightly accented voice that

Eleanor recognized as Liliana, Odile's housekeeper and close friend.

Daniel nodded, but his gaze was still on the papers. "What the hell is this?" he asked. "What the *hell*?"

As the older woman put a soothing hand on Daniel's shoulder, Eleanor saw his body heave. Was he grieving his mother, then? Their relationship had never been smooth. Though Odile visited her son in Europe on occasion, it had taken her death to bring him back to the States for the first time in decades.

Liliana gave Daniel a hug and led him toward the door. "Everything will work out. You'll see. We don't want to be late for our appointment."

"I'm just so confused!" Eleanor heard him still exclaiming as their feet thudded down the stairs.

She emerged from behind the curtain and stood very still, waiting for the tension to dissipate and the atmosphere to settle. Listening for a faint but steady thrum on the edge of her awareness, a rumble that was neither pipes nor heating. Like Odile, Eleanor was attuned to the library's vibrations, inaudible to most people.

But now, standing dead center in the library, straining her senses in the stillness, she detected no reassuring thrum. Nothing. As if the library were an immense machine that had stopped running.

Panic gripped her. *It can't be.*

She hurried to the oak door at the far end of the room and unlocked it with trembling fingers. Here in the librarian's small office, *The Book of Dark Nights* was kept, secure in a safe, its pages alive with the power of the secrets trapped inside, for the library drew its power from the Book. As long as the Book remained there, the library would function.

On top of the safe, she found a sticky note in Odile's strong cursive:

A place of pages,
A subterranean secret,
Where love is shared.
One book brought you together.
Start from there.

Eleanor stared at it for a dazed second. Odile often left literary quotes on sticky notes, but this didn't seem like the style of poetry she would read—or write, if Odile had been a poet.

Then she knelt beside the safe to type in the code. Fumbling in her urgency, she had to enter it twice before the light turned green and she could swing the door open. Eleanor closed her eyes and said a silent prayer: *Please let it be here.*

The Book had been stolen only once, and the results had been disastrous. Eleanor tried not to think about them as she reached into the safe for the cracked calfskin of the Book's binding, bracing herself to feel the usual tingle as her fingers made contact. *Needing* to experience that uncanny suggestion that the Book was alive. To know that it was only Daniel's presence that had made the library feel wrong.

But there was nothing.

She knew people saw her as Odile's mousy, adoring acolyte, hidden away in the library like a relic herself. A perennial student who had never even finished her PhD. A wan spinster, a living history display. Here in the library was the one place Eleanor mattered. *In these books is your future,* Odile had told her long ago. *In these books are all the tools you need to live your life to the fullest.* But all that depended on the magic.

And as she ran shaky fingers from corner to corner of the steel compartment, she found only shadows and a fine, powdery dust that came off on her fingertips.

The Book of Dark Nights was gone.

THEN

February 2, 1995

On the first day of the spring seminar "Exploring the Library of Fates," the professor was late. Six students waited around the library's long table, where half-closed green velvet curtains shielded the books from the glare of a winter afternoon.

Eleanor Dennet sat up as straight as she could. She was here because she had received an invitation from Professor Vernet herself, printed on creamy card stock; no one could enroll without one. To take ENG 237 was to be special, to be chosen, and Eleanor was the type of person who usually faded into the background.

She wasn't tall or confident, like the other two girls at the table, who were chatting as if they knew each other. One boy, wearing a suit and tie like a parody of an Ivy Leaguer, couldn't seem to keep his eyes off the sleek, pretty redhead. Another boy, lanky with dirty-blond hair, was plugged to headphones and zoned out.

The one she couldn't stop looking at was the third boy, the black-haired one with long eyelashes to match. She had been watching him discreetly ever since freshman year, when he flicked a butter pat at her in the Union as she sat innocently reading *The Red and the Black*. He'd been aiming for the high ceiling—or so he claimed, as he apologized and peeled the sticky butter from her long, straight hair with a rakish smile before dashing back to his friends. Despite the grease in her hair, that smile warmed her cheeks.

If he remembered Eleanor now, he gave no sign. He seemed to know the zoned-out boy, though, because he elbowed him and asked, "Got it?" and his friend passed him what looked like a postage stamp.

"Ooh, an amuse-bouche?" the redhead asked, holding out her hand. The zoned-out boy gave her a stamp, too.

"Better not take it just yet," the black-haired boy told her. "Drew's got the good stuff. It'll make you soar."

The other girl, a brunette, refused the tab and giggled nervously. The boy in the tie stuck out his hand. "Hit me, too, Drew."

Were they all friends already? Eleanor sat rigid, not knowing where to look. She wasn't a prude, but she'd learned to keep a clear head for the accidents life was sure to throw at her. Dealing with her mother's paranoia was bad enough without messing with her own mental equilibrium.

She was relieved when, a moment later, the professor swept in with a click of heels and a waft of spicy perfume. Professor Vernet was small, yet she easily commanded their attention, swaddled in an enormous scarf and stylish in a way Eleanor supposed only Frenchwomen could be. The boy's tabs of acid—or whatever they were—vanished into handbags and pockets.

Professor Vernet didn't waste time with small talk, just dumped a book stack on the table with a thump. "Welcome to the Library of Fates," she said, clasping the back of the black-and-gold Harvard chair and looking at them as if she could see their souls.

Eleanor felt her heart patter. Professor Vernet *did* know too much about her. Her greatest fear right now was that the professor would make them share what they'd revealed to her in the diagnostic essays she'd required them to turn in over winter break.

The prompt was a single question: "What is the worst thing you've ever done?" Eleanor had spent some time wondering whether this was a trick, but eventually she decided to be honest.

For embarrassingly superstitious reasons, she didn't want to start the class with a lie. Some people said the library was "magic," though usually in that arch Harvard way that might or might not be serious. Raised on stories of enchanted wardrobes and haunted castles, Eleanor knew that supernatural forces would always find a way to punish you for bad faith, turning your lies back on you.

Just in case there *was* magic—you never knew!—she wanted it on her side.

Her essay began: "My younger sister, Renée, died running across the street on Christmas Day in 1984. She was running from me."

She had told the story before—to her parents, to therapists—but it never got easier. And if these self-assured girls and the black-haired boy heard it and *laughed*, or gave her pitying glances, she would never recover.

Blood roared in her ears. She'd missed the first few sentences of the lecture; she needed to concentrate.

"Until 1980, this was merely a dusty attic," Professor Vernet was saying. "Overflow storage. That year, the renowned Sorbonne literary scholar Julien Theuthet arrived for a visiting professorship here at Harvard College."

Her French accent was just distinct enough to be musical, thickening as she pronounced this name: Tuh-TAY. She gave a dramatic weight to each word that distracted Eleanor, quieting the tumult in her head. Or maybe it was the atmosphere of the library that calmed her—cool and green, ever so slightly musty with the miasma of old books.

They learned that Professor Vernet had been a student of Julien Theuthet at the Sorbonne and was an assistant professor at Harvard when he arrived for his visiting professorship twelve years later. As a thank-you to her for translating his works into English, Theuthet had secured funding for the library, stocking it with volumes chosen by himself and his protégée, including many from his personal collections.

"The library illustrates Theuthet's conviction that human identity is a fabric of signifiers," the professor said with a haughty, capricious air, as if she were used to being heard and obeyed. "If humans are texts, then we can discover our potential among texts. In the books of a well-curated library, we find ourselves—and our fates."

This sounded more like academic jargon than magic to Eleanor. Yet the words made her feel bizarrely hopeful, as if this woman might actually understand why she couldn't just "forgive yourself and move on," as people were always urging her to do.

That afternoon would never stop happening inside Eleanor's head: December 25, 1984. Ten years old, she'd been babysitting while her mother stepped out. Five-year-old Renée had stolen the card that Dad had sent Eleanor, containing a five-dollar bill and a note in his beautiful calligraphy. When Eleanor confronted her, demanding it back, Renée tore open the door and dashed several blocks down Broadway. It wasn't the first time Eleanor had had to chase her sister, who was amazingly fast for her age. But Renée wasn't always careful. The bus hit her on West 110th Street, right before the candy store.

Doubts still tortured Eleanor, keeping her awake at night: *If only I hadn't yelled at her. She knew to look before crossing, but she panicked because of me. If only I'd been faster.*

Sometimes she thought her own story should have ended on that day, too. But instead, she and her mom had moved upstate and lived in virtual isolation in a small house at the end of a long driveway, harried by her mother's constant fears. Eleanor had learned to be quiet and capable, buying the groceries and doing the errands. It was the town librarian, their only real friend, who had finally persuaded Eleanor's mother to go to therapy. She was medicated now and much better, but Eleanor still tried to call and check on her every day. She felt guilty about going to school several hours away, though her father and Harvard were covering the cost.

During all those years alone with her mother, books had been her friends, her peers, her salvation. Books had convinced her to apply to Harvard; books had allowed her to dream. *We can discover our potential among texts*—maybe that was just a different way of describing what she had experienced on every visit to the town library.

The library was very quiet after the professor stopped talking. When the black-haired boy made a soft scoffing sound, they all looked at him, including the professor. "You have something to add, Daniel?" She pronounced his name the French way: *Danielle.*

The boy just smiled lazily and said, "I'm eager to get started on discovering my textual potential."

The redhead stifled a laugh.

The professor didn't dignify this reaction with a glance. "Most of you already know Daniel is my son," she said. "He practically grew up in the library, but I still had to persuade him to take this class, because he thinks he already knows everything there is to know."

No one laughed now. The redhead's cheeks were crimson. Eleanor had never seen a woman wield so much authority before, without even making a fuss about it. She wondered if Professor Vernet was ever afraid of anything.

The next thing she did was give her son an order. "Daniel, ask me to bring you a book."

Daniel stared sullenly down at the table. "I don't do that anymore. You know that."

The professor sighed. When she spoke again, her voice was lighter, coaxing. "Do it for the others' sake, so I can demonstrate how the library works." She raised her head to address the rest of them. "The Library of Fates shows each person their textual potential by bringing them the book they need at that moment in their lives. As the librarian, I am merely its instrument."

Eleanor was dimly aware of the redhead nudging the other girl, eyes wide as if to say she thought the professor was off her rocker. But she focused on Daniel, who still refused to meet his mother's eyes. After a moment he gave in and said, "Bring me the book I need."

Something happened in the library then. Eleanor wasn't sure how to describe it. As the professor rose from her seat and swept her gaze around the shelves, the whole room seemed to throb with a majestic rhythm like a kettle drum. The mustiness of old books intensified like the ozone smell after a thunderstorm, and Eleanor could swear electricity crackled somewhere nearby. She held her breath as her vision blurred, the book spines bleeding together. *I'm imagining it. I must be.*

Or was this the magic? Was it real?

The next instant, everything snapped back to normal. Like a hunting hound released to pounce on its prey, the professor sped to the end of the room facing Widener Library, plucked a book from the shelf, returned, and placed it in Daniel's hands. "This is what you're looking for."

Eleanor glanced around to see if anyone else had noticed anything odd. But they all seemed merely confused or bored—including Daniel, who accepted the book with a resigned shrug. "I have to read it?"

"If you want to succeed in this class, yes," his mother said. "We are embarking on a journey to discover our textual potential. The books we love tell us who we are—and who we might be someday. Look up there."

She pointed, and Eleanor saw a breathtaking mural covering the ceiling. Five jewel-toned panels depicted one woman's journey through ancient Greece, the Middle Ages, ancien régime France, Victorian England, and the American *Great Gatsby* era. The woman looked like a younger Odile. She seemed to be following a thread from one era to the next, reading a different book in each.

"The characters of great literature represent our hopes and fears," the professor explained. "By accompanying them on their journeys, we learn to understand our own lives and predict the consequences of our choices."

The mural reminded Eleanor of Thomas Cole's *The Voyage of Life*, a series of four allegorical paintings her mother had taken her to see after Renée died. But these lacked Cole's creepy focus on God and death. The last panel showed the woman ensconced in a 1920s café with books, espresso, and a croissant, which was Eleanor's idea of heaven.

The boy in the suit raised his hand. He was small with

freckles and a snub nose, not handsome like Daniel but friendlier-looking. *A class clown*, Eleanor thought.

Instead of allowing him to ask his question, the professor said briskly, "You are Will Cheltenham, yes? Your turn. Ask me for the book you need."

Will looked startled, but he said, "Give me a book, please."

"The book you *need*."

"Um, yeah. Give me the book I need."

This time, Eleanor was prepared for the changes in the library: the pulsing rhythm, the slightly blurred vision, the smell, and the lightheadedness. She thought she caught a puzzled look on the zoned-out boy's face, as if he'd noticed, too. But no one else seemed affected.

Once again, the professor took a book from a shelf, this time on the north wall facing the Yard. She placed it in Will's hands. "This is the book you were looking for."

She was performing a ritual, Eleanor thought suddenly, remembering her anthropology class.

A ritual—or a spell?

The professor repeated her script with each student. From what Eleanor could see, each of them received a different book, ranging from ornate, antique-looking tomes to modern paperbacks.

Finally, it was her turn. "Bring me the book I need," Eleanor said in a small voice. "Please."

This time, the whole library seemed to lurch under her like the deck of a storm-tossed ship, yet Eleanor knew nothing had moved. She closed her eyes and listened to that distant vibration: *boom, boom, boom*. Was it only her own heart? Her overactive imagination?

She didn't open her eyes until the professor placed a book in her hands and said kindly, "This is the book you need."

Eleanor looked down and found a paperback short story collection by Ray Bradbury. The cover image was so familiar it wrenched her heart. The library was in focus again, the vibration stilled, but tears clouded her eyes.

Her elementary school library had had the same edition. She'd been halfway through it when the accident happened. When she returned to school afterward, she'd found the book in her desk and recoiled as if it were a cobra, because the cover brought a flood of memories of the innocent *before*. Every single page would remind her of how things used to be before Renée died: their mother humming as she made potato pancakes, Renée sulking because Eleanor wouldn't share her colored pencils, the three-person family they'd been. A vanished world.

Now she stared down at the Bradbury book, her scalp prickling with cold sweat. She hadn't mentioned this book in her essay. She was sure.

"Each of these books," the professor was saying, "was chosen for you by the library because it has something to tell you, whether you realize it yet or not. But you yourselves will discover the next book on your thread of textual potential. Read this book and find a second book to guide you further along the thread. Write a one-page essay justifying your choice."

A hand shot up—the brown-haired girl, whom the professor had called Genevra. "Will we be graded on finding the right book? How many books *are* there?"

"Five thousand, give or take," the professor said. "Look for a second story with a character arc that flows naturally from the first. And yes, you will be graded. If you choose a book at random, or simply for fun, I will know." She paused for emphasis. "The purpose of this quest is self-knowledge, not entertainment."

They all stared back at her. They were worried about their GPAs, Eleanor supposed. Gazing down at the Bradbury book in her hand, she told herself the professor's choice was just a lucky guess.

And yet . . . what if books really could tell you secrets about yourself? Even your future?

Maybe finishing the Bradbury stories, after all this time, would teach her something. How to finally move on from that terrible long-ago Christmas day. How to write her next chapter.

"Follow the arc," the professor told them. "Follow the pathway. How well do you know yourselves? You may, of course, return to the Library of Fates whenever the building is open. Until next class."

From Julien Theuthet, *Reflections on the Well-Curated Self* (1977), Translated by Odile Vernet

There is no escapism in the Library of Fates. Here are tragic arcs, fatal visions, the occasional laborious rise to glory. If pleasant monotony is your goal, you are fortunate, but you have no place here. No one has ever learned to know himself except by weathering the slings and arrows of an eventful life—or death.

Now

September 26, 2019, 1:32 p.m.

Daniel Vernet's mother was dead, and he didn't want to be angry with her, but he couldn't seem to help it. She was playing games with him from beyond the grave.

He was still jet-lagged from the trip across the Atlantic, and returning home for the first time in twenty-four years had made him feel fragile and sentimental. When he'd entered his mother's beloved library a half hour ago and seen all those familiar books bathed in familiar green haze, tears had risen to his eyes. But then he'd opened her folder and read the contents.

Now he paused on the granite steps of Boylston Hall to brandish the folder at Liliana. "Stop trying to calm me down and give it to me straight. Is Mom disinheriting me?"

Liliana wore head-to-toe black except for her usual floral scarf, and grief was evident in the tight lines of her face. She had been Odile's friend as well as her housekeeper—one of only a few intimates, Daniel suspected.

"I found the folder on your mother's desk with a sticky note saying it was for you. I didn't read it myself, Daniel. I assumed it was private. But I know Odile wanted the best for you."

Did she, though? Odile had dreamed of a professor son, not a college dropout who ran an Alpine guiding business. The only aspect of Daniel's life she'd ever seemed to approve of was his daughter, whom she showered with gifts when they met every year or so in Paris. Daniel and Sandrine lived more than five hours away in Annecy, but they took the train to the capital whenever her grandmother visited, because he didn't want Sandrine to grow up the way he had, with one parent and no extended family.

And he'd always imagined things between them would change. Odile was still healthy and vital in her seventies, a towering presence. Sandrine would head to university in the spring; she was studious enough to fulfill her grandmother's academic dreams. Eventually, Daniel had told himself, he would forgive his mother for trying to push him onto that same path, and she would forgive him for resisting it.

The last time Daniel had seen his mom was this past April in Paris. They'd said goodbye at her favorite café, Au Petit Suisse; he could still summon the softness of her cashmere shawl and smell her L'Occitane Verbena as she gave him a brisk hug. He'd been gathering his courage to tell her about his financial problems and attempt to bridge the distance between them. But Odile had been in a hurry to get to the English-language bookstore on the quais.

In July, he had swallowed his pride and emailed his mother to ask for a loan, because he was struggling to pay the mortgage on his inn. She'd sent back an actual letter that consisted of three words: "First come home."

Daniel was busy and annoyed by the way she still ordered

him around, so he'd tossed the letter in a drawer. Now he was home—too late to tell her that he loved her. His mother had suffered a fatal cardiac arrest as two gigantic mobile shelving units converged on her—not in the Library of Fates, as Liliana had patiently explained to Daniel, but in some underground cavern of a library where Odile often consulted Harvard's philosophy collection.

"You knew her better than anyone," he said to Liliana on the steps, handing her the folder. "Can you decipher this for me? It's her will, but it's also, well . . . something else."

The folder contained a handwritten letter, a photo of some bookshelves, and several printed, stapled sheets on the letterhead of a Boston law firm: Odile's last will and testament.

Most of it was no shocker. The contents of the Library of Fates had been a gift from Julien Theuthet to Odile, and she'd left them to her protégée, Eleanor Dennet, who was expected to succeed her as full-time librarian. Aside from a nice little bequest to Liliana, the rest went to Daniel: Odile's house in Porter Square, her bank accounts and stocks, her papers, archives, and other possessions, and her royalties from English translations of the works of Theuthet.

It wasn't a fortune, but it should be enough to get him out of the hole of endless bills—permanently, if he spent it carefully. *I'll figure this out*, he promised his daughter silently as he pictured her back home, on her knees scrubbing guest room toilets. *You deserve your inheritance.*

The only oddness was a little paragraph toward the end:

> ***The foregoing provisions depend upon one condition: the privately printed book entitled*** **Le Livre des Nuits Obscures (The Book of Dark Nights)** ***must reside in the office attached to the Library of Fates. If the Book is not in the library on the date***

> ***of my memorial (as attested by Eleanor Dennet), none of the hereunder bequests may be distributed to Daniel Vernet.***

Liliana sighed. "That old Book—your mother did have strong feelings about it. Superstitious feelings, some would say. But it's already in the library, isn't it? It's always been there."

"That's certainly what I thought." Daniel could tell by Liliana's skeptical tone that she had never witnessed the power of *The Book of Dark Nights*.

He still dreamed about the Book from time to time, and the dreams weren't pleasant. Some of them involved searching frantically for it, which was precisely why his mother's final message was so troubling. He couldn't share those irrational fears with Liliana, though.

"But look at this," he said, passing Liliana the handwritten letter. It was in his mother's cursive, but hastier- and sloppier-looking than usual.

> *9/22/19-Change of plans, Daniel. The Book isn't safe in the library. I'm off this week to France, where I hope to address the problem. But should anything happen to me, you know where I hide things. I showed you before you left.*
>
> *You still have nightmares, correct? Just talk to Eleanor before doing anything. She remembers so much more than you do, not to mention having insights into you that I never did.*
>
> *This photo and my doggerel will offer additional assistance. I think the underlines are important. Trust your instincts. Make sure the last two pages stay blank, and keep the*

Book out of anyone else's hands. Your survival depends on it.

We allowed it to read us. We are all captive to its pages.

Above all, I beg you to forgive me for my dangerous mistakes. And please give my love to Sandrine.

With love, your mother.

The last lines put a lump in Daniel's throat, even on second read. It was so unlike his mother to apologize for anything, let alone beg forgiveness. But why would she make his inheritance contingent on keeping her precious Book in the library and then suddenly decide the Book wasn't safe there? Reading between the lines, it sounded as if she'd stashed it somewhere else.

Could her mind have been slipping away from her?

"Does any of this make sense to you?" he asked. "The part about nightmares . . . well, I know what she means by that." *My dreams about the Book.* "Not the rest."

Liliana looked stricken, too. "I knew she was going to France. She had a ticket for today, as it happens, and asked me to pick up the mail while she was gone. But the rest seems . . . fanciful." She shook her head. "Your mother always seemed so coherent, Daniel. She believed in the supernatural, yes, but she never had wild ideas like this before."

The whole note had a tone of paranoid fantasy. It made Daniel uneasy, as if his vision were tunneling and he were falling through space. "It sounds like she's hidden the Book," he said, "but despite what she says, I have no idea where it could be. Do you?"

Liliana shook her head. "You can search the library and her home, of course, but I fear your mother would never have chosen such obvious spots."

"She says she showed me before I left." He searched his mind. *When would that have been?*

Daniel remembered most of his last year at Harvard just fine. But when he reached the end of spring semester, after Drew's death, details vanished, as if he were stumbling around in a fog bank. Perhaps the vagueness was his brain's way of coping with the trauma of discovering his suitemate's corpse lying in the grass after a fall from their fourth-story balcony in Randolph Hall.

She remembers so much more than you do, his mother had written in reference to Eleanor, the new librarian. So did she expect him to remember the hiding place, or didn't she?

"It's a freaking puzzle," he said, flipping through the notebook. "Suddenly I'm supposed to remember something from twenty-plus years ago? Read her mind? And if I can't, I don't get a cent because of this bizarre provision in the will?"

"Oh, dear." Hand on his arm, Liliana nudged him away from Boylston toward the monumental front steps of its neighbor, Widener Library. "It doesn't make much sense, no. But after you've seen the university police about the accident, you can go back to the library and speak with Eleanor."

Her soothing tone made Daniel ashamed of his outburst. If Odile had hidden her priceless Book because of dementia, the last thing he should do was berate her. Her plea for forgiveness chilled him, along with those strange words: *We allowed it to read us. We are all captive to its pages.*

Around them, the Yard offered a classic Ivy League snapshot: scarlet and yellow ivy against faded pink bricks; the aggressive bulk and puritan steeple of Memorial Church; the darker brick and graceful round bays of Sever Hall. Tour groups and students milled in the grassy quad. Harvard was like Paris or Geneva: a place with history hidden in every corner. To the new students who had just arrived, that New England pinch in the air must be as intoxicating as the first sip of keg beer.

Climbing Widener's steps past clumps of bright-eyed students, Daniel knew even he, raised on campus, had once felt that way.

"I should leave you here," Liliana said when they reached the massive columns guarding Widener's entrance. "I told the associate dean I'd find speakers for the memorial on Monday, and it's like herding cats. But do go see Eleanor next. This isn't one of her teaching days, so she'll be at the library."

"You really think she'll understand what Mom meant?" Daniel asked.

A few steps below him, Liliana swung back around. "Have faith, Daniel. Eleanor understood your mother better than anyone."

4

Then

February 9, 1995

When Professor Vernet dismissed the second seminar meeting, she left disgruntled students in her wake. Will, Genevra, and April—that was the redhead—had released startled gasps as she handed back their papers. Daniel and his zoned-out suitemate, Drew, didn't look happy, either.

Eleanor had an A. She'd slipped the essay quickly into her notebook, hoping no one would see. Being teacher's pet had never gone well for her.

After advising them to take their next assignment more seriously, the professor had lectured them on Julien Theuthet's theory of four personality types that we see in both literature and real life: Meek, Ruthless, Self-Destructive, and Contemplative. The lecture had punctured Eleanor's elation over her grade when she realized that her personality type was Meek.

By ourselves, we're such drab little people, her mother had said once. Eleanor wanted to protest, but she'd heard her father use that same word, *drab*, for the life he'd led with her mother. She had worked hard to get to Harvard, hoping it would decrease her drabness, but here she was in junior year, and she hadn't found a group of friends where she could flourish. She still felt small, timid, unsafe. Meek.

In the library, though, she felt something new—a power in books, which were things she understood.

"How dare she give me a C-plus for identifying with a Margaret Atwood character?" April was complaining, now that the professor had left. "I can tell she thinks I'm Ruthless. People are so much more complex than that!"

"The trick is to find a character who fits *her* vision of you," Genevra said. "Maybe I'll ask her for help choosing my next book."

Eleanor was glad she wasn't the only one who found the characterizations unfair and simplistic. Yet she couldn't help noticing how Daniel's whole attention was on April. Would a Meek girl ever catch his eye?

He chuckled. "Haven't you got the memo, April? My mom thinks you're not a nice person."

"She thinks *you're* a rebel without a cause," April shot back. "And I'm *not* going to ask the professor for help," she added to Genevra. "She'd be so smug about it."

The seminar was beginning to feel to Eleanor like an echo of high school, with clearly defined roles. Daniel and Will were rivals, vying for the girls' attention, though Will usually dominated the conversation while Daniel was prone to smoldering silences. The two girls laughed at everything the boys said, April teasing them relentlessly. Drew was the amiable stoner, friends with everyone and taking no sides.

"You might just have to suck it up if you don't want to tank your GPA, April," Will said, then swung around to face Eleanor. "How'd *you* ace that essay? Did you ask her for help?"

Sharp-eyed Will must have gotten a look at Eleanor's grade before she slid the essay into her notebook. Suddenly ten pairs of eyes were on her, everyone eager to know the secret of her success, and she had no idea what to say about how she'd chosen her second book.

She'd found the Bradbury stories the professor had chosen for her intriguing but not especially resonant—until she reached "All Summer in a Day."

It was about a girl living on the planet Venus whose classmates bully and despise her. Finally, they lock her in a closet on the only clear day in seven straight years of rain, so that she misses her one chance to play outdoors in the sunshine.

That girl was me. All those years after Renée's accident, stuck in the house with her mother, Eleanor had felt as if she were slowly wilting in the dark. The story touched a nerve that had been throbbing inside her for a long time. She felt oddly relieved, as if just having the hurt acknowledged eased it.

But what happened next? The story ended unhappily, and it was up to Eleanor to find the next book on her thread of textual potential.

Alone in the library earlier that week, she had let its atmosphere settle around her like a favorite sweater. Since no one else was around, she had tried the professor's method of choosing books, not expecting magic to happen for her but wishing it could. She'd shut her eyes and whispered several times, "Bring me the book I need."

Nothing pulled her directly to a particular book, the way she sensed Professor Vernet had been pulled. But she did feel the ghost of a vibration, especially when she closed her eyes. It intensified in certain parts of the library and trailed off in others, as if someone were whispering, *Hotter, hotter . . . no, now you're getting colder.* Following that odd resonance around the library, she soon found a title that felt indefinably *right*: *The Haunting of Hill House.*

She'd read most of the slim book that afternoon, curled up in an armchair. The story was about a woman named Eleanor—Nell—who has spent her whole adulthood locked up with her sick mother and desperately wants a life of her own. It made Eleanor shudder and tear up at the end as she thought again of all those years in the little house with her own mother, using books to escape.

"*I see myself in both these books,*" she wrote in her essay's conclusion, "*but I don't want to be locked in a closet, and I don't want to spend eternity in a haunted house. I hope the next book gives me a better ending.*"

Now, forced to explain to the others how she'd gotten her A, Eleanor said, "I didn't ask the professor for help, no. I . . . felt my way through the library. I made a lucky guess," she added because it sounded less weird, although that strange game of hot and cold hadn't felt like chance.

When she glanced up, her cheeks warmed. They were all staring at her.

Then Daniel suddenly spoke. "It's never just about luck here," he said, and she thought she glimpsed something like sympathy in his brown eyes. "My mom says the library has currents, and you have to let them guide you. Most people can't or won't."

"It felt like that," Eleanor admitted, recalling the mysterious sensation of being nudged.

"Creepy! I wish I could feel it." Genevra looked equally unnerved and excited. "Could *you* do what Professor Vernet does, Eleanor? If you can find the right book for yourself, can you do it for us?"

"Why would she be able to do that?" April asked, as if she highly doubted Eleanor had any special abilities. "She only found *one* book."

"Anyway, I already tried asking the library for a book." Eleanor cast her eyes down, embarrassed to admit she'd attempted something that felt like a spell. "But nothing happened."

"You can't ask the question for yourself." Daniel spoke softly. "It doesn't work that way. You can only find a book for someone else."

"The professor doesn't have *magic*," Will countered derisively. "She doesn't read our minds. It's all the power of suggestion."

But Eleanor barely heard him. She was gazing at Daniel, whose generous lips were quirked into a thoughtful expression. "My mom's chosen books for me since I was a kid," he said. "I never saw anybody else do what she can. But you *should* try, Eleanor. Why not? You said you felt the currents."

Why not, indeed? Something inside Eleanor seized on Daniel's words. She already felt at home in the Library of Fates, and if she could do what the professor did, maybe she wouldn't be so Meek anymore.

Telling herself firmly that it didn't matter if she tried and failed, she turned to Genevra. "I think you have to ask me the question first."

"I need the right book so I can get a better grade on the next essay."

Eleanor closed her eyes. *Here goes nothing.*

As Genevra spoke the question—"Could you find it for me, please?"—Eleanor reached down to the place where she still felt the pulsing of those currents, right at the heart of the library. A place of power and knowledge and the strange intuition Odile had shown when she chose books for them during their first class meeting.

At first nothing seemed to happen. But when she opened her eyes, everything had gone gray and blurry—the shelves, the windows, the faces of the others. She saw April's lips move but heard nothing.

What was wrong with her eyes and ears? She knew she should be frightened, but her emotions had gone distant and muffled, along with her normal perceptions of the world. There was only the library, and she sensed it on a different plane than before.

The walls and shelves were pulsing again, just as they had when Odile was choosing books. But now the sensation was stronger, as if she were standing directly above an enormous church organ while it pounded out a hymn.

And this vibration was somehow in motion. It had currents, tides. Like ocean surf drawing a wader deeper, it tugged Eleanor toward one of the shelves on the south wall. The books were all one indistinguishable mass—except for a single spine that stood out in vivid color.

This isn't possible. Eleanor rubbed her eyes, but she couldn't stop herself from following the library's wordless commands. She moved as if in a trance, her feet carrying her to the shelf.

The thrumming of the library was there, too, inside the wood. She felt it as she grabbed hold of the book and brought it back across the room.

As she placed it in Genevra's hands, she heard her own voice say in a strange, flat tone, "This is the book you need."

The words seemed to break the spell. Just like that, as if someone had flicked a switch, her vision snapped back to normal—colors, details. Sounds returned. The vibration faded. Looking at the book Genevra was holding, Eleanor saw it was *Les Liaisons dangereuses* by Choderlos de Laclos. Wasn't that a movie with Glenn Close?

"Whoa, that was weird," Drew said in the sepulchral voice he used sometimes to make the others laugh. "You looked like you were possessed."

"She looked like Professor Vernet." April's tone was tart. "*Just* like her."

"Then maybe this book will get me an A!" Genevra slipped it into her shoulder bag. "That was amazing, Eleanor. Thank you."

"Can you do me now?" April asked seriously. For the first time since they'd met, her gaze lingered on Eleanor, as if she were really seeing her. "Please?"

Eleanor's face was hot again. She had no idea what had just happened, only that she felt less Meek than she ever had before.

She found *The House of Mirth* for April, then *The Picture of Dorian Gray* for Will. At that point, Drew observed that they were late for dinner. "Anybody coming?"

The others followed him, chattering loudly in the stairwell as if they wanted to drown out those strange currents in the library, to remind themselves they lived in the real world. Eleanor was surprised to turn and find Daniel still there.

She expected him to ask her for a book the way his friends had. Instead, he edged closer and said, "That was something."

"You were right," Eleanor said. "It feels different when I'm choosing for someone else." *Strange. Powerful. As if a greater force is moving through me.*

"I kinda grew up here—you'd think if anybody were on the library's wavelength, it would be me. But when Mom asks me for a book, nothing happens." Daniel smiled wryly. "The library won't guide me."

The admiration in his eyes was doing disturbing things to Eleanor. Did he *like* that she could use the library's power?

Her mother always said that men preferred women who made them feel like heroes.

"Maybe you can do it now," she suggested. She wouldn't mind sharing the power with Daniel, she told herself firmly. This wasn't about her ego. "Find me the book I need."

Daniel closed his eyes the way she had earlier. Opened them. Blinked.

"Nah," he said. "I don't think the gods destined me to be a librarian."

The wording made Eleanor laugh out loud. Guys didn't usually kid around with her; they thought she was too uptight. But he didn't seem to mind her quietness, and that encouraged her to creep out of her shell. "I'm not destined to be a librarian, either! I mean, not that I wouldn't *like* to be one. But of my own free will."

Daniel smiled back at her—an easy, radiant smile that melted her usual reserve. "So you *can* laugh. I honestly wasn't sure. You're so . . ."

"Serious. I know!" It wasn't the first time she'd been told that. But how could you explain that smiling and laughing felt like giving away pieces of yourself?

After Renée's death, Eleanor had learned to control her facial expressions, because even passing moments of happiness felt like betrayals of her sister. She showed people what they expected—grief, guilt, maturity beyond her years. And the mask of solemnity had hardened into a protective shield, one she rarely lowered.

"It's okay to be serious, too. God knows, my mom's a pro at the grim stare." Daniel's own smile had faded. But his eyes remained on Eleanor as if he were seeing something in her he hadn't noticed at the last class.

Or maybe he did want her to find him a book, after all?

He didn't suggest it, though, only said, "You live down in Dunster, right? I'm in Adams. Want to walk?"

As they strolled from the Yard into the Square, and then toward the river, Daniel told Eleanor about his summer plan to go to Switzerland, where you could hike and gaze down on green pastures full of brown cows, their bells clanging musically in the fresh Alpine air. He'd used his father's birthday money for a Eurail pass, and he hoped to hit Germany and Italy, too.

His parents aren't together. Eleanor could tell by the way he mentioned his dad, vaguely and with a touch of bitterness. She knew that feeling well.

As they parted, Daniel said, "After graduation, I'll travel the world. No more sitting around and just reading about things. So, you see, Eleanor, I don't necessarily need a book to tell me who I am."

5

—

Now

September 26, 2019, 2:15 p.m.

A knock on the open door made Eleanor start guiltily. She'd been searching the whole library, knowing *The Book of Dark Nights* hadn't walked itself out of the safe but keeping her eyes and hands busy while she considered what to do next. She sometimes had nightmares in which she was hunting for the missing Book, but she'd never expected to be doing it in real life.

"Oh, hi, Will," she said.

Will Cheltenham, Associate Dean of Arts and Sciences, ventured into the room. "You holding up okay? I've been meaning to check on you."

Eleanor accepted his stiff, tweedy hug. "I'm okay. I miss her so much."

Equally proud of his two golden-haired sons, his two golden retrievers, and the collection of model ships he'd assembled himself, Will usually had a platitude or a dad joke for every occasion. He was also always ready with a pointed anecdote about how his boss, Dean Archer Temple, thought the library's space could have been better used.

Right now, though, he seemed genuinely shaken as he patted her back. "Still can't believe it. I thought Odile would outlast us both."

Eleanor relaxed into his sympathy, grateful she wasn't alone. But then she remembered Will didn't know yet about the disappearance of *The Book of Dark Nights*. Dean Temple wouldn't be pleased by the news. The book wasn't insured. Only people very close to the library—past seminar students, Odile's best scholar friends, a few university officials—knew it even existed.

And Daniel Vernet, it occurred to her now.

"I'm still processing," she said as they parted, choosing each word carefully. "I keep expecting Odile to march in here with one of her giant black umbrellas and lecture me about adding new books to the collection."

The note Odile had left on top of the safe kept drifting through her mind. "A place of pages, / A subterranean secret, / Where love is shared . . ." The poem was sentimental, and Odile wasn't. Was it only a random quote, or a message?

"She was a force of nature, right?" Will fiddled with his Uniball, slipping his index finger through the clip. He was twitchier and less polished than your average administrator, but he looked people in the eye and remembered the names of their loved ones, and she'd heard his colleagues call him the "donor whisperer."

It helped that he brought rich alumni to the Library of Fates.

"Her legacy lives on, though," he added. "Thank God you're in charge. Speaking of which . . . well, I know this isn't the right time to bug you with details. We're all still in shock, especially you. But time marches on, and people have schedules, and . . ."

"What do you need?"

"Well." Will released the clip with a loud click. The momentum launched the pen out of his hand, and he bent to pick it up. "I haven't canceled our visit with Belinda Ratliff next week. Do you think you'd still be up to showing her the library?"

Eleanor's heart sank as she remembered the appointment. Belinda Ratliff was an alum and UK venture capitalist whom Dean Temple hoped to transform into a major benefactor of the university. She might need some coaxing, and that was what the Library of Fates was for.

Officially speaking, Dean Temple and his staff saw the Library of Fates as just a quirky tradition. But a few of them—Will, for one—also knew the librarian could hand you a book that would change your life.

Eleanor had performed her role with monied alumni twice or thrice each year, under Odile's watchful eye, and she wasn't proud of it. She much preferred to work with students who drifted into the library: the shy or awkward ones who felt less alone after reading the book she handed them, the aimless ones who gained a sense of purpose, the despairing ones who found hope. One girl to whom Eleanor had given John Keats's collected works had even returned to the library and recited "The Eve of St. Agnes" from memory—the best remedy she'd found for anxiety, she said.

With students, Eleanor let the library choose each book, herself simply an instrument of its will. But when she wanted to, she could exert some control over the power—more than even Odile could. When prospective donors visited, her job was to find a book that would nudge them toward the path of devoting a thick slice of their wealth to their alma mater: a path of reflection, of nostalgia, of contemplating their own mortality and wanting to ensure their legacy.

She always applied *just* a nudge, nothing aggressive. Just showing each donor a facet of their own potential they'd never explored.

"Sure. Thursday, right?" she said now, smiling fixedly and knowing she had to get the Book back by then. Did Daniel see the Book as rightfully his, now that his mother was gone? The safe code was the date of his parents' first meeting, easy for him to guess. And Odile had mentioned recently that he needed money. As far as most antique dealers were concerned, the Book was merely a legend passed down from the eighteenth century, when it had supposedly belonged to Marie Louise Élisabeth d'Orléans, Duchess of Berry. If they discovered it was real, it would fetch a hefty price.

Thursday would give Eleanor enough time to talk Daniel—but *could* she talk to him? Though she knew she should, every part of her cringed at the thought of facing him again.

A book brought you together . . .

"Oh, good!" Will looked relieved. "Belinda's looking forward to hearing all your colorful stories of the library."

And you're looking forward to cashing her seven-figure checks. But Eleanor didn't let her smile falter. It wasn't Will's fault that his boss was eager for those donations.

"By the way, we hope you'll prepare something to read at the memorial, of course." Will blinked rapidly. "I guess I should speak, too. When I think of how we met in that seminar . . . we didn't respect Odile properly, did we? We didn't grasp her brilliance. Except for you."

"You were so young," Eleanor pointed out. "And Odile was strong-willed and opinionated."

She could almost hear Odile's scolding, perfectionist voice

in her head. But she knew the woman critiqued because she cared.

"I just need inspiration. Something to revive those hoary college memories," Will was saying. He paused in the doorway, his eyes narrowing on Eleanor. "Find me a book?"

Eleanor stood frozen.

Here was the moment of truth. Right now, she should have felt Will's need surging through her like a wave, tugging her toward the exact right spot on the shelf.

But she felt nothing. No vibrations, no distant booming. When she scanned the shelves above Will's head, nothing blurred or lost its color. No book stood out more than any other.

The power was really gone. When she swallowed, her mouth was dry as paper.

"Find me the book I need, please," Will repeated, clearly thinking he'd got the prompt wrong.

Surely Eleanor could fake it, picking a book the way other librarians did. But fear had sucked all the titles out of her brain. And she could feel Will staring, because he knew she shouldn't have hesitated.

"What's wrong?" he asked. "Doesn't it . . . ?"

She turned to him. "It's gone."

"Wait. The *Book* is gone?"

Eleanor nodded. "The safe is empty. No signs of forced entry."

"Shit." Will left the doorway and paced the width of the library and back, fingers clawing at his hair. He knew about the Book from their time in the seminar, and clearly he'd deduced it was the source of the library's power. "When did this happen?" he asked, stopping in front of her again.

"This week. Or maybe over the weekend." Today was Thursday, and Eleanor had last been in the library on Monday morning, the day of Odile's death. She didn't recall sensing anything different then, but she'd been busy prepping for class.

"The Book was definitely here on Friday," she added, remembering the familiar hum of the library that day.

Will was pacing again. "When did Daniel get here? Yesterday, right? When I heard he was back from Europe, my first thought was, *Well, he'll do it again. He'll break into that safe.*"

"Drew Pollit was the one who actually took the Book out of the library," Eleanor corrected him, though she also thought Daniel was the likely culprit. "Remember how obsessed he was?"

They seldom talked about poor Drew, and now Will's face froze in a rictus of discomfort. "Yeah, but Daniel was the one who cracked the code in the first place," he said after a moment. "Who showed the rest of us how to get it."

Will was playing with the pen again, his brows bunched. She knew he was thinking that without the Book, there was no way to ensure a substantial donation from Belinda Ratliff or anyone else. His job might be on the line, just like hers. And he had private school tuitions and a sizable mortgage to pay.

He said, "If Daniel did steal the Book again, we have to talk to him. We have to *reason* with him before he, I don't know . . ."

"Sells it?" Eleanor tried not to show how much the idea disturbed her.

"God, I hope not." Suddenly Will's face brightened. "Liliana said he'd stop by in the afternoon to talk to you. Maybe it's about the Book. Maybe it's not too late."

So they'd come back around to the exact conclusion Eleanor had feared: she had to face Daniel. She hoped Odile had been telling the truth when she claimed he barely remembered her, all these years later.

You are only a name in his head, attached to nothing but a vague regret, if even that, Odile had said once.

"I haven't seen Daniel in forever, though," Eleanor tried to object.

"Offer him money if you have to—just not too much!" A canny look passed over Will's face, and she knew he was calculating exactly how much he could squeeze out of Dean Temple. "Forty thousand, say. Daniel's what, an innkeeper now? He might jump for that."

In Will's world, forty thousand dollars was pocket change. But surely Daniel knew the Book might go for millions—if he could obscure its shady provenance. "I can sound him out," Eleanor said dubiously.

Will pulled out his phone. "If you don't have any luck, let me know. I'll invite him to drinks at the Signet Society. With both of us working on him, he'll have to crack. You try first—he always liked you."

"I'll try," Eleanor said, lifting her chin. She refused to be afraid of Daniel Vernet.

6

—

THEN

February 16, 1995

The first time Daniel Vernet ever saw *The Book of Dark Nights* was at the long table in the library, toward the end of their third session. Three hours was a while to sit still, and the class was growing restless when his mother reached into her briefcase and, without warning or preamble, produced a slim black volume with raised gilt bands on the spine.

Everyone went quiet. There was nothing obviously special about the Book except for its age, yet now Daniel could swear the library vibrated with a rich, steady hum. He felt as if he were walking into the museum gallery where the *Mona Lisa* or some other famous artwork was kept, about to see it with his own eyes.

When he glanced at Eleanor, sitting across from him, he could see in her tense, shining eyes that she felt it, too.

Daniel had been twelve when his mother first told him about the Book, though she'd refused to show it to him then.

You should be in college before you touch the Book, she'd said. *In your early twenties, young adulthood, the first thrill of freedom—that's how old I was. That's the exact right age.*

Odile had to know how he'd longed to experience the Book's magic for himself all these years. During his childhood, he could never keep secrets from her. Whenever she wanted to know what was on his mind, she would bring him to the library and order him to request a book. Too often, the library prescribed him one about dead or evil parents or problem kids who ran away from home.

"Still having those fantasies of being an orphan, I see," his mom would say as she passed him *Great Expectations*. Or, when it was *The Catcher in the Rye*, "I suppose we all go through that phase."

But these days, Daniel didn't request books from his mother if he could help it. He preferred keeping his feelings to himself, which was why he'd come to the seminar with a mask of sullen indifference.

When his mother passed the Book down the table toward him, he stared at it coldly, though he itched to touch it. He didn't want to give her the satisfaction of seeing how excited he was.

Eleanor nudged the Book closer to Daniel—and flinched, as if it had shocked her. Their eyes met, and Daniel felt himself blush in a way he hadn't done since high school. Last week, when Eleanor was finding the right books for the others, he hadn't been able to take his eyes off her. She was inconspicuous when she wanted to be, fading into the woodwork. But when the power worked through her, she held her head high and walked like a queen.

"Here is another part of the story of how the library came to be," his mother announced in her theatrical way. "The rest of you will need a translation. Read them the title, *mon chou*."

Daniel drew the volume to him now. The tingle of power under its cover made him gasp. But he didn't snatch his hand away, thrilled by the continuous ripple like a purr building inside a cat's throat. Something was alive in there. No, many things, bound together like the threads of a masterfully woven tapestry.

He opened the Book, keeping his face blank and unimpressed for his mother's benefit. *"Le Livre des Nuits Obscures. The Book of Dark Nights."*

His mother started narrating the Book's history, which Daniel already knew. "It was privately printed in the early eighteenth century for the Duchess of Berry, a granddaughter of Louis XIV who threw famously debauched parties at her Palais du Luxembourg in Paris. She was married as a teenager, lost her husband, and bore several ill-fated infants fathered by the captain of her guard before dying at age twenty-three. You would have liked her, Daniel," she added with a sly glance at him. "I know you dream of running with the fast crowd."

Will and April snickered, but Daniel barely even heard the dig. He'd been holding his breath, focusing on the Book. The frontispiece bore an illustration that looked like the three Fates, spinning the threads of each person's life while constellations burned in the sky above them.

"A single copy exists," his mother continued, "which was believed lost for over two centuries, until the historic protests that shook Paris in May 1968. Hiding from the authorities, a student named Marc Vasselin heard something scrabbling behind a crumbling wall. When he investigated, he found the Book. Someone had bricked it up there."

As always, the story sent a shiver through Daniel. He listened as his mother told them how Marc had brought the old book to his Sorbonne professor, Julien Theuthet, who shared it with two other students in his elite seminar.

She didn't mention that those students had been herself and her best friend, Juliette Aubry.

"The Book inspired Theuthet's theory of textual potential—the idea that books can show us our fates," his mother was explaining. "Show them the frontispiece, Daniel."

Daniel held up the book to show them. An elaborate Gothic font proclaimed: *Ici est le domaine de la Vérité. On ne souffre pas le Mensonge.* "'Here is the domain of truth. Lies are not tolerated,'" he translated.

"Now open to the marker and read."

Daniel turned a page, then another, and leafed to the end. It was exactly as Odile had led him to expect. He saw tantalizing fragments of handwriting, but none of them resolved themselves into words. "There's just one sentence printed on every page—*Laissez-moi vous lire.* 'Let me read you.'"

His mother reached for the Book. After a brief inner struggle, Daniel returned it to her, not wanting to let it go.

It did read us, she had told him when he was younger. *All too well. And it taught us to read ourselves.*

Now she said, "We believe the Book was used in the Duchess's palace as a sort of parlor game—an Enlightenment Ouija board, if you will. It was always kept in a carefully curated library. 'Dark nights' refers to the Catholic notion of a dark night of the soul, when one doubts one's faith and struggles with one's sins. Each player would confess one of their sins on a page of the Book, then close it. When they opened it again, they would find a message in their very own handwriting: a literary quotation that proved to be an accurate prediction of their future. In this way, the Book spoke to them."

Will asked, "*Spoke* to them?"

Odile stared him down, her dark eyes glittering. "Yes, my skeptical friend. Books have been used to divine the future for as long as books have existed. *The Book of Dark Nights* simply makes that divination more precise—for those who use it responsibly. The first step is to reveal their darkest, most secret truths."

She paused for emphasis, and Eleanor suddenly spoke up. "Their darkest truths. The worst thing they've ever done!" Excitement set her gaze alight. "What you asked for in our diagnostic essay is what we'd write in this book."

"I'd rather just read other people's confessions." Will had a sneaky look. "Bet you could get a lot of juicy intel that way."

"Indeed," Odile said archly. "If you could read any confessions but your own."

"Old-timey handwriting is a bitch," Drew suggested. "I can barely read my mom's cursive."

Odile didn't contradict him, but Daniel knew she hadn't been talking about penmanship. The confessions were illegible because the Book's creator had wanted them that way.

"The Book is dangerous to those who think they have more self-knowledge than they actually do," his mother continued. "None of you is ready to write in it yet. Above all, avoid telling it a lie."

Staring raptly at the Book, Genevra asked the same question Daniel had asked his mother when she first told him about the Book, a question she had refused to answer. "What happens if you *do* lie?"

Daniel followed Odile's gaze around the table. Eleanor's eyes had become enormous. Will looked uncomfortable. Drew had a solemn expression that Daniel had never seen on him before.

They all felt magic in the Book, even those who didn't want to.

The Book will bond you, even after death, his mother had once told him. *Those who make their mark there can never truly be parted.*

Daniel hadn't agreed to take the seminar because he

wanted to explore the library or learn the mind-numbing vocabulary of textual potential. He was there for one reason: to experience the Book.

Without the kind of family most people had—grandparents, uncles, aunts, cousins, enough to fill a big table at the holidays—he'd always wondered how it would feel to belong to something greater than himself. Something enduring. When his mother spoke of the time she'd shared in Paris with Marc, Juliette, and Julien Theuthet, she came alive in a way she normally never did. And Daniel knew the Book's bond was more real to her than anything else.

Odile shot them a small smile and stood up, slipping the Book back into her briefcase. "*Lies are not tolerated*," she said. "I've never seen the Book harm anyone, but I suggest you not test it. You are dismissed for today."

***

Eleanor had been thinking about Daniel all week. After class, she pretended to browse the shelves, waiting to see if he'd stay behind again.

The way he'd looked at her over *The Book of Dark Nights*, the way he'd blushed—something had passed between them then, though she couldn't be sure what.

As he sidled up to her now, all lanky grace, her heart thundered.

"What do you think?" he asked, arching a brow. "What secret would you tell the Book?"

When he read the frontispiece of the Book, his French accent had been flawless, yet now he sounded as American as she did. Before she could stop herself, she was imagining him as Julien Sorel in *The Red and the Black*, speaking whole fiery sentences in French.

Eleanor swallowed, trembling a little in the bright light of his attention. Of course she wasn't going to tell him about Renée—not yet, anyway. "I don't know. What about you?"

Daniel's smile had a wicked edge. "I'd confess that I've never loved anyone, not in the romantic way. I've hooked up with people. But I haven't been in love. Does that shock you?"

It did, just a little, but only because she was so far behind him in experience. "No," she lied, then tried to hide her embarrassment with a lofty, abstract tone. "True love is overrated—I mean, look how it turns out in books and plays. Somebody usually dies. Anyway, I thought you were supposed to confess something you'd *done*."

"Hooking up counts, right? I mean, that was a sin back in the Book's day."

Eleanor hoped the library's shadows camouflaged her blush. "Hooking up without *marriage* was a sin in the eighteenth century," she corrected him. "Love was optional. Seeing love as redemptive is more of a modern thing."

The truth was, Eleanor had spent much of her adolescence fantasizing about a romantic love that would give her whole life meaning. What her parents had shared wasn't love, in her opinion, but the affection of a gardener for an exotic flower. Her dad had discarded her mother as soon as someone more exciting came along.

In middle school, she'd favored the shadowy, strong-armed lovers in paperback gothic and fantasy novels, and in tenth grade, she scribbled *Mrs. Fitzwilliam Darcy* in all her notebooks. But no boy seemed interested in even so much as kissing her, so she eventually soured on those dreams and turned to stories of love that was doomed or unrequited or hopelessly compromised. They felt more true to life.

"I never thought of it that way." Daniel's smile faltered.

"You felt something, didn't you? When you touched the Book?"

He sounded dead serious now, the teasing tone gone, so she nodded the same way. "It's those currents you were talking about, the ones that run through the library. They were . . . stronger inside the Book."

"Do you think they come from the Book?" His voice had fallen almost to a whisper, though they were alone.

"I don't know. Maybe." Eleanor wanted to understand those currents better, but it was hard to focus on anything else with Daniel standing so close. "Do you think your mom actually believes the Book makes words appear? And punishes people for a lie?"

"Sure. She takes the Book really seriously, which is why she locks it up very securely in her safe." He tucked a strand of hair behind his ear, his gaze falling to the side, and Eleanor sensed he wasn't telling her everything. "Wanna walk again?"

As they left the library, Eleanor could almost feel the Book straining after them. The professor had taken it into her office and locked the door. But it was still in there, marvelously alive, waiting for someone to return and make their marks on its pages.

7

Now

September 26, 2019, 2:46 p.m.

Over the years since he'd left Harvard, Daniel had sometimes dreamed of Boylston Hall. Made of giant slabs of gray Rockport granite with a dark-shingled roof, the building stood out like a goth cousin to the red-brick rest of campus—a fitting hiding place for his mother's secrets.

In his dreams, the Book was lost and he was chasing it, dashing downstairs from the library into the Yard. But he never found it. Now he traced that path in reverse, marching up the steps of the building, and hoped his night visions weren't prophetic.

His conversation with the campus cops had been depressing and tedious. All he'd learned was that they considered his mother's death an accident, even though someone else had apparently pressed the button that closed her aisle in the mobile stacks—unintentionally, they'd assured him. When he asked who had *unintentionally* killed his mother, they'd admitted no one had come forward or been caught on camera. They'd even politely implied that, by climbing the shelf to find a book rather than using a step stool, Odile was partly responsible for her accident. And she must have been aware she had a life-threatening heart condition. Surely he knew all about that?

Daniel did not know that. His mother had always insisted that her daily constitutionals kept her "healthy as a horse." He wasn't surprised she had hidden her health worries, but it gave him a stab of sadness, because it was just one of too many things that had gone unspoken between them. Maybe she'd feared he would see her weakness as a burden.

He paused outside the main entrance to tug out his phone. His daughter had texted him a link to an article about Odile's death in the *Boston Globe.*

She was crushed by shelves??? A horrified emoji. *You didn't tell me.*

Daniel cursed himself for trying to spare Sandrine the details. She wasn't a child anymore, and of course she would google. *Not crushed!* he typed frantically. *They only closed halfway, but she fell and had a cardiac incident.*

They're making jokes in the comments. "Librarian killed by books." Fuckers.

I know. Call you soon, okay? Just need to handle some things here.

Sandrine asked him to call her tonight, because she was headed out on a weekend hike with her friend and might be out of cell range. *Tried to cancel, but it's Katrin's last chance before going back to Bern.*

When Daniel didn't immediately reply, she added, *Don't worry! I'm an adult now, remember?*

You just turned eighteen last month—but no, he wouldn't remind her of that. He remembered being eighteen.

Have a good hike, Daniel wrote instead, then scrolled quickly through his inbox. A tour reservation, a bill, a guide's request for vacation time, another bill, the front desk clerk lamenting that a party of carousing Germans had trashed the main suite and broken some furniture. And that would be another whopping bill to add to the pile.

He swore softly to himself, thinking of the looming mortgage payment. Why couldn't his mother have written an ordinary will?

That note of hers kept revolving in his head. *Make sure the last two pages stay blank, and keep the Book out of anyone else's hands. Your survival depends on it.* What sort of dark delusions had Odile been having?

As he entered the building and crossed the foyer, achingly familiar from his childhood, he knew it was more than the money that bothered him. It was the fact that he was still even thinking about money, when he'd just learned from his mother's message how deeply troubled she'd been in the days before her death. If he'd been in touch, he would have known while she was still alive, could have done something to help. *I beg you to forgive me*, Odile had written, as if he didn't have just as much to be forgiven for. The words felt as if they'd been branded on him—her last wish.

He climbed the stairs past students speaking German and Italian, struggling with the memories and echoes triggered by every step. In his dreams, the three flights sometimes stretched into infinity.

Nightmares—he shouldn't call them that. They'd never been all that bad, had they? In some of them he was alone, searching for the Book, but in others he had company—his mother, his old friends, even poor dead Drew.

He reached the third-floor landing, a little winded by the climb, and paused in the doorway of the library. The afternoon sunlight had intensified. The glare made Daniel squint, and he could barely make out a slight shape by the windows that faced the Square.

For an instant, he thought he was seeing his mother. Somehow he'd slipped into the timeless world of those ominous dreams, where the dead returned to life and the Library of Fates never changed.

Then he realized that the woman approaching across the green carpet was his own age. The person he'd come to see—the new librarian. Eleanor.

Do you ever miss Eleanor? his mother had asked him a year or so ago. When he'd reminded her that no, he didn't recall ever meeting her protégée, Odile had gazed at him as if she pitied him for his memory, so much weaker than her own steel-trap one.

Eleanor wore a scarf knotted chicly around her slim neck, as his mother used to, and she seemed perfectly *right* in the library. As if she'd been in his dreams, too. Or maybe she'd been in the seminar? He recalled his mother saying something to that effect. Daniel remembered most of the other students: Drew, of course, and the boy who always wore a suit and the brown-haired girl and April, who'd reached out to him on Facebook several years ago asking for Grenoble restaurant recs.

"Daniel," Eleanor said. "Liliana said to expect you."

"Uh, yes. Hello, Eleanor." He extended a hand, feeling clumsy. "Been a while."

She took his hand, her expression unreadable. Daniel searched his brain for memories of her—the strawberry-blond hair, slipping out of a bun and falling in a shiny curtain on her pale cheek. The sharp nose, the gaze that flitted around the room to rest on him with unnerving intensity.

He thought he remembered a girl with those features, seated across the seminar table from him. But the memory went vaporous when he tried to grasp it. Maybe he was confusing her with a phantom from his dreams.

"I'm so sorry about your mom." Eleanor spoke politely, yet the set of her chin was almost hostile. "She meant a great deal to me, too."

"You were a huge help to her." Although Daniel had been raised bilingual and still spoke English often with his clients, the words felt stiff and unwieldy in his mouth. He'd come here to demand answers, but now he felt out of his depth.

She remembers so much more than you do, not to mention having insights into you that I never did, Odile's note had said.

"Odile told me you run a hotel now? In the Alps?"

"That's right! Well, a B and B, anyway." As a tour guide, Daniel had learned how to tell his story in a friendly, entertaining way, and he launched into the capsule version. "I dropped out of college after junior year—well, you probably know that. I had a Eurail pass for the summer, and when fall came, I just stayed."

He didn't give her the details of how his twenties had passed in a whirlwind of long-haul flights and adventures—hiking and climbing, savoring the adrenaline rush of clinging to icy cliffs. Falling in with a loose society of daredevils, he summited Denali and took up cave diving in Mexico and Thailand. When he made France his home base, it was only because of Sandrine. A grad student in Grenoble, with whom he'd had a one-night stand in the Caucasus, had called to tell him she'd given birth to their daughter.

Neither of them wanted a relationship, but Daniel was determined to be part of Sandrine's life, because he knew how it felt to grow up without a father. He got a steady job with an adventure tour company. When his daughter was four, her mother died in a car crash, and then he was a single parent, saving to open his own business.

"Odile told me about your daughter," Eleanor said, seeming to soften as she broached the subject. "She was so proud, and always excited to see the two of you in France."

"Yeah, she was a great grandma." How was he going to tell her about Odile's note? It seemed too intimate, like airing family secrets, yet his mother had implied he should do so. "Sandrine is eighteen going on thirty now. She's studying for her *baccalauréat*. You have kids?" he asked, trying to warm Eleanor up a little.

She shook her head, her mouth hardening. "Not unless you count the students who come through the library."

Wrong question. "I'm hoping you'll come to the house and catalog my mom's papers while I'm here," Daniel said, taking another tack. "You're probably the greatest living expert on the library."

Eleanor gave him a flat, assessing glance. "Daniel, why are you here? Just to pay your respects? I do appreciate it, believe me. But . . ."

"But what?" What had Odile told her about him—or what did Eleanor remember that he didn't? Clearly nothing good, but frankness was often the way to win someone over.

He hoisted his backpack onto the table and unzipped it to fish out Odile's folder. "I guess you think I'm an ulterior-motive kind of guy, and you're not wrong this time. My mom left a message for me that I find . . . disturbing. I need to ask you about *The Book of Dark Nights*."

Now he had Eleanor's full attention. She stared at him, hazel eyes widening until he saw notes of green. "What about it?"

She does know something. With a rough jerk, Daniel tugged the folder out of his backpack and spilled the contents on the table.

"The Book's not in the safe anymore, is it?" His voice was louder than he meant it to be, sending shock waves through the serenity of his mother's library. The traffic noise outside shrank to a hum. "My mom took it out and hid it, God knows why. And I hope you know where. Because until I find it, my daughter and I won't inherit a cent."

Eleanor leaned over the will and the note, adjusting a pair of tortoiseshell reading glasses. She didn't look angry with him, just focused, her hooded eyes darting from word to word.

But she pressed a thumb to one corner of her mouth as she read, and he suspected the note troubled her at least as much as it did him.

When she straightened up, she had a strange expression, as if she weren't sure whether to be happy or sad. "No one stole the Book," she said. "That's a relief."

"So you agree she hid the Book? Where?"

"*You know where I hide things*," Eleanor quoted softly, then raised her eyes to his. "You don't remember what she meant, then?"

"Your guess is as good as mine."

Her eyes glazed, as if she were recalling something. When she blinked, they cleared again. "Odile's right, isn't she? You still have the nightmares?"

Daniel didn't like how sharply she was looking at him. He shrugged, then pointed to the image of bookshelves that Odile had clipped to her message. "Do you know where this is? She wrote, *This photo and my doggerel will offer additional assistance*."

"The photo is Dunster House Library. And doggerel is bad poetry." Eleanor was frowning intensely down at the note again. "Oh," she said after a moment, her face brightening. "Oh!"

"What?"

But she was already turning from him and striding briskly across the room. "I found something on top of the safe after the Book disappeared," she called back to him as she unlocked the office door. "It's in Odile's handwriting. I thought maybe it was a quotation she'd copied, but if this is what she meant by *doggerel*, then I guess she wrote it."

She ducked into the office and returned, her boots clicking on the oak, with a blue sticky note in hand. "See if you can make anything of this."

Her cheeks were pink as she handed him the note. Wondering why, Daniel read:

A place of pages,
A subterranean secret,
Where love is shared.
One book brought you together.
Start from there.

He stared at the words. "One book brought *who* together? Who's this even for?"

Eleanor's blush had deepened to crimson, and she wasn't meeting his eyes. "Based on where Odile left it, I would guess . . . she meant me to find it. And since her message told you to talk to me, I would guess maybe she meant it for you, as well. *You* means us."

8

——

Then

February 16, 1995 (later)

Daniel's mother had drawn the library curtains halfway through the seminar meeting, perhaps to set the stage better for her grand presentation of *The Book of Dark Nights*. So he and Eleanor weren't expecting to emerge from Boylston Hall that evening straight into a snowstorm.

The weather was such a surprise that it felt magical. They looked at each other, snowflakes catching and sparkling in their hair, and Eleanor's smile held nothing back this time.

She likes being with me, Daniel thought.

Soft, muffling flakes fell steadily as they walked, and there was no wind. This time, he accompanied her all the way down to her own House by the river.

He'd been planning to spend the evening hanging in the suite with Drew, whose mom had recently been diagnosed with breast cancer. But now those plans drifted away, and he promised himself he'd catch up with Drew later. He couldn't bear to end whatever had started when his eyes met Eleanor's over the Book this afternoon.

The silence between them was comfortable, and he let Eleanor be the one to break it. "I thought about what you said last week," she said. "About not needing a book to tell you who you are."

Daniel's own words sounded juvenile when she quoted them to him—especially now, after he'd seen and touched *the* Book. "I didn't really mean it that way," he said. "I just don't love it when my mom chooses books for me. Do you know she's been doing it since I was nine? Sometimes I feel like she's inside my head."

They'd reached the Dunster entryway, the House a featureless hulk in the snow. Daniel asked, "Wanna go a little farther? Along the river?"

Eleanor nodded, and he could tell she felt what he did—the warmth growing between them, like a newly caught fire eating away at its first log.

Snowflakes flew fast on Mem Drive, driven in the wake of whizzing cars. The city's grime vanished under the snow. They had to dash across, and when they were safely on the river side and had caught their breath, Eleanor asked, "So what book did your mother give you on the first day of class, if she's been doing it all these years?"

"Are you going to use the theory to classify me? Don't bother. I already know she thinks I'm Self-Destructive," he said, trying to sound blasé about it all. "The book she gave me was *The Red and the Black*. Wait, why's that funny?"

They'd paused on the bridge, watching snow fall on the color-coded cupolas of the Houses—red Dunster, blue Lowell, aquamarine Eliot. Eleanor ducked her head, so he got only a glimpse of her suddenly beaming face. "It's just . . . well, the first time I saw you, back in freshman year, I was reading that same book. You wouldn't remember."

Daniel didn't recall ever seeing her before the seminar, but he wasn't going to admit that. "Did you like it? Me, I kinda think Julien Sorel is a weepy tool."

Eleanor reacted as if he'd insulted a close friend. "He's not weepy! He's angry. He's an abused peasant determined to succeed in a society that's set up to screw him over. His family treats him like garbage, like a changeling, because he'd rather read than chop wood. He knows there are good things out there in life, and he wants them."

Daniel was a little shocked by the vehemence with which she glared up at him—and a little turned on, as if *he* were the one she was defending instead of a fictional character. "I see what you mean," he admitted, resolving to give the book another chance. "But the romance part is all fucked up. First he's with the mayor's wife, who's old enough to be his *mom*, and then he's trying to seduce a rich girl."

Eleanor gazed into the dark water that roiled below them and swallowed the snowflakes. "He has feelings for both of them. He tries to be cold and manipulative—Ruthless—but he isn't good at it. When you come from nothing, you have to invent yourself, and often you make a mess of it."

There was a slight throb in her voice, a tenderness in the way she shaped the words, that gave Daniel an impulse to throw his arms around her. Was that how she saw him? Or was she the one who was inventing herself?

"I guess that explains why *The Red and the Black* is my mom's favorite book. She invented herself, too." The phrase resonated, but he didn't dare to probe into Eleanor's past—or to admit that he felt the same need to create himself from nothing. A boy without a country, without a father.

It was easier to talk about his mother than himself. "She always says she never felt at home anywhere until she studied at the Sorbonne. When her friend found the Book, and the four of them confessed to it—her, Marc, Juliette, and my dad—it was like they made their own family. Using the Book bonded them for life."

As they crossed busy Soldiers Field Road, Eleanor turned away from Daniel, and she kept her face averted as they wandered through the business school campus, the buildings fuzzy humps in the night.

"What?" he asked her.

When she looked back at him, he could tell she was perplexed. "When the professor was talking about the Book today, she said Theuthet and three of his students used it. One student was her, and you mentioned two other names. Was there another? Your dad?"

Daniel's breath caught as he realized he'd made a stupid slip. He racked his brain for an explanation, but the truth was, he didn't want to lie to Eleanor.

"No, my father wasn't a student." He sighed. "My father was—is—the professor. Julien Theuthet."

For a few minutes, they walked in silence, retracing their steps across the white-blanketed park to the bridge, tears of melting snow running down their cheeks. "That seems like a strange thing for Odile to leave out of her story," Eleanor said at last, and Daniel could tell she'd chosen the words carefully.

One of the first things he'd ever learned was never to tell anyone his father's name. That entry on his birth certificate was blank. But the secrecy was his mother's idea, and now that he'd told Eleanor, suddenly he found himself aching to explain.

Because the bridge was dark, and she couldn't see his face, he let it all pour out. How his father had a wife and four daughters who knew nothing about him. How Odile had promised they would never disturb the great professor's *real* family.

The first time Daniel ever met his father, he was four or five, crying and fretting in a gloomy room of the Harvard Faculty Club while a strange man plied him with pastries and toys. *This is your papa!* his mother insisted in a whisper. *He's giving you presents. Smile for him!* When he hid his face in her coat, trying to escape back into the private world they shared, a world where she loved him and only him, his mother had apologized to this stranger.

He heard Eleanor's sharp intake of breath—not shock but sympathy. "How are things when you see him now?"

"He's fine." Daniel struggled to describe a man he barely knew. "Polite, considerate, asks the right questions." *Gives good presents on birthdays and Christmas.* "He's just not *there*. But to her, he's everything."

Daniel always knew when his mother was talking to his father on the phone by the way she caressed each word, practically crooning it—no longer the strict, lecturing professor but a woman speaking to her lover, eager to do anything he asked of her.

All because of the Book. According to Odile, it had brought her and Julien closer and turned their student-teacher relationship into a romance that transformed their lives. She believed the Book had somehow predicted their love, Daniel's existence, the library—all of it.

Eleanor didn't speak until they had left the bridge and crossed Mem Drive. Then she reached out and caught Daniel's hand in the dark. "It was worth it, then, if it all led to you."

He squeezed her hand. "I'm not sure I even believe in fate. I mean, when I touched the Book today, I felt power for sure. But maybe it's all just chaos and randomness. The power of chance."

"Maybe it's neither fate nor randomness," Eleanor said softly. "Our choices matter, don't you think?"

They were at the Dunster entryway again, but she didn't tug her hand from his. "If you want to come up, there's a coffee maker in my suite. My roommate's gone for the break."

***

They didn't end up drinking any coffee. The first time Daniel bent to kiss Eleanor, his long lashes were still dusted with snow. When he said, "I've been wanting to do this," his voice was thick with emotion.

"So have I," she whispered.

Eleanor thought about the Fates, who measured each human life and decided whether its arc would trend up or down. Because they had cut short her sister's thread and left her feeling responsible, she second-guessed every gift from them. When Daniel brushed a lock of damp hair from her forehead and swept her into his arms, she knew he might end up hurting her.

But every instant with him was worth it, so she made a choice that sent her down a new pathway. She let herself melt into him.

And later, as they lay entwined under her comforter while the snowy world wended its way toward dawn, she didn't regret a thing.

Now

September 26, 2019, 3:01 p.m.

Together Eleanor and Daniel gazed down at the sticky note covered with Odile's "doggerel." From their perch at the top of Boylston Hall, the sounds of traffic in the Square came to them distant and disembodied, as if the library were a secret garden. As if all of Harvard were.

> *A place of pages,*
> *A subterranean secret,*
> *Where love is shared.*
> *One book brought you together.*
> *Start from there.*

There were many "places of pages" in Eleanor's life. *The Book of Dark Nights* had brought her and Daniel together, but since it was missing, she couldn't very well *start from there*. Maybe Odile was referring to *The Red and the Black*? One night when the two of them were tipsy on sherry, Eleanor had gotten sentimental and told Odile all about the role of that novel in her ill-fated relationship with Daniel.

She'd better figure it out, because Daniel was staring expectantly at her, clearly hoping she could decode Odile's coy hints and secure his inheritance.

He was still the boy she'd given her heart to. Older, yes. But every confident step, every volatile flash of his eyes or expressive arch of his brows, revived painfully vivid memories. She felt as if she'd been straining her ears all this time for the particular throb of his voice on the low notes, seeking it in other men—dates, podcasters, randoms on the street—but finding an exact match only in her dreams.

Meanwhile, to him, she was a stranger.

Eleanor had been reluctant to believe Odile when she said Daniel remembered almost nothing about her. But now she could see for herself. There was no recognition in his dark eyes, none of the awkwardness she felt on her side, no intense curiosity about how she had turned out.

"I think your mother's referring to a book we discussed in the seminar. A book that brought us together," she said, hoping he would think she meant *all the students* and not *us two.* "I'm not sure what she means by a *subterranean secret,* but the photo shows Dunster House Library, which is certainly a place of pages."

They'd shared love in Dunster House, too, but he didn't need to know that.

Daniel's eyes lit up. "So maybe she hid the Book there? Could we go check?"

"Of course, we can look there." Eleanor scooped up the sticky note and crumpled it into her pocket. Then she went to lock up the office, feeling very aware of his gaze following her. "But knowing your mother, I doubt it's that easy. She liked her puzzles and secrets."

"I knew you'd be able to help," Daniel said as she led him to the door.

He sounded so grateful—the way one would feel toward a stranger, without any baggage. Eleanor wanted to scream. His bland friendliness hurt more than she had ever imagined it would. Instead, she made a special effort to be breezy and kind to him as they walked downstairs. *Normal.*

Their route took them past the bulk of Widener, through the gate in the red brick wall that enclosed the Yard, across Mass Ave toward the river. It was the exact same way they'd walked on the snowy night in 1995, the first time they slept together.

"How long have you worked in the library?" Daniel asked her, still making small talk.

"Twelve years. And before that, I did my doctoral coursework here with your mother."

He whistled. "Now, that's commitment."

Commitment . . . or lack of real options. Eleanor didn't tell him how she'd tried to leave back in 2004, taking a teaching job in Cleveland that didn't require a completed dissertation. Independence had felt good. But the place was bleak compared with Cambridge, and she was expected to lecture to gigantic classes of students who were fulfilling a requirement and had no interest in literature.

Three years in, she'd received a call from Odile—in a panic, sounding utterly unlike her normally controlled self, because an old friend had visited and made some alarming demands. Odile sounded older, too, quavering as she said, *I worry about what will happen to the library when I'm gone.*

Eleanor flew to Cambridge on her next break and stayed with Odile for a week, keeping her company. She hadn't realized how much she'd missed the Library of Fates. By the end of her visit, she was looking at rentals in Arlington and Somerville. That spring, she quit the job and said goodbye to a sweet but uninspiring man she'd met online. Though she told her colleagues she was returning to Harvard for dissertation research, she no longer felt motivated to finish her degree. She packed up everything and returned to Odile's world, determined to help keep it intact.

Some people, she knew, might see this choice as defeat. But to her it felt like coming home. Once you had wielded the power of the library, giving people the books they needed, how could you ever be satisfied with the tired flatness of ordinary life?

She'd always wanted to teach the seminar in the Library of Fates, while Odile had resisted giving up any control. But after some haggling, they worked out a coteaching arrangement: Eleanor graded the essays and delivered most of the lectures, and Odile made dramatic entrances and exits and introduced students to *The Book of Dark Nights*.

"When's the memorial again?" Daniel asked as they crossed Mount Auburn Street. "I'm supposed to return the Book to the library by then."

"Monday." That gave them just four days, counting today, and a week until Eleanor was expected to use the Book to coax a donation out of Belinda Ratliff.

She wondered if Daniel remembered that the library's power could do more than just meet people's needs. It could persuade people, change people, in subtle ways and occasionally less subtle ones.

Back in college, he hadn't been happy about that at all.

They'd left the larger streets behind and were snaking their way toward the river. "Did Mom tell *you* she had a heart condition?" Daniel asked. "Because I didn't know."

Eleanor shook her head, though she'd had her suspicions. Odile was forever popping pills with her tea. "Your mother didn't like to admit when she was weak. If she told anyone, it was probably Liliana."

"She asked me to come home this past summer." Daniel's brows lowered, his eyes glittering with anger mixed with undeniable grief. "I told her I couldn't. It's my busy season."

You never wanted to come home anyway. For twenty-four years he hadn't crossed the Atlantic, and Eleanor imagined he had his reasons.

"But now I wonder," Daniel continued, "if I had, would she have told me she was sick like a normal person, instead of creeping around and hiding her possessions? Would she have given me and Sandrine a chance to say goodbye?" He came to a standstill. "Eleanor, was my mom even in her right mind?"

Eleanor was very aware of his height and the span of his shoulders. She heard mourning in his ragged voice, regrets that were perhaps akin to her own. When he left the US, he'd been eager to escape his mother's control. But she doubted he'd ever entirely lost the need for Odile that he'd had as a small, fatherless boy.

"Yes." She hoped the assurance would set his mind at rest. "I didn't know about her heart, Daniel, but I would have known if she wasn't mentally all there. I never saw her less than fully sharp and alert, and I saw her often. The morning of the day she died, in fact."

"But why that note, then? I don't understand any of this!"

"I don't either—most of it."

For example, why would Odile say that Daniel's survival depended on keeping the Book out of anyone else's hands? That seemed melodramatic. So was *We allowed it to read us. We are all captive to its pages.* The words chilled Eleanor, reminding her of dreams in which she was imprisoned in a cathedral-like space with a throng of shadowy people, only some of whom she recognized.

Whenever she saw that crowd in her dreams, Daniel was part of it. She could never speak directly to him or make contact, but she heard his voice sometimes, and his presence was unmistakable. She wondered if she appeared in his dreams, too.

He hadn't denied having them when she asked, back in the library.

There was the small red dome and spire of Dunster, rising above Cambridge's forest of red bricks, reminding her of their shared past again. It seemed almost cruel of Odile to drive them together this way—but maybe Odile had thought she was doing a good thing for both of them.

Eleanor said half to herself, "Odile wanted us to work together. She wanted me to give you insights into yourself."

"Insights!" Daniel laughed, perhaps at the lofty language. "I can always use those. What did Mom use to say—that I'm Self-Destructive?"

Even in recent years, Odile had spoken to Eleanor of her son as a tragic figure, like some haunted fugitive from an existentialist novel. *He is a willfully unfinished story, like so many Self-Destructive people*, she'd say. *Distracting himself with childish pursuits, postponing his inevitable crisis, his dénouement. Like Proust without the genius.*

Crisis, dénouement—Odile always talked about people as if they were literary characters. Personally, Eleanor thought Daniel had mellowed with age. He didn't have the sarcastic edge she remembered, the neurotic desire for attention. When he spoke of his daughter, you heard the commitment in every word.

He was better off without Eleanor. Back in 1995, when she and Odile had discussed Daniel's reasons for leaving, they'd agreed on this point, even if a small, stubborn part of Eleanor had tugged her in a different direction.

She wasn't meant to be part of his story, nor he part of hers. Yet here they were again, still living out the consequences of his very first theft of the book, so many years ago.

10

THEN

February 23, 1995

Seeing and handling *The Book of Dark Nights* could never be enough for Daniel. He needed to know why his mother had made it the centerpiece of her life, to understand the unbreakable bond between her and his father that seemed to have no room for him. He needed to write in it.

His new closeness to Eleanor had distracted him, wrapping him in a pleasant haze, but soon his determination resurfaced. After the next class meeting, while Eleanor was busy finding books to help the others improve their essay grades, he slipped into his mother's office. She'd left it unlocked.

The office was little bigger than a closet, with one heavy desk, two filing cabinets, and the safe wedged between them. Daniel knelt beside it, knowing the code was his birth date.

He felt the power of the library throbbing in the walls around him as Eleanor drew on it, bringing another student the book they needed.

Now he knew his mother wasn't the only one who could use the power. Given how tightly she liked to control her little realm, she might not be happy with Eleanor playing her role, but he wasn't going to tell her.

Maybe their new status should remain a secret, too, from his mom and even from the others. He could just imagine the comments Will would make—and Odile would be even more intrusive. He didn't need her advice on his love life.

As he entered his birthday on the fancy electronic keypad, it occurred to him that he'd never told a girl the truth about his father before that night. Even Drew didn't know. It was easier just to shrug and say *My dad's out of the picture* rather than admit that his parents were very much in the same picture, but he didn't fit in the frame.

From the library, he heard scattered applause as Eleanor placed a book in someone's hands. "Woo-hoo!" Will said.

Will and April still didn't take the power seriously, Daniel suspected. They thought Eleanor was simply skilled at channeling his mother's preconceptions about them. But Genevra seemed awed by the process. And Drew had admitted to Daniel that Eleanor's choice for him—Simone de Beauvoir's memoir about witnessing the death of her mother—had struck him as a disturbingly apt fit when, a few days later, he'd learned of his own mother's diagnosis. At first the book had made him angry. It seemed like a bad omen. But as he read, Drew realized that facing his worst fears made the future less daunting.

Daniel wondered how it would feel to contemplate his own mother's possible imminent demise. Drew's mom was open and loving, offering her children unconditional acceptance. Daniel couldn't imagine Odile doing anything but critiquing him, even on her deathbed, but she still deserved his love, didn't she?

Once he got away and had a life of his own, things would work themselves out between them. But first, the Book.

"What're you doing in there, Danny-boy?" Will yelled in his annoying way.

"Just a sec!" The lock's mechanism whirred. A red light turned green.

The safe door opened with a tug, and there sat the three-hundred-year-old book, all by itself in the shadows of the steel box. Light glinted on the raised golden bands of its spine, and again Daniel felt that urge to hold it.

He grasped it very carefully, electricity shivering through his fingertips, and brought it back into the library to show the others.

***

As Daniel placed *The Book of Dark Nights* on the table, he looked straight at Eleanor, and a tickling warmth spread from her cheeks down her chest. In the week since *that night*, they'd met for muffins at the Italian bakery and held hands, and they'd had two long, intimate phone conversations. He hadn't treated her any differently from the others in class today, and she'd followed his lead. But now she knew something about him that no one else in this room did—that Theuthet was his father. That his parents had fallen in love over the Book.

Daniel sat down and beckoned the rest of them to cluster around him. They all obeyed, yet Eleanor felt a twinge of misgiving. She wished he'd told her he was planning to sneak the Book out of the safe, and she wasn't ready to confess in front of the others. Odile had suggested the Book couldn't be read, but what did that even mean? More importantly, she wasn't sure *what* to confess anymore. At first, her guilt over Renée's death had seemed like the obvious thing. But for the Book's prediction to be meaningful, maybe she needed to confess something she had done on purpose, knowing it was wrong.

Daniel opened the Book with great care, the way the professor had. Gazing down at the first handwritten page, he said solemnly, "It's true what she said. You can't read other people's confessions."

Will and April elbowed each other to get a good look, while Eleanor hung back. She watched as Daniel leafed slowly through the pages and the others peered down at them, clearly struggling to decipher the confessions of the living and the long dead.

When April stepped away, looking unnerved, Eleanor took her place and saw that most of the Book was already full of writing. The early pages were marked with what looked like a quill pen, their original black faded to rust. She squinted, but the archaic scribbles refused to resolve themselves into recognizable words. On the later pages, the handwriting turned to ballpoint, and Eleanor spotted the professor's familiar cursive. She had no problems reading Odile's handwritten comments on her papers, but this was different. From a distance, she could swear she glimpsed familiar letters and words, yet they dissolved when she got closer. It wasn't another alphabet; it wasn't inverted. It simply refused to be read.

Her heart fluttered, and the handwriting swam before her eyes. The Book was just as magic as the library, maybe more. Who had created the Book, she wondered suddenly, and how had it been lost all those years?

Genevra was frowning. "I could swear I see letters, and then I *don't*."

"We're just spooking ourselves," Will said. "I'm gonna write something in there to prove we *can* read it."

"Ooh, yes! Confess something!" Genevra cried, nudging him. Those two had been getting closer, Eleanor had noticed.

Will reached for the Book, but Daniel tugged it away from him. "I stole it from her safe," he said firmly. "I go first."

As he spoke, he glanced at Eleanor again. The contact was brief, but she sensed his anticipation—and his reassurance that if she wanted it, she would have the next turn.

She still wasn't sure, but Daniel's quiet excitement was contagious. *This is the start of something for us*, she found herself thinking as he lowered his eyes and turned to a blank page. *The real first chapter of our story.*

After all, the Book had brought them together last week. If they hadn't both felt the life inside it, they might never have walked in the snowstorm at all.

There were twenty or so blank pages at the end. *Let me read you*, each said. While Daniel bent low over a page and wrote, Will babbled in his usual way. "I did a little research on this Duchess of Berry who used to pass the Book around at her parties. She dropped dead at twenty-three, but she did a lot of living first, and I'm talking about scandalous living. Voltaire went to prison for starting a rumor that she was pregnant by her own father."

"It's like an eighteenth-century royal soap opera," Genevra said, "and we're just nobodies. What are we even supposed to confess?"

"Sins," Drew suggested. "Dark nights of the soul. Next to the duchess's, ours will be like parking violations."

Eleanor stood a few paces off, trying not to stare as Daniel's pen scratched across the rough, ancient paper. Was he confessing about meaningless hookups, the way he'd said he would? Or did he have deeper and darker secrets she didn't know about?

After no more than a minute, Daniel set the pen down. "Well, *I* can still read it. Can any of you?"

Eleanor stayed where she was, her throat tightening because she did and didn't want to know. But April, who was closest to Daniel, bent over the page. "How'd you do that?" she asked.

The others were scrutinizing the page, too. "It's like the other confessions." There was a note of awe in Will's voice. "Unreadable."

Drew reminded them, "Only the people who wrote them can read them."

He looked very serious. So did Daniel as he said, "Notice exactly how much I wrote. Four lines."

A humming rose in Eleanor's ears that seemed to come from everywhere—the bookshelves, the walls—and drowned out their voices. It made her think of bumblebees in her mom's garden on a sunny day. A pleasant, sleepy, satisfied sound.

Maybe Daniel heard it, too, because he tugged the Book away from the others' eager hands and picked it up.

Eleanor could swear she heard words deep in the humming—almost distinct, almost human, but not quite. Her brain shaped them into something that made sense: *Close me. Let me read you. Open me again.*

Feeling as if she might be dreaming this whole scene, she watched Daniel close the Book, press it briefly against his chest, and shut his eyes. Before she had time to wonder if he also heard and was obeying that humming command, he opened the Book again.

He placed it down on the table, so they could all see words on the page that hadn't been there before. The four lines of the confession, illegible yet recognizable as his handwriting, were now followed by a swarm of more unreadable words written in his exact same hand.

Eleanor breathed shallowly, cold prickling on the back of her neck.

All he did was shut the Book and open it. Though she'd used the library's magic herself, there was something especially uncanny about what they'd just witnessed. As if the Book had reached into Daniel's head and heart and used its intimate knowledge to impersonate him.

"Still can't read it, can you?" Daniel's face was calm, but he bit off the words as if he were unsettled, too.

"No." April looked queasy.

Will's features had frozen, as if he'd realized he would never manage to make a joke out of this.

"It's evil," Genevra said softly.

"It doesn't feel that way. But that's some *X-Files* shit right there." A deep furrow had appeared in Drew's brow.

Softly, wanting an answer to her question and fearing it at the same time, Eleanor asked, "Can *you* read the prediction, Daniel?"

Daniel nodded, then read aloud in the cadence of poetry:

"Let us alone. What is it that will last?
<u>All things</u> are taken from us, and become
Portions and parcels of the dreadful past."

"'All things' is underlined," he added as he looked up at them.

The humming was fading. But Eleanor still felt as if reality had shifted and mutated in the library when Daniel left a piece of himself between those pages.

Will stepped back from the table, tugging Genevra with him, an arm around her waist. "I'm never writing in that fucking thing. It's alive."

His voice was huskier than normal, and it took Eleanor a moment to realize why. He was afraid. They all were.

***

That night, Daniel dreamed he was in his mother's office again, opening the safe.

But this time there was only emptiness inside. *The Book of Dark Nights* was gone, and a piece of him with it. He'd barely noticed the constant vibration at the heart of the library, steady as his own pulse, until it went still.

Now the world was panic. Nothing made sense, walls swelling and floors billowing like something out of a Dalí painting. When he glanced at his watch, the hands were spinning wildly. He couldn't draw a full breath or form a thought.

A strange girl appeared beside him. She was small and wispy like Eleanor, but she wore a skirt and laced-up bodice, her hair caught under a grubby kerchief. She latched on to him with cold, sharp-tipped fingers, her foul breath wafting in his face, and croaked out words: *Find it, get it back, keep it safe.*

Daniel ripped himself free of her and pounded down three flights of stairs into the Yard, which was deserted under a black sky marbled with strange golden clouds. He had no idea where the Book could be. But it had to be somewhere—someone must have stolen it—so he kept running . . .

And woke to find himself sitting straight up in bed, dripping with sweat, pulse racing. It took him a moment to realize he was safe in his room in Randolph Hall.

Just a dream. It was almost dawn, delivery trucks rumbling in the wintry distance. He reminded himself that his parents and their friends had all confessed to the Book with no ill effects.

They'd become part of something larger. And now he was, too.

11

Now

September 26, 2019, 3:53 p.m.

Daniel hadn't lived in Dunster House when he was at Harvard. But as they entered its library, with its two-story windows facing the river, he remembered admiring this place. Glossy, golden-brown bookshelves rose far above their heads. A chandelier scattered light on tall window bays, carved garlands and pillars, tables and armchairs.

Music drifted from a grand piano by the windows—a Chopin nocturne, played so quietly and meditatively that the students bent over their laptops seemed undisturbed by the notes that tumbled like raindrops through the sunlight. Back in his undergrad days, Daniel used to meet a friend in this library—who? That detail was fuzzy, but he thought there'd often been a pianist playing Chopin in a similar quiet way.

Eleanor strode briskly to the back wall and stood on tiptoe to examine the book spines. "We'll need the ladder."

One book brought you together. / Start from there, Odile had written in her "doggerel." Earlier, in the library, Eleanor had suggested the lines referred to a book they'd read in the seminar, one that had brought the class together. But Daniel only remembered them all reading different books, following their separate threads of textual potential.

Luckily, Eleanor's memory was better than his. He could see why his mother used to call her a "little mouse." She had a dry, academic vibe, in her sober skirt and turtleneck and boots, but the toss of her shimmering hair and the shy glints of her eyes hinted at something more under the surface. If she'd been one of his clients, he would have felt confident in her ability to cling to a slope through sheer determination, and he might have been a little curious about how she'd be in bed.

Not an appropriate thought, he chided himself. He was here to secure his daughter's inheritance, not to hit on his mother's successor. And if he'd glimpsed a girl with hair like hers in his dreams—well, dreams meant nothing.

Glad to have something to do, he found a stepladder attached to a rail at about head height and slid it over to Eleanor.

The music broke off abruptly, mid-measure, as if the grating of the ladder had disturbed the player. Daniel saw the pianist staring at them from his bench, owlishly startled: a small man with horn-rimmed glasses on his nose and a few tufts of gray hair, wearing a faded flannel and jeans as if to blend in with the much younger people around him.

Eleanor was looking at the pianist, too. But she only said, "You hold, I'll climb" so authoritatively that Daniel obeyed, though climbing things was his forte, not hers.

She scaled the ladder until her feet were at his eye level. When she held on with one hand and craned dangerously out to remove a book with the other, Daniel had to remind himself she wasn't a client he was guiding up a perilous slope.

He was relieved to hear that Eleanor thought Odile had been in her right mind when she died, yet that only made his mother's message more mysterious. And it bothered him that he couldn't remember Eleanor when she obviously remembered him. His well-practiced friendly small talk hadn't warmed her up. She seemed to be holding herself aloof from him on purpose, her sidelong glances freighted with meanings he couldn't decode.

She was paging through the book she'd selected, propping it on the rung she was holding. "Which book?" Daniel asked, hoping the title would spark memories.

A subtle scraping noise made him turn for a quick survey of the library. Students were peacefully typing at tables and napping in armchairs. But the pianist who'd been watching them was gone.

Eleanor's gaze was tight on the book. "*The Red and the Black*," she said as if divulging a secret. "Not your favorite, was it?"

"Not really." Daniel recalled plowing through Stendhal's realist classic, which his mother adored. A book about a boy with no family, a boy who had to invent himself.

He watched her flick pages, wishing he could ask her to tighten her grip on the ladder without being patronizing. But then her face brightened. "Oh yes. Odile's been here!"

"Could she have hidden the Book next to Stendhal?" Daniel suggested. But Eleanor didn't seem to deem this worthy of a response. While she shut *The Red and the Black* and returned it to its spot, he scanned the shelf for the distinctive raised golden bands on the Book's spine.

He recalled the Book having a special feeling to it, a

charge that was palpable even when you weren't making physical contact. But he suspected all his memories of it were heightened by his own youthful excitement and naïveté. He'd been so eager to believe in the magic, so avidly curious about this artifact that had always been his rival for his mother's affections.

After Drew died, Daniel had renounced that curiosity. The promise of a glimpse of the future had spun him and his classmates in circles and turned them against each other. It was safer and more sane to live in the present.

Motion on the ladder caught his eye. Eleanor was descending again. She was halfway down when her boot slipped on a rung, and he darted in to grab her around the waist, saving her from a fall.

She went still immediately, every muscle rigid under his hands. Through the thick knit of her sweater, Daniel felt her trembling.

There's something wrong here. Once she had her footing again, he quickly released her and stepped clear. It was a stupid thing to be bothered by, he knew, but women didn't usually react that way to his touch. They trusted him.

What does she remember that I don't? Did I hurt her?

When Eleanor reached solid ground, her expression was composed—perhaps too much so. She reached out, and for an instant Daniel expected to be slapped. But she only thrust something in his face: a saffron-colored sticky note stapled to a photo that looked clipped from a magazine.

The image showed a gracefully arched brick footbridge across the Charles River, one Daniel knew he'd traversed in the past. The note, like the one Eleanor had found in the library office, bore a message in his mother's distinctive handwriting:

My Creed is Love and you are its only tenet-You have ravish'd me away by a Power I cannot resist.

"Does that mean anything to you?" he asked. *Where love is shared*, the other note had said. There was a theme here, even if it perplexed him.

"It's John Keats. A letter to the woman he was obsessed with, Fanny Brawne." Eleanor held her gaze pointedly averted as she led him back to the door by which they'd entered. "I wonder what that has to do with the footbridge, though?"

Outside the library, a hall brought them to the landing of a wide stairway. Sunlight from a high window momentarily blinded Daniel, darkening the stairwell's shadows by contrast.

"Mom can't have hidden the Book on a bridge—too much traffic," he said as they started down. He tried to imagine his mother poking around the brick span. If anything, the Book seemed frustratingly further away now, caught in the web of Odile's mysterious clues.

Deep in these thoughts, he nearly plowed into a slight figure who stood at the bend of the stairs, directly in their path. It was the pianist from the library.

"Nice playing," Daniel said, attempting to detour around him. But the small man darted backward and blocked their way down.

"Daniel Vernet, isn't it?" he said with a disturbingly avid expression, as if he'd been waiting to ambush Daniel. "Back after all these years to bury your mother. I warned you not to write in that Book, but you didn't listen. I hope you plan to do something about it now."

12

—

THEN

February 24, 1995

Since the snowstorm, Daniel and Eleanor had often walked at night, with or without a destination. It was still too cold to pause anywhere for long, but the darkness of Cambridge's narrow streets and alleys hid them from observers. She liked seeing his breath mist, holding his gloved hand, inhaling the faint musk from his wool coat, absorbing the vibrations of his voice.

The day after Daniel's confession to the Book, they wandered past the towering brick spire of St. Paul's Parish and the darkened storefronts of Mount Auburn Street, past Eliot House, down to the red roofs of the Boathouse looming over the silent river, and then back up the hill. Daniel was talking about places he wanted to explore—the Andes, Angkor Wat, the piney wilderness of Vancouver Island. This summer, the Alps; after graduation, the world.

"You don't want to go to grad school?" Eleanor asked. She was dreading senior year, when she would have to cement her future plans and acknowledge she couldn't afford to be an eternal student. But surely Daniel, with his mother's connections, had more options.

He laughed and squeezed her hand. "Not in a million years. I was hoping my prediction would be about travel. It did mention ditching the past, so that's something."

Am I part of your past? Will you ditch me? Eleanor had a feeling she wasn't built for travel the way Daniel was. All her life she'd only wanted a safe nest in which to curl up and read about adventures, like the library.

They were approaching the Lampoon Castle, their feet squelching in slush. Randolph Hall was just beyond. Shyly, hoping he'd invite her up to his suite, she said, "I've never seen *your* room."

"Soon! It's kinda a mess." After a moment, Daniel added, "Also, maybe we should keep this between us for now. Not tell other people in the seminar. What do you think?"

Eleanor's heart lurched. He didn't even want Drew to know. Was he ashamed of her?

She couldn't speak. But maybe Daniel sensed how his words had sounded to her, because he added, "You've seen how my mom is. She'd notice, and then we'd have to deal with her watching us like a hawk, every class. Trying to fit . . . *this* into her theory."

With a flush of relief, Eleanor saw his point. It would be awkward, and Odile might even think less of Eleanor for letting Daniel distract her from her studies. She longed to impress the forbidding professor on her own merits, not because she was involved with Odile's son.

She was about to concede he was right when a voice called out: "Daniel? Daniel Vernet?"

Both of them wheeled around, but the sidewalk was empty. It took Eleanor a moment to spot the glowing end of a cigarette above the steps leading to the Lampoon's clownish purple-and-yellow door.

A slight man sat smoking on the balustrade, his face in shadow. "You two come this way a lot," he said. "I've been watching."

Daniel's grip on Eleanor's hand tightened reassuringly, and she was glad she wasn't alone. "I think you're mistaking me for someone else," he said, then turned to walk on.

"Wait!" the stranger called, his voice low but penetrating. "Daniel, have you written in *The Book of Dark Nights* yet?"

Eleanor was shivering. As Daniel halted, he dropped her hand to wrap his arm around her waist, his warmth bleeding into hers. "Sorry, but who the hell are you?" he asked the stranger. "A friend of my mom's?"

"I used to be her student, actually." The small man hopped down from the balustrade and extended his hand. He looked even shorter on the ground, with a hunch to his shoulders, and Eleanor saw him better now—perhaps in his mid-thirties, with a grubby windbreaker and what looked like a fluffy mullet. "Emerson Carlyle, graduated '82," he said. "I attended one of the very first seminars in the Library of Fates. We met in '81 when I helped your mother move some boxes."

Eleanor gave Daniel a nudge. "It's okay! He's the piano player from Dunster," she whispered. Carlyle was something of a campus legend, having lived in Dunster House almost continuously since his undergrad years with the blessing of the administration. Though some students engaged him in conversations about music and art, Eleanor knew him only from a distance. She'd never imagined he was one of Odile's former students.

Daniel didn't accept Carlyle's hand. "I don't remember meeting you when I was seven, no. Why've you been *watching* us?"

Carlyle ignored the question. "Have you confessed yet?" he demanded again, tipping his head up, birdlike, to look into Daniel's eyes. "I was hoping to talk to you before you did. Warn you not to."

Eleanor felt Daniel's body tense against hers. There was something dreamlike about the whole encounter, with the whimsical turrets and gables of the Lampoon outlined above them against the stars. When Carlyle said those last words, his voice dropped to an ominous baritone, as if he'd planned to deliver the warning for a while.

He was one day too late.

"Why shouldn't we confess?" she found herself asking, recalling her own mixed feelings. How had Carlyle even known Daniel had a way into the safe?

Carlyle's head swiveled. His eyes fixed on Eleanor, surprisingly keen through the dark. "The dreams," he said.

"Dreams?"

Daniel swung Eleanor around, his grip still firm around her waist. "He's got problems," he whispered in her ear as he tried to march them both down the street.

But Carlyle was still talking, words pouring out of him as if he seldom had an audience. "Odile told us we weren't ready to confess to the Book," he was saying. "Not enough self-knowledge, she said. And then one day after class, she left the office door open and the Book out where we could get it. *Accidentally*, we all thought."

And you couldn't resist. Suddenly Eleanor wondered if Odile had deliberately programmed the safe with a code Daniel could guess.

"Three of us confessed that night, out of seven," Carlyle continued, even as Daniel tried to pry Eleanor away. She resisted. "We were just kids like you. We thought we were rebelling. We had no idea it was exactly what our professor wanted."

"Why?" Eleanor wrenched herself free of Daniel, momentarily forgetting everything but her need to understand. "Why would she want students to confess?"

"To power the library, of course." Carlyle's index finger drew a shaky circle in the air. "The library has no power without the Book, and the Book has no power without fresh confessions from young, impressionable minds." His voice had gone singsong, as if he were reciting a lesson. "So now you know, and you won't do it, will you? Either of you? A glimpse of the future isn't worth it."

The library has no power without the Book. Eleanor had felt the connection between the two herself, the similar vibration, but it hadn't occurred to her until now that confessions were somehow *required.* Or that Odile could have manipulated her students.

Ice tickled her spine, and she decided Carlyle was being paranoid. He might be right about the power's source, but she couldn't imagine Odile telling bald-faced lies.

"For every prediction, there's a price," Carlyle called as Daniel led her away, sounding more unhinged than ever. "Every one of us who confessed in that class, we still dream about the Book to this day."

13

——

Now

September 26, 2019, 4:28 p.m.

"I warned you not to write in that Book, but you didn't listen," the pianist said to Daniel. "I hope you plan to do something about it now."

Emerson Carlyle. Until this moment, Daniel hadn't connected the man in front of him with the one who'd ambushed him on the street back in college. Time had blurred the details of that encounter—had he been alone? But he couldn't forget Carlyle's warning about nightmares, because it had come true.

Eleanor seemed even more familiar with Carlyle than he was. Before Daniel could say a word, she'd linked arms with the small man and drawn him to one side, as if he were merely a harmless eccentric. "Emerson, Daniel's jet-lagged, and he's on the trail of something for Odile's memorial. Could we talk another time? Will we see you there?"

Carlyle's watery blue eyes darted between them, and he

laughed in a dry, mirthless way. "You're asking if I'll attend the memorial of my revered former professor? The one who gave me nightmares that stunted my life?"

They aren't that *bad*, Daniel thought. *At least not for me.* As he traveled the world, the dreams had waxed and waned, sometimes not troubling him for months at a time. He had come to terms with them as a residue of his strange upbringing, which had led to his choice to confess to the Book and the unsettling, lingering sense of having left a piece of himself behind in its pages.

Carlyle was a special case: someone who blamed *The Book of Dark Nights* for everything that had gone wrong with his life.

Suddenly Odile's message made more sense. She could have been trying to hide the Book from Carlyle.

Daniel looked at Eleanor to see if she'd had the same thought, but she was still focused on the pianist. "Emerson, you know that's not true," she said patiently, as if the two of them had similar discussions in the past. "Dreams can't hurt you."

"So you always say! But she had her hooks in you, Eleanor." Carlyle tugged his arm from her grip, his tone sharpening. "Still Odile's loyal apprentice, aren't you?"

With two nimble steps, he dodged around Eleanor to confront Daniel, who backed away from his stink of tobacco smoke and perspiration. "*You* saw the danger, didn't you? Even if it was too late? When your roommate died, you knew the Book was to blame."

"Drew's death was a suicide," Daniel said, shaking his head. It still hurt to pronounce those words, because they brought back the chaotic events of that night in their suite. But he knew no book had pushed Drew off the balcony.

Carlyle's watery gaze had turned to ice. "No, Drew was obsessed with the Book. It got inside his head, and then it killed him."

Daniel opened his mouth to reply that Carlyle didn't know the first fucking thing about his friend. But Eleanor shot him a warning glance and stepped between them. "Daniel just lost his mother, Emerson. Please let him be."

She touched the man's arm. Carlyle winced like a startled animal, but the pinched expression of his blue eyes relaxed a little as she added, "Come to the library sometime soon and let me find you a book. You know it helps."

"It does. But Eleanor . . ."

"Later, Emerson. I promise." With a last soothing pat, she turned and continued downstairs. Daniel lowered his gaze and followed, hoping she'd defused the situation.

Carlyle wasn't done, though. He called down to them, "Remember your friend Genevra? Do you want to end up like her?"

Genevra. The brunette from their class, the one whose nightmares had so upset her. Daniel stopped in his tracks. "What do you mean?" he shouted back.

Eleanor was plucking at his sleeve, her expression telling him Carlyle wasn't going to start making any more sense. He ignored her. "Did something happen to Genevra?"

No answer came to them except the dull thuds of Carlyle's feet, retreating upstairs. For a moment, Daniel considered chasing the pianist and making him explain himself.

But Eleanor seemed determined to leave, so he followed her instead. Once they were outside in the street, he asked, "What did he mean about Genevra?" *How do I remember her and not you?*

"I saw Genevra just a year ago when she came here for a conference. She visited the library. Maybe she told Emerson something that set him off. I'm sorry," Eleanor added, leading him down Cowperthwaite Street, between Dunster and the brutalist bulk of Leverett Tower G. She seemed as baffled as he was, yet he sensed she was holding something back. "Emerson's okay generally, but he has these . . . fits sometimes. His old obsession coming back. I should have known to keep you away from him."

Golden sunlight slathered the faded bricks of the buildings and sidewalks, gilding Daniel's hometown into a tourist brochure. But the encounter had shaken him, sending images of Drew's death looping through his head.

"You were so patient with him," he said wonderingly. Carlyle had been dismissive of Eleanor, calling her his mom's *loyal apprentice*, but she hadn't seemed to mind. "Do you think he's the person my mom hid the Book from?"

Eleanor pointed across the roaring traffic of Memorial Drive at the glittering Charles River. "There's the footbridge from your mom's photo. See?"

When she halted and turned to face him, there was something hard about the set of her jaw. "If Carlyle were going to steal the Book, he would have done it long ago. He was never as bold as you were."

Was she there when I stole the Book? Daniel remembered placing his mother's treasure on the seminar table, proudly showing it to the others: April, Drew, Genevra, the boy in the suit.

When he focused on the memory, he could *almost* see Eleanor there, too: younger, staring at the Book with enormous eyes, feeling its power as strongly as he did.

"It's strange how easily I just slipped out of your mind after college," she said.

Daniel snapped out of the memory to find her gaze pressing on him, making him uncomfortable, her eyes full of secrets he couldn't fathom. That twist of her mouth—did it hint at regret?

He had too many questions. But before he could formulate them, she was turning away from him to greet a middle-aged bureaucrat type who was approaching briskly from the direction of Leverett House. "Will!"

Daniel froze, the name catapulting him back into the past again.

Will always wore a suit—they used to tease him mercilessly about it. He was still wearing one, but now it looked more expensive, and he had salt-and-pepper hair and an obsequiously polite grin.

He greeted Daniel with a hug and a clap on the back. "Danny! I was hoping I'd see you before the memorial. I'm so sorry about your mom, man. It's been too long."

He always called me Danny, and I never liked it, but I let it pass. He always says "man," and it always sounds ridiculous from him. Daniel felt a brief flood of nostalgia as he stepped out of the hug. Will had been a friend—not remotely as close as Drew, but someone who made him laugh.

Will had been there when Drew died. Carlyle hadn't, which made his claims about Daniel blaming the Book all the more absurd.

"I'm late for a drink with donors at the business school," Will said, gesturing with his briefcase toward the river, "but let's touch base tomorrow or the next day. It's been too long!"

Daniel nodded and smiled. The forced sociability grated on him. As soon as he had a minute, he decided, he would do a little research on Genevra. Then he would message April Carraway, the only person from the seminar he'd kept in touch with, and see what she remembered about Eleanor—or, more precisely, about him and Eleanor. He couldn't ask Will with Eleanor right here.

Of course, he could also just ask Eleanor. But it would be mortifying to admit how thoroughly he'd forgotten her.

"Will's at the top of the Harvard pyramid now," Eleanor was telling him. "Associate Dean of Arts and Sciences. He's always having sherry with the dean or beers with the Fortune 500."

"Shut up! I'm still a nobody from Omaha who wears a suit well." Will gave Eleanor a teasing smack on the shoulder, suggesting a long acquaintance, and then hugged her—holding her a little longer than necessary, Daniel thought.

"See you both soon! Wish it hadn't taken something like this to get us back together, Danny!" Will released Eleanor and went off toward Mem Drive, his smart loafers tapping on the pavement, flashing Daniel the universal symbol for *Call me.*

Daniel was feeling hazy with jet lag again, and he wanted to touch base with April. "Shall we call it a day? Or do you want to, I don't know, explore that bridge? It doesn't seem like a *place of books* to me."

Eleanor had a curious expression on her face, as if she were trying to repress laughter or tears. "I just had an epiphany. Let's walk over to the business school. There's a bench there that . . . well, it's a place where love was shared, I guess you could say."

14

Then

March 3, 1995

Drew's voice rang out across the library. "Eleanor, please bring me the book I need."

Eleanor had been focused on Daniel, wondering why he was quiet today. The library's power caught her unawares, as if she were slipping abruptly from waking life into a dream.

She had no control over the shivers of electricity or the eerie, booming vibration filling the library, as all the books faded into one monochromatic mass. Energy funneled around her like wind or water, squeezing the breath from her lungs. Only one thing mattered: *Drew needs a book.*

Where was the current tugging her? She wouldn't know the title until she saw it, but she could tell already it would be another book about death. And that seemed almost unfair. Of course Drew was worried about his mom, but didn't he deserve a little relief from thoughts of the grave? A little distraction?

Without thinking, she did something she'd never tried before: She resisted the current. She pushed back.

There was an odd hitch or hesitation in the library's vibrations. Then Eleanor seemed to be caught in an eddy, her head whirling, panic strangling her breath. She'd made a mistake. The forces working on and through her felt so much older and stronger than she was—strong enough to rip her apart.

Focus! She thought of the Book in the safe. Carlyle had said the power emanated from there.

Finding a book was almost like giving someone a prediction. There were so many books here, so many potential pathways through life, each linking to other pathways. Surely she could find another one for Drew that was just as valid as the grief route she'd given him last time.

Where did one pathway become another pathway? At a turning point. Eleanor remembered the pivotal moment when she'd invited Daniel up to her room, a moment that had changed her life, and a thought popped into her head. *Love is the enemy of death. Love gives people hope.*

Just as she had Daniel, Drew should have someone to take his mind off his worries. The warm comfort of being close to someone. She summoned that feeling, and before she knew it, the whirling sensation was giving way to the flow of a new current. This time she yielded and let it carry her along.

Now she saw the exact book Drew needed, crystal clear on the shelf. Her legs carried her straight to it.

"This is the book you need," she said, placing it in his hands.

It took her a moment to return to herself. She still tingled with the rush of letting the power work through her and knowing she could also navigate it now, like a surfer who'd ridden an enormous wave to shore.

Will, April, and Genevra had dissolved in laughter, and shortly she realized why. The book she'd found for Drew was *The Idiot* by Fyodor Dostoevsky.

Drew guffawed, too. Eleanor tried to apologize, red spreading over her cheeks. How was that a romance? Had the library made a mistake, or was the power mocking her attempt to exert control over it?

Drew shushed her in his friendly way. "I bet it's not what you think," he told the others. "It's actually a book about someone who's smarter and wiser than all of you put together."

April wiped her eyes. "We'll see!"

Only then, when the others were distracted, did Eleanor dare to glance over at Daniel. Had he sensed anything different about the way she'd used the power this time?

He sat on the windowsill with his arms crossed, unsmiling and intent, as if she'd scared him a little.

***

The evening was unseasonably warm. Around midnight, they walked across the footbridge to the business school campus, just as they had the night of the snowstorm. It was nice to be in public yet know you wouldn't run into any acquaintances. On a backless concrete bench in the corner of a quiet quad, Eleanor read aloud to Daniel from Nietzsche's *The Gay Science*, which she'd been assigned for a Core class. He stretched out with his head in her lap, which distracted her so much she barely knew what she was reading.

As they walked back toward Dunster afterward, he finally brought up what had happened in the library earlier. "What did you do to Drew today? He's acting weird."

"I . . . found him a book." Eleanor didn't want to admit she'd tried to redirect the library's choice, especially since she wasn't even sure she'd succeeded.

"Yeah, and he skipped dinner to read! When I left, he was holed up in his room, smoking a bowl with his nose stuck in that *Idiot* book like it was actually interesting." Daniel was grinning, but there was worry in his tone. "Reading these dark books about death, philosophical books—maybe he shouldn't dwell on such heavy shit when he's already freaking out about his mom."

I tried to give him something different! But Eleanor feared she'd been messing with forces she couldn't comprehend, let alone harness to her will. "Reading books like that can be therapeutic," she pointed out.

"Right. Or maybe you brainwashed him. Turned my stoner friend into a Dostoevsky-loving goth."

Daniel said this in such a deadpan way that Eleanor looked sharply at him. But he laughed and swung an arm around her. "It's sexy when you use the power," he said, kissing her forehead. "Have I ever told you that? Just a little freaky, too."

A few hours later, in her room, he woke her by thrashing in his sleep. "*C'est pas juste, Mariane,*" he cried out angrily, elbowing her against the wall. "*Laisse-moi*—leave me alone!"

"Shh, it's okay." Eleanor hugged him close. "Just a dream."

Daniel opened his eyes, damp with sweat, shuddering in her embrace. "I thought . . . never mind."

She tried to calm him back to sleep, but he stayed wide awake. "When I confessed to the Book, I told it I don't know how to feel anything but hate in my heart for my father. I wish it weren't that way." He turned to her, a world of trouble in his eyes. "I shouldn't have written that."

"You were just being honest. Feelings can change." Eleanor kissed his throat. The fact that she could do this now, touch him this way, still gave her a dizzy thrill, but she was remembering uneasily what Carlyle had said about nightmares. "Do you often have dreams like that?"

"Like what? I've already forgotten it," Daniel said.

15

Now

September 26, 2019, 5:07 p.m.

Their bench was still there. Over the years, Eleanor had sometimes visited it on her runs, in a rarely frequented corner of the Harvard Business School campus. She'd watched as the slender silver birch above it rained down leaves each fall. She'd seen it hedged in by snowbanks and bordered by pink-and-white tulips and golden mums. The rough concrete slabs of the bench's seat and legs seemed to darken a shade each year, but it had changed in no other appreciable way.

In her mind, the bench still belonged to her and Daniel—but not this Daniel. The Daniel who would have remembered her.

"What are we looking for?" Daniel asked. He sat down on the bench and glanced around at the surrounding buildings, the empty paths. Then he bent to peer into the narrow space between the seat and the ground. "You think she could've hidden the Book here?"

Eleanor stood where she was on the aggressively mown grass. "Maybe the Book. Maybe another clue."

In her memory, it was a March night in 1995. Moonlight shone through gauzy clouds. She sat on one end of the bench with that paperback of Nietzsche's *The Gay Science*, reading passages aloud. He lay with his head in her lap. The seat was uncomfortable and the position awkward, but she didn't want to move.

When they left, she'd tucked the book under the bench so it would belong to that moment forever, at least in her mind. It was still there when they returned a few days later, so she'd pulled it out and kept reading. Three times she'd done that. Then had come the cold snap and Drew's death, and she'd never looked for the book again.

Her clues are about us. First the book that had brought them together. Then the place where they'd shared both love and a book.

But how had Odile known about the bench? It seemed unlikely that Daniel had told her, and Eleanor was sure the subject had never come up in their conversations.

Then it occurred to her. Her novel. Eleanor had put the whole story of the bench in it, trying to immortalize it, only she'd changed the Nietzsche book to Keats's letters to make the scene more romantic.

The novel had taken her fifteen years, and its heroine was a woman who devoted herself fiercely to a small-town library but ultimately chose love and freedom instead. It read like an alternate pathway for her own life—a tantalizing might-have-been.

Odile had called the novel "self-indulgent," but clearly she had been paying attention. By pairing the Keats quote with the footbridge photo in her clue, Eleanor believed now, she'd meant to reference *their* bench. Eleanor hadn't made the connection until Will mentioned the business school, though, because she had never *actually* read Keats's letters on this bench, only imagined doing it in her novel.

Her clues are about us, but Daniel doesn't even know who I am. When he'd touched her to keep her steady on the ladder, just now in Dunster House, she hadn't been able to stop herself from shying away. To him the touch meant nothing, while for her it roused far too many memories.

Had he even noticed her reaction?

She knelt beside him to examine the underside of the bench's seat. *A subterranean secret / Where love is shared.* "Maybe she buried it?"

"The Book?" Daniel was on hands and knees, running his fingertips over the sparse grass and sandy earth under the bench.

He seemed absorbed in the search, and Eleanor hoped Carlyle hadn't spooked him too much. A few times a year she tried to meet the older man for coffee, to discuss his nightmares and soothe his old resentments, showing him that the librarian did care about every student who had ever left a confession in the Book and contributed their energy to the library's power.

Carlyle had called her Odile's *loyal apprentice* as if it were an insult. But she'd never been his enemy, or even that different from him—she had the nightmares, too.

Eleanor was getting grass stains on a good pencil skirt. They'd searched all over and under the bench, and they weren't finding anything. She was deciding how to phrase her apology to Daniel for the wild goose chase when he began scrabbling furiously in the loose dirt. "Found something!"

She watched as Daniel used the butt of his Swiss Army knife to carve grooves in the earth, as if he were outlining something. "I never knew your mother liked scavenger hunts," she said to hide her nerves.

Please let this be the Book—undamaged.

Will didn't know yet that Odile had hidden the Book. When he'd hugged her on the street just now, he'd whispered in her ear, *Does he have it?*—meaning Daniel.

No, but I have a lead, Eleanor had whispered back.

"Can't you just see her out here in the dead of night, on her knees, digging a hole? It's a good four or five inches deep, too." Daniel's cheeks were pink with exertion, but he seemed more at ease now than he had earlier. Grinning with the relish of a small boy hunting earthworms, he uncovered one corner of what looked like a box. "White Owl Cigars! This is her, all right."

His excitement was infectious, and Eleanor crawled over to help him free the other end. Sure enough, it was one of the vintage red-and-white cigar boxes Odile had inherited from her father and used to store odds and ends.

Not big enough, Eleanor realized with a lurch of disappointment. Whatever was in here, it wasn't the Book.

The lid was sealed down with duct tape, but Daniel slit it deftly. He lifted out some folded pages—photocopies, by the looks of them. "What is this? Looks like some old document."

Eleanor peered over his shoulder.

It was a letter in French, dated 1718. Shivers coursed over her as she read the salutation: *Monsieur de Voltaire . . .* "*Oh*," she whispered.

"What?" Daniel's phone was buzzing. He handed the photocopy to Eleanor and stood up to answer, knees creaking. "Liliana, hey!"

The spidery, archaic handwriting of the letter wasn't easy to decipher, especially because the hammering of Eleanor's heart kept her from holding it steady. Barely breathing, she flipped to the second page and found the signature: *La Sorcière Mariane.*

"It can't be," she whispered to herself, her teeth chattering in the evening chill. The Mariane letter, after all this time?

The woman who had created *The Book of Dark Nights* was more legend and conjecture than anything else. But Odile had always insisted she'd seen a letter proving her existence.

On the second page of the photocopy was one of Odile's sticky notes:

Go next where she hid the Book.

Eleanor scrambled to her feet. Daniel was sitting on their bench, phone in his palm, staring into space. "You need to see this," she said, vibrating with her need to read the letter.

He didn't seem to hear her. "Liliana says someone ransacked my mom's house while I was out."

"Ransacked?" She struggled to shift gears.

"Turned it upside down." When Daniel looked up at her, his expression had a disturbing hollow quality, as if he'd received a shock. "Whoever did it, they left a note saying they want us to bring the Book to the library by five on Sunday. And . . . there's a picture of my daughter. Seems to me like a threat."

16

——

Then

March 7, 1995

"What're you reading?" Drew asked, startling Eleanor out of her reverie.

She sat up and stretched, cramped from hours in the armchair by the window. It was a lovely spring day outside in the Yard, but she'd barely glanced that way, absorbed by the heavy hardcover in her lap. Carefully keeping her place, she closed it to show Drew the title: *Vie de la Sorcière Mariane* by Juliette Aubry. "*The Life of the Witch Mariane*," she explained. "The only book ever written about the creator of *The Book of Dark Nights*." Mariane, the name Daniel had cried out in his sleep. It couldn't be a coincidence.

Drew's eyes widened. "I thought the Book was privately printed for a duchess or something. The creator was a freaking witch?"

Eleanor nodded, excited by the new knowledge she'd just absorbed. After fruitless attempts to research the Book's background in Widener, she'd asked Odile, who had handed her Juliette Aubry's book with an admonition to keep it in the library because it was a rare, out-of-print edition.

Juliette is one of my dearest friends, Odile had added. *But she has scant respect from the scholarly community. They say she concocted a good story for academic advancement. You'll notice that few of her claims are footnoted, making her book perhaps as much fiction as fact.*

Eleanor didn't care about footnotes. The story in Professor Aubry's book enthralled her.

In a rush, she told Drew the outlines. Marie Louise Élisabeth d'Orléans, Duchess of Berry, had had the young Voltaire imprisoned for a scandalous libel. Mariane, an ambitious peasant who supposedly had learned witchcraft from a wise woman in her rural village and then studied philosophy with Voltaire—according to some sources, while sharing his bed—was working as a servant in the palace. She hatched a diabolical scheme to get revenge on the duchess by giving her a book that predicted your future, but only if you told it a dark secret from your past.

In the château's library on rainy nights, Mariane would perform for the entertainment of the duchess's guests. First she would use the Book's power to pick out books for them; then she would invite them to confess and see even clearer glimpses of their future. But her secret motive was to coax the duchess into confessing something that could be anonymously leaked and used to shame her.

Drew sat down on the windowsill, listening intently. "I thought only the confessor could read the confession."

Professor Aubry speculated that Mariane had ways around her own spell. "Like, maybe the Book becomes legible if you read it reflected in a water basin at the full moon."

As Eleanor read about Mariane, she had felt the Book's power humming softly through the library, through Juliette Aubry's book, through her own body.

Remembering her own experiment with steering the book-choosing process, she was intrigued to learn that the power seemed to give Mariane a certain control over others. For instance, one of the duchess's guests was unlucky in love and asked her for a book to help him forget his sweetheart. Mariane plucked out Homer's *The Odyssey* and read him a passage. From that moment on, the guest no longer even recognized the face of the woman he had so desperately adored.

Eleanor imagined the duchess's library: marble walls, ceiling frescos, smoking candles. She shut out the distant sounds of city traffic and heard the delicate strains of violin and harpsichord. She saw men and women in powdered wigs and stiff, paneled garments, speaking courtly French and following labyrinthine etiquette rules. An alien world.

That world had a dark side, too. According to one especially salacious broadsheet, Mariane had crafted the paper for the Book's pages from the discarded garments of criminals who had died on the scaffold or the breaking wheel, sucking power for her spell from their final agonies. When gilded young aristocrats wrote their secret confessions on the pages, they had no idea they were linking their fates to those of the wretched beggars and thieves they despised.

In modern times, no one had seen Mariane as anything but a rumor, an attempt to discredit the great skeptic Voltaire by associating him with witchcraft and superstition. But when Professor Aubry was cataloging the philosopher's more obscure correspondence for an archive, she'd found a letter addressed to Voltaire from "La Sorcière Mariane," or Mariane the Witch, that described the Book and its purpose. The professor claimed the letter had been stolen from her Paris apartment before she could have it photographed or authenticated.

Drew scowled. "That kinda makes it seem like this professor made the whole thing up."

"Maybe the letter, but she didn't invent the Book!" Professor Aubry claimed *The Book of Dark Nights* had been lost in the eighteenth century and never reappeared. "And we know that's not true!" Eleanor added, tripping over her words in her eagerness to reach her conclusions.

Daniel had told her that Juliette Aubry and Marc Vasselin were the two other people who'd known about the Book besides his parents. "So Juliette knew perfectly well Odile had the Book this whole time!"

She just didn't want anyone else to know. Even as she wrote her biography of Mariane, staking her own claim to literary celebrity, Juliette had kept the Book's secret.

And now it was their secret, too. Eleanor recalled how Daniel had called out Mariane's name in his sleep, as if confessing to the Book had brought him so close to its creator that her ghost was invading his dreams.

She shuddered, but it was a pleasant kind of shudder, because Carlyle's talk of nightmares scared her less in the daylight. She hadn't confessed yet, but now she found herself wanting to. By joining the tiny circle of people who had written in the Book, she would be closer to Daniel. She could keep wielding the power of the library. She would always have somewhere to belong.

Drew's attention was wandering, his gaze drifting out the window to the blue sky, the still-bare trees, and the grassy squares where students were enjoying the sunlight. "That Book should be in a museum somewhere," he suggested absently, "where everybody can see it and learn its story. Not locked up in a safe."

No, it should stay here. If Carlyle was right, the library's power depended on keeping the Book close by. Eleanor knew that was selfish reasoning, though, so she kept it to herself. "Don't tell Daniel that! The professor would be upset if she knew he even took it out."

"I guess so." Drew was giving her a strange look, head angled. "Don't you think he kinda wanted to piss her off, though? Isn't that why he took the Book?"

Eleanor knew now that Daniel had wanted much more than that. "I think he'd like to understand himself better. It's hard growing up without one parent—you wonder who you are deep down."

"You really care about Daniel, don't you?"

Bile rose into Eleanor's throat, and she had to drop her pen and retrieve it to hide her burning cheeks. Had Daniel told Drew about them? After refusing to bring her to his suite because he wanted to keep things secret?

Drew clearly sensed the turmoil inside her, because he added hastily, "Daniel didn't say anything! I saw you guys one night on Bow Street, that's all, when you didn't see me."

If anyone in the seminar had to know, Eleanor supposed she preferred it be Drew, because he was a good friend to Daniel and had always been kind to her. Still, she couldn't meet his eyes. "Does *he* know you know?"

"Nah, don't worry, I won't spill the goods." Drew was gazing off across the Yard again. "I know how it feels when you're at the beginning of something like that—like you're tipsy all the time, and you gotta be real careful not to trip over your own feet."

He sounded wistful, as if he'd been in love, too. Or as if he were right now? Remembering her reckless attempt to choose a new pathway for him in the library, Eleanor had to wonder.

By choosing books for people, Mariane had changed them.

Eleanor rose to stand beside Drew, following his sightline. Across the Yard, April and Genevra were talking to a couple of tall guys outside Weld Hall.

"Maybe," she said, thinking aloud, "the Book will tell me."

Drew looked sharply at her. "Tell you what?"

Whether Daniel and I are meant to be together. Whether I'm meant to use this power. How it will all end. But she only shrugged and said, "My fate."

17

——

Now

September 26, 2019, 6:42 p.m.

Odile's home in Porter Square was usually tidy but lived-in, with decades-old appliances and vintage film posters on every wall not already covered with books. When Daniel arrived yesterday from the airport, he'd paused for a long moment in the mudroom, breathing in the subtle smells of his childhood and fighting back tears as he realized he would never again see his mother serve Lapsang souchong tea or hear her beloved Edith Piaf records.

It was jarring now to find the house in disarray. The shelves were bare. The floor was a sea of books: hardcovers with their dust jackets askew and large, slippery foreign paperbacks that Daniel and Eleanor kept tripping over.

And sticky notes and scrap paper were littered everywhere. Liliana had explained yesterday that Odile feared slipping into dementia so much she'd left herself reminders about everything from checking the stove burners to dusting behind the television, plus some notes that were literary quotes or just plain indecipherable. Daniel couldn't help finding it touching: Though Odile's own parents had been stolidly rational into their eighties, her greatest fear was losing control of the world around her.

But now the notes were scattered all over the Persian carpet and sagging armchairs like confetti. While Eleanor hurried from room to room, assessing the damage, Daniel sank down on the living room sofa, shell-shocked.

The note had been left on the coffee table, just as Liliana had said. *Bring the Book to the Library of Fates Sunday @ 5. No police—after all, you don't own it, do you?*

Beneath the printed message was a photo of Daniel and Sandrine with a background of snowy peaks, both of them wearing belaying harnesses—an image Odile had posted on her public social media last year. By itself, it seemed innocent enough. But in Daniel's mind, the threat was clear. Whoever had left this knew his daughter's welfare mattered immeasurably more to him than any book, magical or not.

While Eleanor drove them here, fighting rush-hour traffic, he had managed to reach Sandrine by text. She'd talked him down with repeated assurances that she hadn't seen anyone lurking around the inn, and she hadn't received any odd communications. When Daniel suggested she cancel her hike tomorrow, she'd pointed out that only she and her friend knew their route, and she never posted her whereabouts on social media. All in all, she was so calm and matter-of-fact that Daniel hung up feeling a little ashamed of his fears.

How had she become the one who offered reassurance? When Sandrine was a little girl grieving the death of her mother, living with him permanently for the first time, she'd decided there was a monster hiding in the closet of her room in their shoddy apartment. Daniel would sweep open the closet door and challenge the monster to a duel, then shadow-box until she forgot her fears and dissolved in giggles.

As she grew up, she'd stopped telling him about her terrors. Whenever they both got jittery as she faced a driver's test or a sheer rock face, Sandrine would dispel her nerves with dark jokes and encourage him to do the same. Under that show of toughness, Daniel knew, part of her was still the little girl who'd cowered from noises in her closet, haunted by the specter of her mother's unexpected and inconceivable death. But he still marveled at her steely quality, which reminded him of Odile.

Walking the Harvard campus, he'd recalled stray remarks Sandrine had made about wanting to visit her grandmother here and see her presiding over the Library of Fates. Now, because he'd dragged his feet, she would never have that chance.

Eleanor's descent from the second floor interrupted his thoughts. Judging by the ease with which she navigated the house, she knew it well. "There's a window cracked open in the downstairs pantry. That must've been the entry point," she said. "You haven't called the police, have you?"

"Not yet, but I think we should. It's got to be Carlyle, don't you think?" Daniel suggested. If Carlyle had left the note, he seemed erratic enough to have left fingerprints on it, too. "He's obsessed with the Book, and he said flat-out that he wants me to *do something about* it. He's probably feeling bolder now my mom's gone. Unless someone else has been nosing around?"

Eleanor sat down in the love seat opposite him. "There's at least one other possibility. Do you remember Marc Vasselin?"

Daniel recalled a bald man with a loud laugh whom he'd met a few times on childhood visits to France—one of his father's students and his mother's friends, part of the charmed circle of four who had confessed to the Book. "He was the guy who found the Book after it was lost for centuries, all bricked up behind a wall."

"Right." Eleanor tucked a strand of hair behind her ear and crossed her tall boots, looking chic and at home in his mother's living room. *Why do I barely remember her?* he wondered again. Maybe she'd simply been mousy, but in the fragmentary memories he'd managed to retrieve over the past few hours, she felt *important*, as if he'd been paying special attention to her.

She said, "Twelve years ago, Marc visited Cambridge and tried to persuade Odile to give him the Book. He pointed out that, since he had basically looted it from the Palais du Luxembourg in Paris, she had no legal claim to it."

"Neither did he!" And then Daniel remembered the wording of the note: *After all, you don't own it, do you?* Maybe Marc was working on the finders keepers principle.

"I haven't seen Marc since I was a kid." He shuffled through memories of conversations with his mother, wishing he hadn't so often tuned her out when she got on the subject of her old friends. "He and Juliette Aubry were a couple, right? Married?" Bonded by the Book, his mother used to say—just like her and Julien, who hadn't been able to marry. "I think they split up at some point. So you think Marc still wants the Book?"

Eleanor leaned forward, and he saw tension in the set of her shoulders. "I think he wants it badly, and he knew Odile wouldn't give it to him while she was alive."

Badly enough to fly to the States and break and enter? Marc Vasselin had to be well into his seventies. "Why, though?" Daniel asked, trying to keep a lid on his skepticism. "Does he think the Book is evil, like Carlyle does, or does he want to use it to start his own library, or is he just desperate for a prediction?"

Eleanor reached for something on the coffee table—the cigar box they'd found under the bench on the business school campus. The news of the break-in had made Daniel forget all about his mother's clue, but clearly she hadn't.

She removed the papers inside and spread them out. Daniel saw the faded, wavery lines of a quill pen, poorly captured by a photocopier.

"I wondered the same thing," she said. "But that was before I knew your mother had the Mariane letter—Mariane's letter to Voltaire. The one that was supposedly stolen from Juliette Aubry's apartment. Your mother was full of secrets." Her mouth hardened, and she lifted her chin, as if she were having trouble stomaching Odile's silence. "All this time she kept it from me."

"She was like that, even with her family." Daniel's eyes skimmed impatiently over the nearly indecipherable French words of the letter. He could almost see and feel the yellowed paper of the original document, though he didn't recall his mother ever showing him such a thing. "So, you think Marc Vasselin wants to steal the original of this letter, too? I imagine it's worth something."

When he glanced up at Eleanor, a fever shone in her eyes, rousing more of his disconcerting, disconnected memories. "That's not what I meant."

Through the window behind her, Daniel saw the backyard blanketed in the deceptive peace of twilight. The sugar maple had strewn its scarlet leaves on the circlet of carefully tended lawn, just as it had every year of his childhood.

He wanted to mourn his mother and call the cops about the break-in. He didn't want to have to chase down *The Book of Dark Nights*. In Eleanor's eyes he was beginning to see an obsession that reminded him of Carlyle—and before that of poor Drew, who'd been convinced the Book could set his fears about the future to rest.

Nothing good ever came of that obsession. But without the Book, without his inheritance, Daniel wasn't sure how to give his daughter the future she deserved. She was so bright, and her English was nearly fluent. Harvard was a place she would thrive, if only he had the means to send her there.

"What *did* you mean?" he asked with a sigh.

Eleanor handed him the photocopy. "Read it, Daniel. If this letter is authentic, then *The Book of Dark Nights* might have a purpose your mother didn't tell us about. One we never dreamed of."

Squinting to make out the handwriting, Daniel read:

Paris, 2 April 1718

Monsieur de Voltaire,

I, your loyal servant, have been giving thought to this matter of how to write the All-Things Book. I realize you are a skeptic of all religions, Monsieur, and you may give scant credence to the means I have employed, methods taught to me by the wise woman of my village and by certain practitioners of the lost arts here in Paris.

But I ask you to grant me a hearing before you dismiss me.

I have created a book like no other, The Book of Dark Nights, a book of rag and bone and despair, whose pages are still blank. You will know in whose hands to put it. This Book devours confessions. In return, like a carnival fortune teller, it spits up predictions of dubious value, which should appeal to its frivolous new owner. Only you and I need to know what this Book is truly for.

A word to the wise, Monsieur: You will not be able to read it yourself. None can read it until it is full.

Let the unwary confess their sins therein. Warn them not to lie, for the Book is like God and sees into their hearts. We shall harvest their guilty, tormented souls like full-ripened grain. Remorse, grief, melancholy, joy, envy, spite—such are the makings of every story in the world. Even death cannot release those who have left pieces of themselves on these pages.

When this Book is full, when no blank pages are left—then, and only then, you may sit down and read it at your leisure, Monsieur. After you have read it, tear out every page—this step is essential.

And when you rise afterward and go to your desk and pick up your pen, the first thing you write will be the All-Things Book. The book to end all other books. The book to secure your immortality. All the souls you have collected in this Book will be only characters in that epic story you shall author.

This power I give you. Use it well.

Votre très humble servante, Monsieur,
La Sorcière Mariane

From Eleanor Dennet, *A Student's Guide to the Thought of Julien Theuthet* (2011)

The most fascinating yet mysterious idea in the entire oeuvre of Theuthet is the "All-Things Book."

The theory of textual potential teaches us that books mean different things to different people. The book that becomes one reader's inspiration or comfort leaves another reader cold. Another might hurl it against the wall. No book can ever be loved by every reader—except the All-Things Book.

The All-Things Book is not real but a hypothetical concept: an imaginary book that fulfills every possible reader's needs. Everyone who reads it is cheered or inspired or moved to tears or whatever they seek from a book—and not just on the first reading, but every time, because the All-Things Book rewards infinite rereadings. It keeps readers company, answers their everyday questions, and guides them safely through the travails of their lives. No one ever hurls it against the wall.

If the All-Things Book actually existed, it would drive all other books extinct. Writers would cease to write and publishers to publish. Who needs a library if a single book fulfills all your needs?

Luckily (some would say), the All-Things Book does not and cannot exist. No book can transform itself to suit every reader. When internet use first became widespread, some said it would make all books and libraries redundant, similar to the All-Things Book, but clearly they were wrong. And so, because the All-Things Book can't exist, we keep following our threads through the countless books that do exist, learning to write our own unique stories and braid them into the fabric of every story that has ever been told.

18

—

THEN

March 9, 1995

One day after class, when the others had already escaped into the almost-spring air, Professor Vernet said to Eleanor, "You live down by the river in Dunster House, don't you? Would you like to stop for tea at Pamplona?"

At the start of the semester, Eleanor would have been ecstatic about the invitation. Now her anticipation mixed with dread as she and Professor Vernet left the building, crossed Mass Ave, and continued down Bow Street.

She knows I've been using the power. Her *power. She knows about Daniel and me.* Those two possibilities were all she could think of, though she managed to make polite small talk about her plans for spring break.

By the time they reached Café Pamplona, tucked in the basement of a neat red clapboard house, Eleanor had decided she would deny nothing. Daniel wasn't the professor's property, and neither was the power. The books in the library might belong to Odile, but the Book was another matter.

Pamplona was a Harvard Square institution, but Eleanor had never ventured there by herself. She was surprised by how cramped the basement room was, with its rough plaster walls, black-and-white checkerboard floor, and low ceiling. There was room for only a dozen people or so, and all of them looked very glamorous as they conducted urgent conversations in languages she couldn't always identify.

Professor Vernet led Eleanor to a table against the wall. When the waiter came over—a handsome, scornful-looking young man in a spotless white shirt and black pants—she ordered a large pot of Lapsang souchong and a plate of shortbread and then waved him away. "You do like tea, don't you? Or should I call him back and order an espresso? They make them almost as well here as in the Latin Quarter."

Eleanor assured the professor tea would be fine, bracing herself for an accusation.

None came. Instead, Professor Vernet asked if she had ever been to Paris. Eleanor admitted she had never been out of the country, and Odile cried, "Oh, but you must, soon! I can't imagine. Harvard has an excellent postgrad scholarship for study in France. You could attend Theuthet's lectures at the Sorbonne."

Paris. The Sorbonne. Tantalizing, postcard-perfect images rose before Eleanor's eyes.

No, she was being absurd. Postgrad literary studies in Europe sounded like something a person with a trust fund would do. "It must be very competitive," she said politely.

Odile waved the objection aside. "Not if I write you a recommendation. I'm friends with the whole committee. I know what it's like to come from a stultifying background, Eleanor—Paris changed my life."

By the time the tea arrived, Eleanor had learned that Odile had been born in Brittany to a French father and British mother, attended a "very stuffy" English boarding school, and then fled to the Sorbonne, where she "went a little wild, smoking all night in cafés on the boulevards, arguing about Sartre," before being enticed into the intellectual world of Julien Theuthet.

"I met him in the Luxembourg when the chestnuts were blooming—May 14, 1968, the day after the general strike, when the whole city was in disarray. My throat was hoarse from days of protesting, and he brought me to a café and fed me tea with honey. He convinced me to study with him, and I took one course, and then another and another," Odile said, pouring the tea. "I was a young firebrand, fed up with abstractions. In my other literature classes, we had to pretend books had nothing to do with ourselves. But in Julien's, we used them to *know* ourselves. We spoke passionately of our connection to characters. It was exactly what I'd dreamed of when I was languishing away in that boarding school in Sussex, devouring every book I could get my hands on."

Eleanor could relate to this. Her other Harvard English professors never wanted to talk about how books affected you personally either; everything was simply *text* to them. But with Odile, you could talk about yourself *through* books, and that was often much less painful than telling the blunt truth.

"My parents had expected I would be a housewife. Or teach snot-nosed brats! Over my dead body." Odile nibbled delicately at a shortbread. "Try these. They're scented with lavender. Instead, I obtained my doctorate and devoted my life to translating and transmitting the theory of my mentor. The '60s were an intoxicating time in Paris, Eleanor—you have no idea. It was a letdown to come here to Cambridge and find dull puritan propriety still ruling the day."

Thanks to Daniel, Eleanor knew what Odile wasn't saying—that Theuthet had been much more than her professor. She wished she could hear the story from Odile's perspective, but she couldn't think of a tasteful way to broach the subject. Instead, she asked, "Your friend discovered the Book in 1968, didn't he? Thank you for Juliette Aubry's book about Mariane—I learned so much from it."

"Even if Mariane's mostly apocryphal, she's a fascinating figure, isn't she?"

"Yes!" There was so much Eleanor wanted to know, but she couldn't let on that she was using the power herself. "She found books for people the way you do—but she didn't *only* give them what they needed, did she? She changed people. As if they were under her spell."

"Who really knows?" Odile said with a wave of her hand. "If she did ensorcell anyone, I imagine she would have done it to please Voltaire. He had her under *his* spell."

Eleanor couldn't resist making a sly insinuation. "Do you really think they were lovers, the way some people say? I mean, a man and woman can have a mentorship relationship without having sex."

Odile stared at her for an instant. Then she laughed a deep, witchy laugh that caught Eleanor off guard. "They can indeed. When they choose. Oh, my dear, are you curious about my son's father? I think you are. I hope I'm not shocking you," she added as a blush spread across Eleanor's face.

Eleanor hadn't expected Odile to guess what she was really saying. She stammered, "I didn't mean anything like that."

"Are you sure you haven't been making certain speculations?" Odile twisted the ornate ring on her left hand, her lips quirking impishly. "You're not the first student to do so. I'm not ashamed. With Daniel's father I found passion, a meeting of the minds, and enduring friendship. But he was already married with four daughters, and his wife was devout and quite psychologically fragile. Too many other people would have been hurt. So when I learned I was pregnant, I applied for the position at Harvard. And Daniel and I have done quite well on our own." She met Eleanor's eyes, as if daring her to object. "Wouldn't you say?"

Nodding, Eleanor took a sip of the rich, smoky tea. She thought of how Daniel spoke of his father, how much bitterness he held. "Daniel's very smart."

"Smart and Self-Destructive, you mean?" Odile smiled slyly, as if she and Eleanor were sharing a secret. "Believe me, I know he resents my guidance. But he'll grow out of it. When I met Theuthet, I was Self-Destructive, too, but the years have made me Contemplative, thank God."

So the personality types weren't fixed for your entire life. Eleanor had wondered, since this was one of the many issues Theuthet's books cloaked in obscure language. And now she found herself bursting out, "So can I grow out of being Meek? I don't want to be Meek."

"Who said you are?"

"You! No, I mean the library. Obviously." Eleanor put the teacup down. "My father left my mother for a beautiful actress, someone who's always the center of attention," she confessed. "He called my mother drab, and she sees herself that way—as a mousy woman living an unfulfilled life."

Sometimes when Daniel was bantering with April, who had all the charisma of that actress, Eleanor couldn't help wondering if the only reason he'd even noticed her was that she could use the library's power. For the first time in her life, she was having a real effect on other people. Even Drew had told her that reading *The Idiot* was making him think differently about everything in his life. But by herself, could she ever be enough for Daniel?

Odile fixed Eleanor with piercing eyes. "Who says the 'mousy' girl is unfulfilled? Sometimes the Meekest people hide the most fiery determination."

"I guess." And Eleanor was determined, but what would happen when the seminar was over, and she had to leave the library? When Daniel went off to Europe this summer, would he forget all about the Meek girl he'd left behind? "I want to have a full character arc," she said. "I want a climax. I want catharsis. I don't want to live my life locked in a closet away from the sun."

Odile put her cup down with a loud clink. "Did you even understand the Bradbury story, Eleanor? Why do you think they locked the girl in the closet?"

"Because she was weak. An easy target."

"No. Because they envied her. Because she was born on Earth and knew what sunlight was, and they were born on Venus and did not."

Odile was right, Eleanor realized with a jolt. The Bradbury book reminded her of her ten-year-old self, so she had been reading it with a ten-year-old's limited understanding.

"I guess," she said again in a small voice.

"Don't just guess at your worth. *Know* it. You've already experienced life more intensely than most of these overgrown children can ever dream of doing." Odile waved contemptuously around the café. "You've known grief, Eleanor. You've known loss. And from those things comes knowledge."

"Knowledge." Eleanor thought of those tall bookshelves and the power thrumming through them. Contemplative people had knowledge, but they were usually only supporting characters, the seminar had taught her, because they were too busy Contemplating to take action. "What good is that if I can't have a story of my own?"

"Would you rather be part of a story, or *tell* the story?"

Odile clicked her tongue. "My personal theory is that Mariane herself was a Meek and bookish sort. Repression creates enormous potential energy. Sooner or later, it will burst forth and become power. That's why I chose you for this seminar—you remind me of my younger self, a bookish girl yearning to be special. You understand the library so much better than the others."

She does *know what I've been doing!* Eleanor barely dared to blink, waiting for the accusation.

But it didn't arrive. Odile poured the dregs of the tea, winter sunlight glinting on her silver rings. "You would be surprised, *ma petite*, at the power a good librarian can have. Watch me and learn. I can help you get to Paris—and return here for your doctorate, if it's what you wish. An assistant in the library would be very helpful to me. A potential successor."

Was that an *offer*? The view that suddenly opened in Eleanor's mind's eye—study in Paris, a career in the Library of Fates—took her breath away. She imagined not having to settle for a life that was merely small and safe, the way her mother had. "You really think I could do what you do?"

"Of course. Learn to tell other people's stories, show them their threads, and eventually you'll come to know people so well you'll never be sad or alone . . . or besotted with a Self-Destructive boy."

She knows. She disapproves. The words had doused Eleanor's enthusiasm instantly. "I . . . I'm . . . not," she protested hopelessly.

"You are. Don't be ashamed." Odile reached across the tiny table to touch Eleanor's hand. Her dark eyes behind the glasses had a warmth Eleanor had never seen in them before. "We all go through phases, as I said. Both of you will mature. Tell me, have you written in *The Book of Dark Nights* yet?"

The sharp question took Eleanor by surprise, and she blurted out, "No. Why would I? I thought you didn't want any of us to do that."

"It's been known to happen in my seminar from time to time." Odile summoned the waiter with a flittering of fingers. "Students get curious and sneak into my office. I wouldn't be surprised if Daniel had done exactly that."

Eleanor wasn't going to betray Daniel, of course. But as she gazed steadily into Odile's eyes, playing innocent, she had a strange feeling that Odile already knew everything, from Eleanor's fears about losing Daniel's love to her temptation to confess.

"Confessing to the Book can form a powerful bond between people," Odile said. "It did between Daniel's father and me—even separated by an ocean, I often feel we're together. And physical separation is necessary sometimes for people to grow and come into their own."

The professor propped her chin on one palm, her gaze not releasing Eleanor. "Many students aren't mature enough to confess and receive the Book's prediction, it's true. But you . . . I think you're ready."

19

Now

September 26, 2019, 7:52 p.m.

Fear had a smell, Eleanor had learned after Renée died—rank, stomach-churning. Sometimes even worse than the fear of a known danger was the dread of something subtly out of place, like a wrong-shaped shadow or an unfamiliar car on the block.

She felt that uncanniness now, watching Daniel read Mariane's letter in the living room as daylight ebbed. A disturbing sense of the long-dead woman's closeness, as if Mariane's ghost were passing and brushing them with the edge of her spectral cloak.

From the way Daniel's face darkened, she could tell he was unsettled, too. She recalled that long-ago night when he'd thrashed in his sleep and told Mariane to leave him alone. Eleanor thought she'd also glimpsed Mariane now and then in her nightmares over the years, though she couldn't be sure.

"The All-Things Book," Daniel said, raising his head from the photocopy. "That's part of Theuthet's theory, isn't it?"

Eleanor nodded. The All-Things Book was one of many topics she'd struggled to explain in simple language when an academic publisher had commissioned her to write a student's guide to Theuthet. It was complicated because it was a useful construct, like Schrödinger's cat in physics, that couldn't exist in the material world. An idea divorced from reality.

"Part of your *father's* theory," she said, emphasizing the word so that Daniel wouldn't think she didn't know.

Did he still avoid telling people about his father? From the way his eyes narrowed on her, she suspected so. But they needed to acknowledge his connection to Theuthet, because she suspected his father could help them. Theuthet might have information they didn't.

She went on quickly, feeling uncomfortable with Daniel's scrutiny: "What if one book could be all things to all readers? Some religious people see their holy text as a book that has all the answers and makes every other book redundant. The All-Things Book is a secular version—a book anyone could spend their life reading and never need another one."

Daniel's attention had left her while she spoke, his gaze wandering. "I thought the whole point of the theory was to find the books that speak to *you* personally, that show you *your* pathway and no one else's."

"Exactly. The All-Things Book goes *against* the theory, which is why it can't be real." Or so she'd always assumed. The idea of a world in which only one book existed—or needed to exist—hurt her brain. What would happen to libraries then?

"So, according to this letter, the witch Mariane gave Voltaire a recipe for the All-Things book." Eleanor nodded, and Daniel continued in a tone tinged with skepticism, "Which involves filling *The Book of Dark Nights* with confessions. You read it, you tear out all the pages, and then, abracadabra, you have the ability to write the book to end all books. Voilà, you're the greatest author on earth—or just the last."

His eyes returned to her, but now sarcasm twisted his mouth. "You believe any of this?"

The whole point of the All-Things Book was that it wasn't possible in the real world. No one could write a book to end all books. But Eleanor had witnessed the magic of the Book and the library for herself, countless times, and she felt she couldn't rule anything out. "I don't know. I just know anyone who *does* believe it might have a strong motive to want the Book. Someone like Marc Vasselin, a failed academic who never attained the fame your father did. Especially because . . . well, last I checked, the Book had only two blank pages left."

Daniel's face sobered. "It's almost full. The confessions are almost ready to be 'harvested.' If Marc *does* believe all this, do you think he could be dangerous?"

"He never was before." But maybe Marc's bond with Odile had held him back while she was alive. Or . . . "He could have been waiting for the Book to be full of the right kind of confessions," Eleanor said, thinking aloud, recalling how Odile had always said that young people's confessions were the most powerful because they were just embarking on their life pathways. All these years, Marc Vasselin might have been biding his time.

Surely Odile herself hadn't believed in the All-Things Book as *The Book of Dark Nights*'s end game, though. To her, the Book mattered for one reason: It made the library powerful.

Daniel pulled out his phone. "Let's see what we can find out about our suspect. If he's threatening my family, though, he's gonna have much bigger worries than not writing a book to end all books."

While he searched Marc Vasselin, Eleanor went to the kitchen and made tea. The righteous rage in Daniel's tone had reassured her that he was taking this seriously. She needed him to, because she could already tell the third clue would take them farther afield than the first two had. If they wanted to find the Book, they both needed to be committed.

But Daniel's anger was disconcerting, too, because she would never forget the one time when it had been directed at her. It was a memory that still woke her at night sometimes, sweating and shaking—not because she feared any sort of violence from Daniel but because she knew that his accusations had some truth to them.

It was a good thing *he* didn't remember.

She brought out the tea tray. Daniel was still hunched over his phone, frowning, knuckles pressed to lips. He didn't look up as she entered.

Seeing him like this, without the polite façade, brought back too many memories. She had to resist an impulse to stroke his hair as she set down his cup, knowing exactly how the short, fine strands in back would feel against her palm.

"Not getting recent hits for Marc Vasselin," he said, reaching for the cup. "I think he's retired. Juliette Aubry, though—I was hoping she could give us some help, but she died in August."

"Yes, I was so sorry to hear that." Eleanor recalled Odile debating whether to fly over for Juliette's funeral but ultimately deciding simply to send flowers. Could she have been worried about encountering Marc?

"When I was in France on my fellowship," she added carefully, because she was about to broach something she knew Daniel wouldn't like, "Juliette was kind to me. She even showed me the spot in the Palais du Luxembourg where Marc found *The Book of Dark Nights* in 1968."

Daniel looked incredulous. "He found the Book where the French Senate meets?"

"No, in the cellar of the palace's orangery, actually. The building is a museum now." Eleanor picked up the sticky note that Odile had attached to Mariane's letter and brandished it at him. *Go next where she hid the Book.* "I think that's where Odile wants us to go."

Daniel stared at his mother's message. "I don't get it. Who says Mariane hid the Book? I thought it was just lost all those years."

"Whether Mariane hid it or not, it *was* hidden," Eleanor pointed out. "And we know where. If I were your mother, and I were hiding the Book now, that's the kind of place I would choose. Remember the little poem she left on the safe? 'A subterranean secret' sounds like a cellar to me."

A subterranean secret, / Where love is shared. Love had been shared on the bench where they'd found the second clue. What love was shared in the palace's orangery? Did Mariane and Voltaire have their affair there?

Daniel was nodding. "You think she wants us to go to Paris. She hid the Book there?"

"Maybe." There was one big problem with that idea, from Eleanor's point of view: She could sense the Book's absence from the library, and she hadn't sensed it for very long. It had to have been removed recently, probably just this week, and Odile hadn't flown to Paris since last spring. She might have used a friend's help to relocate the Book, but none of her friends had visited recently.

Regardless, the clue was clearly sending them to the orangery. And Will had already suggested she bribe Daniel to return the Book. There must be sufficient discretionary funds available to pay for two plane tickets. She would just need to call him and remind him that donations like Belinda Ratliff's were at stake.

"Either way, we need to go to the Book's original hiding place." It was time to broach the issue she'd been avoiding, because she knew he would object. "And, because of what happened here—" she gestured around to encompass the house's disorder "—I think we should also talk to your father, Daniel."

Daniel's demeanor changed instantly, his face closing up in the sullen way it always had when someone mentioned his absent parent. "We're not in touch. I haven't seen him in almost a decade—haven't bothered."

"But you could get back in touch, couldn't you?" Eleanor made her voice gentle, almost pleading. "Julien knows Marc better than either of us does. He'll know how much of a threat he poses. Maybe he can explain Mariane's letter, too, since we know now it was the source for his theory of the All-Things Book."

She'd known her suggestion would be a sticking point, and it was. Daniel sighed heavily. He rose from the sofa, went to the window, and surveyed the backyard as if he expected to catch Marc Vasselin lurking there.

He drew the curtains with an angry jerk, then went to the front windows and closed those drapes, too. When he faced her again, his expression was obdurate. "I have reasons for not seeing my dad," he said. "He's been asking my mom about Sandrine, telling her a whole sob story about how he needs to meet his granddaughter just once before he dies. Fuck that. He never cared until now."

His eyes flashed, and Eleanor remembered all the stories he'd told her on their long walks around Cambridge. Growing up, he'd seen his father no more than once a year, always somewhere impersonal like a restaurant or café, watching his mother fawn over her lover while the man treated him with the politeness of a stranger. His fascination with the Book was also a desire to unlock the secret of the bond between his parents and why it excluded him.

Daniel despised his father so much that Eleanor had braced herself to find Julien Theuthet a cold and forbidding person when she went to Paris after graduation. To her surprise, he'd been warm and kind, introducing her to his colleagues as *Odile's most brilliant student.* When she wrote the simplified guide to his theory for students, he had praised it effusively and sent her a bottle of champagne.

But her own father, too, had always been pleasant when he was around. It was his absence that stung, with the silent rejection it implied. *I'm not good enough for him*—that was the belief that had haunted Daniel through his life as well.

Julien Theuthet could help them now, though. Daniel had to understand that. Eleanor could always arrange to meet the old professor by herself, but she had a feeling his son's presence would make everything easier.

"You can see your father without making him any promises," she said. "He's a reasonable person, Daniel. I'm sure he understands why you're hesitant to let him have a relationship with your daughter."

Daniel sat down again, head hanging. "I never wanted Sandrine to grow up like I did, with a two-person family." He picked up the teacup as if he'd forgotten what it was for. "But we muddled through . . . or I thought we did."

The words reminded Eleanor of what Odile had said in Café Pamplona about the absence of Daniel's father. *Daniel and I have done quite well on our own.* The echo filled her with a strange, blunt pain, because Odile's show of pride had hidden insecurities that she'd confided to Eleanor only years later. Did Daniel really have to live out the same story as his mother, worrying that he hadn't done enough?

She wished she could sit down beside him and reassure him with a touch. But she limited herself to saying, "You did more than muddle through, Daniel. You've been a great dad—that's obvious. I know how you feel about Julien. You grew up thinking you didn't know how to have anything but hate in your heart for him. But . . ."

She broke off. Daniel was staring at her, his eyes burning with confusion.

"That's what I confessed to the Book," he said, "using exactly those words. That I couldn't have anything but hate in my heart for my father. How did you know?"

Words shriveled in Eleanor's throat. She'd made a stupid slip. She couldn't say that Daniel himself had told her about his confession in her bed in Dunster House after she woke him from a nightmare—not without informing him just how much he'd forgotten. And she wasn't ready to do that.

I'm making such a mess of this—but it's my own fault, isn't it?

"There are ways of reading the confessions in the Book, Daniel. Your mother just didn't tell you about them." It was true, but Eleanor herself had never read any of the confessions. She rose stiffly, slinging her handbag over her shoulder. "Marc wants the Book by Sunday. The will specifies Monday. I'm going home to do the legwork for a trip to France tomorrow night. You can come with me or not, as you choose."

"Of course I'm coming! That Book is my daughter's inheritance." Daniel sprang to his feet to follow her into the mudroom, and she saw from his puzzled frown that he hadn't been satisfied with her explanation.

"You know me too well," he said in a low voice, confronting her from the doorway as she found her coat, "and I don't remember you at all . . . or barely. Why is that?"

Their eyes met, and she could tell he hated admitting he'd forgotten her. He didn't want her to feel slighted—and that one small observation of his goodness made her quiver with shame.

"In the library earlier, when I stopped you from falling, you trembled like a leaf," he added, and she thought she caught an expression she'd never expected from him: raw, unchained regret. "As if I'd done something to you."

His visible emotion touched something deep inside her that had been untouched for too many years, and she longed to stay and explain. But if she did that, he might never go to Paris with her. They might never find the Book.

Eleanor made her voice razor-sharp as she said, "Maybe you didn't *want* to remember." Then she tugged on her coat and turned crisply to the door, trying to be as matter-of-fact as the clicking of her heels on the oak boards. "Let's just find the Book, Daniel," she said. "And try to sleep off that jet lag, because crossing the Atlantic again won't help. I'll see you tomorrow."

20

Then

March 16, 1995

Maybe it was the impending spring break and the warmth in the air that made everyone a little reckless that day. Whatever the reason, as soon as Odile had dismissed class and left the building, Drew asked, "Isn't it time to write in *The Book of Dark Nights* again?"

Eleanor was grateful he'd brought it up. Ever since the conversation in Café Pamplona, when the professor had suggested she was "mature" enough to confess to the Book, she'd been dwelling on the idea with a jittery excitement.

Daniel's words were in the Book now. Would confessing bond them, as Odile said it had bonded her and Theuthet? Her natural caution told her to beware, yet she couldn't help wanting, just once, to throw that caution to the winds.

Looking around the room, she saw a range of reactions. To her surprise, Daniel frowned at Drew, as if he'd been hoping the topic wouldn't come up. But April, who was wearing a flippy floral skirt and radiated confidence, tossed her shiny hair and said, "I'm first."

Will stepped back from the table as if someone had proposed human sacrifice. "Count me out."

"I'm not scared," Genevra said in her soft voice. "Could we do it, please?"

Genevra's was the deciding vote. Despite his obvious reluctance, Daniel didn't argue. While he found the office key and got the Book, Drew offered Eleanor his take on *The Idiot*, now that he'd finished it. "I don't think this Prince Myshkin is actually an idiot at all. I think he's Contemplative. And so am I! That's what I wrote in my essay."

Eleanor felt intensely relieved that the book had resonated with him. Daniel's joke about "brainwashing" had made her doubt herself. The book didn't seem to have made Drew fall in love, as she'd intended, but it hadn't made him any more morbid, either.

Now that Eleanor had become more sensitive to the library, she could almost feel its energy rippling around Daniel as he emerged with *The Book of Dark Nights*. Drew grabbed for it, but April got there first and clutched it to her chest. Sitting down in a chair and opening the Book on the table, she asked slyly, "Has your prediction come true yet, Daniel?"

"Still waiting." Daniel grinned in his old easy way, but his jaw was tight, Eleanor noted, and his eyes were fixed downward.

April's face turned serious as she brought her pen to the ancient page and began to write, her hand flowing silently over the rough paper. As Eleanor watched, a shiver of anticipation ran over her. *Let me read you.* Once she let the Book read into her soul, how would she change? What would it tell her?

Will and Drew also seemed to be observing April closely, but Daniel had walked over to gaze out the window.

Genevra fiddled with her cross, her tension palpable, as if she felt tempted to go next but also conflicted. "My grandma would say there's a demonic entity in the Book that makes predictions appear."

April closed the Book and reopened it gingerly, as if it might bite her. She gazed down at the page for a long moment. Eleanor realized she was holding her breath and released it quietly.

At last, April read aloud in a tight voice, as if the Book had unnerved her, "'Haven't I told you that your genius lies in converting impulses into intentions?' And *lie* is underlined. Not *lies*, just *lie*. Daniel, didn't yours have an underlined part, too?"

Lie—the one thing they weren't supposed to do in the Book. The late-afternoon chill slipped under Eleanor's sweater. Surely April hadn't lied?

Daniel didn't turn from the window. Why did he seem so perturbed? "Don't remember."

All things had been underlined in Daniel's prediction. *Let us alone. What is it that will last? / All things are taken from us, and become / Portions and parcels of the dreadful past.*

Daniel had confessed that he struggled with his hatred toward his father. The Book had urged him to let the past go—or so Eleanor interpreted the prediction.

"It's from *The House of Mirth*," Eleanor said now, recognizing April's quote. The first book she'd given April from the library when the power was working through her. And April did remind her of Lily Bart in the book: a brilliant, beautiful girl whose charisma could turn any gathering into a party. Lily acted on impulse, following her instincts; that was both her "genius" and her tragic downfall.

What had April confessed? Was she like Lily—torn between different men and different priorities, between love and a life of luxury?

April didn't seem to hear Eleanor, or she was distracted. Drew loomed over her, reaching for the Book. But April rose with a bounce, elbowed him aside, and handed it to Genevra instead.

"It was my idea," Drew lamented as Genevra sat down to write.

"You'll have your chance," April said tartly.

Daniel left the window and returned to them. Daylight had faded from the library as clouds covered the spring sky, just two lamps in the corners fending off shadows.

Eleanor tried not to look directly at Daniel as he hovered at the head of the table; he was clearly on edge, and too much attention would annoy him. Meanwhile, Genevra wrote and wrote, covering much of the page.

Would they walk together tonight? Sit on their bench? She wasn't looking forward to being separated over spring break—a whole week in her mother's dreary house listening to the tick of the radiator.

At last, Genevra closed the Book. She held it against her chest and shut her eyes for a few seconds, as if she were praying, before spreading it wide open again.

"It's in French!" she cried, as if the Book had cheated her. "Daniel, translate this for me?"

Daniel stayed where he was, his expression stony. "I can't read your page, remember?"

"I'll show you." Genevra yanked out a notebook and transcribed a few lines painstakingly into it. Still hunched over the Book, as if she were afraid someone would take it, she passed the notebook to him.

Eleanor watched Daniel's face as he read Genevra's prediction. He flinched, a muscle leaping in his jaw.

But when he returned the notebook to Genevra, his face was blank again. "I'm not sure that *is* French, actually. Or maybe you mixed up some of the letters. It doesn't make sense."

"Are you sure?" Genevra compared her notebook to the Book page, her worried eyes wide. "I need to know what it says."

Will leaned close to Genevra and whispered in her ear, slipping his arm around her waist with easy intimacy. Genevra didn't bridle at the touch, though she did blush again as she said, "But I want to *know*. Who's next?"

"I am," Eleanor said. She feared that if she waited any longer, she'd miss her chance, like the girl in the Bradbury story whose classmates locked her in the closet so that she missed the only day of sun.

Rather than waiting for Genevra to hand her the Book, she reached across the table and seized it. Waves of energy spread from her fingertips through her body, making hairs stand up on the back of her neck. She remembered everything she'd learned from Juliette Aubry's book. Imagine being able to read the secret confessions of the Sun King's granddaughter! *I read the duchess's soul*, the Book seemed to whisper to Eleanor, *and I can read yours, too. Take your place in history. Let me read you.*

Eleanor longed to obey the command. If she poured out her soul to the Book, her thoughts and feelings would live on there after she died. Her inconsequential little life would have meaning at last, part of a greater whole.

But before she could turn to a fresh page, Daniel darted forward and brought a firm hand down on top of the Book, holding it in place. "No. Not you."

Eleanor's first reaction was outrage. How dare he stop her from confessing when she had the strongest connection to the library of anyone here? "Why not me?"

Drew asked, "Yeah, why not her?"

Daniel's eyes were deep, dark pools, nothing readable in them but refusal. "Two confessions per day, max. We don't want to tire out the Book," he said.

That wasn't one of the rules. He'd just made it up. Did he really think she couldn't handle some dark prediction?

Or did he not want that kind of bond with her?

Eleanor held fast to the top edge of the Book, resisting his pull. The longer she maintained the contact, the more she could swear it felt different from the last time she'd touched it, as if each new confession altered its essential nature. Daniel, April, Genevra—each of them had woven a thread in the tapestry of the Book. Each of their pages had its own distinct color, texture, and frequency, part of Mariane's miraculous creation.

I want to be part of it, too. Why not me?

But Daniel was stronger than she was, and if they played tug-of-war with the Book, the brittle pages might tear. She relinquished it, feeling as if he'd slapped her across the face. "Why don't you want me to confess?" she demanded.

Daniel's cheeks had reddened. The others were all looking at them.

Drew said in a low voice, "He thinks it's dangerous."

"What, only for *her*?"

"Nothing like that." Daniel tucked the Book under his arm. "I just got a weird feeling about it. The rest of us can confess next time."

While he hustled the Book into the office, the others got ready to leave—all but Eleanor, who sat frozen.

When she looked up, Will and Genevra were gone, Drew was browsing, and April was giving her a penetrating look, as if she were putting two and two together. "Daniel thinks you're *special*," she said, drawing the word out mockingly.

Did Daniel tell her about us? Eleanor might not have minded, but April's tone mortified her.

"We can't all confess at once," she mumbled, grabbing her coat and handbag. Then, not wanting to face April or Daniel, she lowered her head like a charging bull and wheeled toward the door.

She hurried down the three flights of stairs, her heartbeat a frantic stampede. Through the foyer she staggered, barely missing a knot of students who were conversing in Italian, and down the steps into the Yard.

But right at the bottom, someone caught up to her. A large hand closed on her arm, yanking her to a standstill. "Eleanor, please! I'm sorry!"

Daniel was in just his jeans and sweater, having left his coat and scarf in the library in his haste. He said breathlessly, "Remember what Carlyle said."

"I don't believe him." She shook him off and kept walking, into the narrow, tree-lined pathway between Boylston and its hulking neighbor, Widener. Delicate crocuses striped with white, purple, and gold poked from carefully tended beds.

"I do. Remember how I cried out in my sleep? Since I confessed to the Book, I've had these creepy recurring dreams." He was beside her, keeping pace with her. "They're not so bad, but . . . I don't want you to have them, too."

"But you let *them* confess!" Eleanor couldn't believe this was the real reason. *He doesn't want to have with me what his mother has with his father.*

"I know, and I feel like shit about it." Daniel's voice was rough, as if he desperately needed her to believe him. "I should've said no. We should leave that thing alone."

As Eleanor reached the corner of Widener, he seized her hand and drew her into an alcove formed by the giant library's façade. "Ever since my mom told me about the Book, I've wanted to be part of that special circle of people who've confessed. But when you reached for it, it was like everything snapped into focus. I couldn't risk letting it hurt you."

"Hurt me? Because I might get bad dreams?" His touch brought warmth to her cheeks that spread down her neck into her chest.

Had he really only been trying to keep her safe? He should have known she could never fear the Book; its power was already as familiar and welcome to her as his touch. As for the nightmares, meeting the Book's ghostly maker in her dreams seemed more desirable to her than frightening.

She touched Daniel's cheek. He looked very beautiful just then, with his cheeks and lips flushed and his eyes wide and wet, and she said, "Don't worry about me. If you really want, I won't confess. But I *want* to, and not just for the thrill or even for the prediction. I feel like you're part of the Book now. I want to be there with you."

Suddenly his arms were around her, warm and steady, and his voice was husky in her ear. "I feel like I'm part of the Book, too. But in the dreams, sometimes I'm *trapped* . . . it's hard to explain." His voice broke. "Maybe you're right. Maybe it's fine. But will you still promise me you won't do it? Just as a favor?"

They'd edged off the path and were almost against the wall of Widener, concealed by a clump of bare bushes. Eleanor shook her head. It was impossible to refuse with him so near she could almost feel his heartbeat. She heard herself whisper, "Yes. I promise."

"Thank you." Daniel cupped her face in his hands. Every muscle in Eleanor strained toward him, like the library's power surging inexorably within her as it carried her to the right book.

When he kissed her, she met him fiercely, pressing her

whole body against him, conveying the ferocity of her need. Her hands roved over him, pulling and tearing at his sweater, and soon he was doing the same to her.

Somehow they ended up in the heart of a bush, their hair full of twigs and their clothes of cedar chips. And it felt so good to be close to him—not in the pages of the Book, but in the flesh—that Eleanor didn't regret her promise.

21

Now

September 27, 2019, 1:05 a.m.

Eleanor had told Daniel to get some sleep, but that was easier said than done.

He hadn't contacted his father, as she'd suggested. If it was really necessary, it could wait until they got to Paris. But as soon as Eleanor left, he'd messaged April Carraway on Facebook, where they'd stayed in touch, with a carefully worded inquiry:

> Hi! This is going to sound strange, but maybe you heard my mom just died and I'm back in the States to wrap up stuff. Maybe you know that Eleanor is now the librarian? From our seminar? Anyway, I don't have the clearest memories of that year, probably because of Drew, and I seem to have forgotten Eleanor in particular, which is pretty embarrassing. I'm wondering if you could give me a crash course on anything I should know.

He endeavored to think of a funny, charming way to close the message, one that made him seem less insensitive or deranged, but nothing came to mind.

No reply so far. All his attempts to sleep ended with him sitting up in a cold sweat thinking he'd heard movement downstairs, as if whoever had searched the place was back.

It was just the unfamiliar soundscape of a house where he hadn't lived for decades, but he couldn't convince his half-conscious mind of that. So he got up and went into his mother's study, where he spent hours searching through the chaos, examining sticky notes with quotes in French, English, German, Italian, Russian. Nothing that seemed likely to help.

Where would you hide the Book, Mom? Why did you think I would know?

His eye caught on a book that had been knocked halfway under the desk, with a striking black-and-white photographic cover. It was a paperback, cheaply bound: *Broken Thread: A Novel* by Eleanor Dennet.

Daniel picked it up. The cover showed a young girl in a motion-blurred cityscape. Opening it, he found an inscription: *To O.V., the mentor who gave me the courage to tell my own story.*

Odile had encouraged Eleanor to write about herself? He didn't mean to start reading, but suddenly he was leafing through the book, his eyes sliding easily over the lines. At this point, any story was a desirable escape from the unrest in his head.

The novel opened with the wrenching tale of two young sisters living on the Upper West Side of Manhattan. The younger one ran out of the apartment on Christmas Day and was killed by a bus before the older one's eyes.

Everyone said it wasn't my fault, Daniel read. *I pretended to agree with them. But it had to be my fault, because if not mine, whose?*

On this page, he found his mother's bold handwriting:

Self-pitying. Still not finding her own path.

His heart sank. Odile could be so cruel sometimes. He skimmed more pages, watching the grieving older sister become a sullen teen and then a college student. One snowy night, she takes a walk with a handsome classmate, and he ends up back in her room.

Oh.

Reading the scene was like seeing himself in video footage shot by someone else, with a slightly distorting lens. Yet clearly it *was* him. The dark eyelashes, the overbearing professor mom, the absent father.

And there was something painfully familiar about Eleanor's description of the snowstorm and their walk across the river. As if it really had happened.

A few pages later, the couple kiss on a bench in the dark. The boy puts his head in the girl's lap; she reads to him from the love letters of John Keats.

Daniel's breath caught as he recognized the place where they'd found Odile's latest clue. Was it possible that somehow his *mother* knew more about his college love life than he did?

All this time he'd thought his memory loss was a fog bank—college recollections gradually slipping away. But apparently part of his past was a blackout, abrupt and absolute, a velvety darkness where anything could be hiding.

Maybe you didn't want *to remember,* Eleanor had said when she left earlier. Now he understood why she'd sounded so bitter. Even if they'd only shared your standard short-lived college romance, he shouldn't be able to forget things like that.

Daniel had accepted many years ago that he wasn't made for long-term commitment. Anyone who got too close made him feel crowded, reminding him of his mother's creepy devotion to his father. And he didn't like having to explain the dreams that sometimes woke him at night, thrashing and flailing.

Over the years, he had gone from fling to fling. Some of his clients were eager for no-strings encounters, and he'd always been up-front with his intentions and tried to be respectful and give everyone a good time. When he met a former lover years later, he never drew a blank on a face or name. If he'd been intimate with Eleanor, he *shouldn't* have forgotten her.

Yet seemingly he had.

More and more unnerved, he flipped pages, looking for mentions of himself. There was some kind of fight or betrayal, which confused him, and then the "black-haired boy" didn't reappear until the second-to-last chapter.

Decades have passed. Disillusioned and no longer young, the heroine takes a week's vacation in Paris, where she encounters him by chance at a café outside the Jardin du Luxembourg. She says, "I haven't forgiven you," and he replies, "I didn't expect you to." They walk through the park together as dusk thickens under the trees.

> He stopped. Turned to me and took both my hands in his. "I was told I was self-destructive, and that's what I've been. The moment I get any happiness, I want to toss it away. But are you any better? You're afraid to even chase happiness, I think."
>
> His grip felt warm and oddly safe, as if at last I'd unwound the thread of my life and come home to the girl I'd once been, the child who hadn't yet been afraid to live. The woman who hadn't renounced real happiness in favor of the knowledge in books.
>
> "You don't have to be this version of you," he

said, squeezing my hands. "And I don't have to be this version of me. We both could have been, should have been, someone else."

There in the Jardin, just for a moment, we became the people we should have been.

Blood flamed in Daniel's cheeks, the words swimming before his eyes. Well, *that* part certainly hadn't happened. And if the college part were all true, why hadn't Eleanor said something much earlier? Why had she allowed him to treat her like a stranger?

He remembered how Eleanor had shied away from his touch in Dunster House. The intense way she'd looked at him earlier this evening, as if she'd been waiting all this time for him to come to his senses and return to her.

She even knew what he'd confessed to the Book. Something he'd always believed he hadn't told a living soul: that he couldn't find anything but hate in his heart for his father.

What happened between us? After telling her that, how could I have let her go?

He didn't *want* to believe he'd forgotten so much, yet something deep inside told him he had.

Bold, Odile had written in the margin of the Jardin du Luxembourg scene, *and revisionist history. But perhaps she's right.*

***

Daniel woke to the jarring noise of his ringer. He'd fallen asleep on the downstairs couch with the lamp still on. Now its pallid light vied with the sun flooding through the sheer voile on the windows, making him blink as he dived for the phone.

"Sandrine?" he asked woozily.

But an American voice answered—a woman's voice, low

and cultured and confident. "Daniel, it's April Carraway. You messaged me last night."

"April, right! Thanks so much for calling." Remembering the message he'd sent her, he felt like the world's biggest clown. Did she know all about him and Eleanor? How many people did? "Sorry, my message was a little weird."

"No, *I'm* sorry about your mom. What a shock." April spoke briskly, though, as if she wasn't particularly sorry. "So, I have to ask, what's going on with Eleanor? Why are you asking about her? Is she acting weird or controlling or something?"

Daniel found he had no idea what to say. He didn't want to tell her that the Book was missing, and he didn't know how to ask his real question: *Do you remember Eleanor and me together?*

April seemed to take his silence as a prompt. "Whatever you do, don't ask her for a book when you're in the library," she said, "even if she asks you to. You haven't, have you?"

"Um . . . no." Could Eleanor find books for people the way his mother had? He'd always thought that power belonged to Odile alone.

"Will thinks I'm delusional, but I absolutely don't trust Eleanor. Especially after what happened to Genevra."

"Genevra?" Then Daniel remembered what Carlyle had said to them in the stairwell. *Remember your friend Genevra? Do you want to end up like her?* He'd meant to look into it, but in the excitement of the break-in, he'd completely forgotten.

April sighed. "Oh, jeez. Odile didn't tell you? Well, I guess she wouldn't have bothered." When she spoke again, her voice was sharper, almost tart. "Genevra died two months ago. She parked her car on the median of the 405 and stepped out in front of a semitruck. You can tell me that has nothing to do with her nightmares if you want to, but I know it does."

"Oh, shit. I'm so sorry." Daniel rubbed his eyes. Birds were caroling in the shrubbery outside, oblivious to the darkness of their conversation. A leaf blower howled in the distance, straining his fragile nerves. "Her nightmares were worse than ours, I remember that, but I never thought . . ."

"Yeah, her nightmares were so bad she needed about five prescriptions to handle them," April said, wearily now, as if she were an adult trying to explain something to an obtuse teenager. "That seminar changed Genevra's life, and not in a good way. Odile claimed the books expressed our deepest selves, but actually they sometimes pushed us in new directions. I mean, *Dangerous Liaisons*? It's about an innocent, deeply religious woman falling for a worldly man and getting her heart broken so badly she ends up dead. Genevra was a Catholic schoolgirl. She read it, and suddenly she was jumping into bed with Will Cheltenham. Who *did* break her heart, just like every other guy she's been with since."

A trickle of perspiration made Daniel tug at the neck of his sweater. "I feel responsible. I'm the one who gave you all the Book."

"You were just a kid—we all were. You couldn't have known." April's voice had softened a little. "I didn't mean to guilt you about that. Honestly, sometimes I've wondered if everything to do with that Book and the library was just our overactive imaginations. Mental illness was certainly a factor, with Genevra and Drew both. The Book just gave them a focus for their obsessions."

Daniel remembered how upset Drew had been by his mother's diagnosis, how disturbingly hungry for a prophecy from the Book to reassure him about the future. And April seemed to be suggesting Genevra could have used the Book as a convenient scapegoat for her relationship issues instead of addressing her mental health.

"But," he asked, "what does any of that have to do with Eleanor?"

"I'm getting to that." April's tone hardened to flint again. "Honestly, the main thing I remember about Eleanor is that she could find books for us. The library worked through her, I guess you'd say. I haven't seen her since that class. But last year, Genevra flew to Boston for a conference, and she told me she planned to go to the Library of Fates and ask Odile about a cure for her nightmares. She wanted answers about the Book. To know how it all worked."

Daniel was suddenly very aware of blood pulsing in his temples, a headache taking shape. *Were* there any answers? From his point of view, Mariane's letter about the All-Things Book had only made everything more confusing. "What'd my mom tell her?"

"She didn't!" April sucked in a breath, as if she were straining to describe what had happened in a way he'd understand. "When I called Genevra after her trip, she said she hadn't even seen Odile. Instead, Eleanor met her in the library and badgered her into asking for a book. And when Genevra did . . . well, I'm not sure what happened, but Genevra wasn't acting normal after that meeting. She seemed almost dazed, like she'd been hypnotized. She said the nightmares were gone. I think Eleanor gave her a book that brainwashed her."

"Brainwashed her!" Daniel couldn't repress a gust of nervous laughter. It was just so absurd. He'd grown up in his mother's library. Though he'd often felt unsettlingly known and seen by her book choices for him, he'd certainly never been brainwashed.

"Are you suggesting," he asked, "that Eleanor used a book to make Genevra suicidal? Why in the world would she do that?" However little he knew about Eleanor, she couldn't be a murderer.

"I don't know! To protect the library, maybe. I realize it's just a hunch." Another sigh. "All I'm saying, Daniel, is that if Eleanor gives you the big-eyed innocent act, and she asks you to do anything for her, think twice."

The innocent act. Was that what Eleanor had been doing? Until now, it had never occurred to Daniel that she might wish him any ill, even when he'd resisted her suggestion to reconnect with his father. After all, she was right—Julien's knowledge could be useful.

"April." He drew a deep breath and shoved his pride aside. "What I was really wondering was . . . did I have a thing with Eleanor, back in college? Were we together?"

"A *thing*? Not that I know of." To his relief, April sounded only intrigued, not shocked by his lapse of memory. "I mean, sometimes I thought she had a crush on you, and you flirted with her, but you flirted with everybody. Why do you ask?"

"Not important." Maybe the two of them had been secretive about their relationship, which meant no one could help him but Eleanor herself.

And could he trust her? Though he didn't understand April's story about Genevra, it had shaken him.

"Maybe just tread carefully with her, Daniel," April said. "From everything I've heard, all she cares about is the library. She'll do anything to keep its power."

22

——

Then

March 29, 1995

The week after spring break would always hold a special place in Eleanor's memory.

Spring was arriving at last, daffodils and tulips blooming in every yard in Cambridge. The evenings lengthened, with majestic sunsets washing the sky red. The bushes between Boylston and Widener, where Daniel and Eleanor had argued and then not argued, burst forth with a riot of forsythia.

They fell into a habit of meeting at nine or ten most nights in the Dunster House Library. Nothing was arranged, but she would be sure to study there, and suddenly Daniel would appear. They'd cross the bridge and roam the business school campus, deserted by night, where their special bench or a secluded stretch of new grass became a make-out spot. Fresh air sharpened the excitement. She became very well acquainted with the smell of his aftershave, the texture of his wool coat, the occasional very French hand gestures he made when he was talking about something that excited him.

He told her how, in first grade, he had "practiced being American" to avoid ridicule. She told him about her sister's death, her mother's mental illness, how bleak and interminable spring break in that small town had been.

Daniel was still the only student who had never requested a book from her. Eleanor understood he'd come to see his mother's power as an intrusion, a form of spying, and she couldn't blame him, but she was still a little disappointed. Although the library's power didn't give her a direct window into anyone's mind, there was an intimacy about it, as if she were the channel through which the library read their deepest desires. And she wanted to know if she was right in the intuition she'd had after he stopped her from confessing to the Book—that he really did care for her.

If he asked for a book, she wouldn't try to steer the power the way she had with Drew. That was playing with danger, she'd decided.

They were passing Adams House on one of their nighttime walks when April barreled into them—coat half on, hair tangled. "I was just looking for you!" she said, grabbing Daniel by the arm. "Genevra's in the old pool, and she's freaking me out. She says you were lying when you said you couldn't translate her prediction."

Eleanor glanced at Daniel as they followed April into Westmorly Court, past the empty dining hall. It hadn't occurred to her that he might have lied about the French prediction, but he *had* looked cagey that day. She sensed his discomfort as April led them downstairs into the basement, hurriedly explaining that Genevra was also upset because she had "done some things" with Will that she now regretted. "I told him to be careful of her feelings! She's so sensitive."

Adams House's basement swimming pool was a relic of the Gilded Age, recently drained and closed for safety reasons. Drew had bought a key off a maintenance guy, Daniel whispered to Eleanor as April unlocked the door and took out a flashlight. Since the place was off-limits, switching on the overheads was risky.

The flashlight illuminated tantalizing glimpses of a corner of campus Eleanor had never seen before. A nest of giant wooden beams rose overhead, and two elegant stairways curved down to the pool, with its intricate black-and-white tiling.

As they approached the yawning cavity that had once been filled with water, a shape reared up out of it. Eleanor barely managed not to scream. But it was only Drew, dressed in a flannel and jeans with sandy hair tumbling in his eyes. "You didn't find Will?"

Shaking her head, April dragged Daniel toward the dark maw of the pool. "You need to tell her the Book's predictions are random, okay?" she ordered him fiercely, just loud enough for Eleanor to hear. "Will laughed at her when she said she felt like they'd committed a sin, and then that stupid prediction convinced her she's actually doomed. She has nightmares about being in hell."

Nightmares. So Daniel wasn't the only one having them. Eleanor remembered Carlyle's warning, and suddenly the darkness seemed full of phantoms. She couldn't help a nervous glance behind her before she lowered herself into the pool and followed the others to the deep end. The flashlight beam bounced off a grotesque statue, some kind of river god with a pipe protruding from his laughing mouth.

They found Genevra curled up in the far right corner, hugged by a graceful curve of the concrete. When she saw them, she turned away and said in a choked voice, "Told you, just wanna be alone."

"And we just want to help you." April draped a protective arm around her friend, while Eleanor stood awkwardly in the rear of the group. "Look, Daniel's here."

"Daniel?" Genevra's head jerked upright, her eyes glittering. Her gaze swept around the room, alighting briefly on Eleanor before fixing on Daniel. "You lied to me before, didn't you?" She ripped something from the pocket of her jeans and held it out to him. "You said you couldn't read my prediction. I found somebody who speaks French in my Heroes for Zeros class, and she translated it for me. It says I'm going to die! And 'death' is underlined."

Daniel took the grubby scrap from her trembling hand and unfolded it. His elbow nudged Eleanor in the dark, and she felt him shivering, too.

"'The fatal truth enlightens me,'" he read, "'and allows me to see nothing but an assured and imminent death whose path is traced for me between shame and remorse.'" He looked up, grim-faced. "You're right, I lied because I didn't want you to know." After a moment, he added, "But the Book is like tarot, right? You can't take it literally."

Did he believe that? Eleanor wondered. His own prediction had been vague, merely hinting at escaping the past, but he hadn't laughed it off.

Not reassured, Genevra buried her face in her hunched knees, her shoulders shaking. "It was meant for me! I *do* feel shame and remorse for what I did with Will, and the Book could tell."

April and Drew hovered over her, Drew promising to punch Will the next time he saw him while April insisted that the Book was a stupid parlor trick, nothing more.

Yet the supernatural manifestation of those predictions couldn't be explained away. Eleanor glanced at Daniel again. He was staring into space, brows bunched as if he were working out some problem.

"Maybe we should talk to Professor Vernet," Drew suggested. "I mean, the Book *was* supposedly created by a witch, according to the book Eleanor read. But if it's all bullshit, the professor might know—"

"Shut up!" April sprang to her feet. "Don't encourage Genevra," she whispered furiously at him. "She already thinks our nightmares are proof dark magic trapped our souls in that Book. Talking about witches doesn't help."

Our nightmares—Eleanor hadn't missed that. April was having them, too? Carlyle's warning hadn't been paranoid after all—confessing had consequences.

Although she sympathized with Genevra's reaction to the grim prediction, she couldn't help also feeling excluded. Now, Daniel, April, and Genevra were all linked to each other, while she and Drew stood outside the circle.

Be grateful, she told herself. Judging by Genevra's terror, she and Drew were the lucky ones.

Odile had warned them that the Book's predictions were dangerous to those without self-knowledge. Could Genevra's real problem be her mental instability, her ambivalence about her own choices? Maybe, but April and Daniel were trying to deny she had anything to worry about, and that didn't strike Eleanor as especially enlightened, either.

As they coaxed Genevra out of the pool, Eleanor felt sneakily glad that Drew had backed down from his suggestion. If they complained to Odile about dire predictions and nightmares, she was sure to cut off their access to the Book.

It doesn't matter to me. I promised Daniel I wouldn't confess, no matter what. But she was relieved, just the same.

23

Now

September 28, 2019, 6:23 a.m.

Eleanor was in a dark, dark place. Underground, where the cold of the earth seeped in. Dirt floor under her feet, candlelight dancing on rough stone walls.

She held the candle in one hand and *The Book of Dark Nights* in the other, clutching it tight to her chest. Skirts rustled and then pooled around her as she knelt and set the candle on the floor of the narrow passage.

Here the old masonry wall had crumbled, leaving a small, dark cavity. Reaching in with her free hand, she felt the cold damp of natural limestone. When the wall was repaired with new bricks, a gap would remain hidden behind it.

The Book vibrated madly against her bodice. It was stuffed with confessions, but not sated. Never, until every page was full—and then what?

She had made a terrible mistake, and she would pay the price. But not in her lifetime. Ignoring the throbbing of the

Book, even though it felt as urgent and intimate as her own heartbeat, she placed it in the cavity and shoved it out of sight.

With any luck, no one would ever find it.

Then she was opening her eyes and startling upright to find herself belted into an uncomfortable economy seat, surrounded by the rumble of an Airbus crossing the Atlantic. Dim but steady lighting, temperature-controlled air, the distant beep of some electronic device—all the comforts of the twenty-first century.

Where had she been just now? It had been familiar and yet not.

She stiffened again in surprise as she realized that Daniel's head was resting on her shoulder—then relaxed, not wanting to wake him. He needed the sleep.

They'd stayed apart most of Friday while Eleanor made the travel arrangements, and their drive to the airport for the evening flight had been awkward. She hadn't dared ask him whether he'd contacted his father about meeting in Paris, but she also didn't feel comfortable reaching out to Theuthet without his blessing.

For his part, Daniel didn't ask her any more questions about what had happened between them in college. But she sensed his wariness of her. Every now and then she turned around—at the TSA check-in, for instance—and caught him gazing straight at her with brows furrowed, as if he were starting to remember.

Please let it happen slowly, not all at once. Maybe his remembering was inevitable, but she feared what it would mean for finding the Book. For the moment, at least, they needed to be allies.

The weight of his body against hers felt familiar and good, as did the tickle of his hair on her neck. When she concentrated, she could sense each even breath pulsing through him. He was sleeping soundly for now, without nightmares.

Unlike me. But Eleanor's nightmare, if it was a nightmare, hadn't been typical. In the years since her confession, she'd had some dreams in which she was searching desperately for the lost Book in a surreal and chaotic setting, and others in which she and a throng of people—including Daniel—were trapped in a hellish space that might be the Book itself. But in this dream, she had been *hiding* the Book. And all the details suggested she had been Mariane. *Go next where <u>she</u> hid the Book*, Odile's sticky note had said.

But why would Mariane hide the Book? That was what they still didn't know. In the dream, she'd seemed to be trying to fix a terrible mistake.

And she hadn't wanted the Book to be found.

***

"Don't look now," Daniel said as they climbed the stairs from Luxembourg Station, "but the boy in the white tee has been tailing us since the airport."

Eleanor couldn't keep herself from glancing the way they'd come. The Latin Quarter stops were popular and crowded. But she managed to pick out a young man with a big, square face and butter-blond hair.

She turned back quickly as they emerged into the sunlight, remembering the threatening note they'd found in Odile's ransacked house. If Marc Vasselin was behind that, he might certainly have coconspirators in Paris.

When Eleanor spoke with Will yesterday, securing the money for their trip, he'd mentioned getting a weird call from someone with a French accent, claiming to be an antique dealer who wanted to buy the Book on behalf of a client. They seemed to think the university owned it. When Will had referred them to Daniel, they'd hung up without giving their name.

She, Daniel, and Will somehow weren't the only ones who knew the Book was missing. Other parties were sniffing around.

She checked her watch—a half hour till their appointment at the Musée du Luxembourg, part of the palace that had once been Party Central for the Duchess of Berry. The building's cellar was normally off-limits to visitors, but Odile had been friendly with the curator, who was saddened by the news of her death and all too happy to do a favor for the bereaved son.

"Let's cut through the park," Eleanor said, turning away from the traffic of Boulevard Saint-Michel toward the wrought-iron fence of the Jardin du Luxembourg.

All around them, people were pushing and shoving and pointing, some blocking the pedestrian flow to gaze in fascination at the eighteenth-century apartment blocks with their gables and garrets and delicate lacework balconies. Behind the fence, a breeze swept rusty leaves from the groomed branches, promising tranquility.

Eleanor had forgotten how overwhelming Paris was, even to someone accustomed to the bustle of Harvard Square.

She had studied here with Julien Theuthet the year after she graduated, thanks to the scholarship Odile had secured for her. Her stay had been expensive, cold, and lonely—even lonelier than her senior year at Harvard without Daniel. But spring in the Jardin du Luxembourg almost made up for it. She'd spent hours under the sculpted trees in the warm sun, savoring the scent of blossoming chestnuts and the colors of serrated tulips, dreaming up ideas for a novel of her own.

And when she finally did write her book, she had ended it with a fantasy of reuniting with Daniel in the Jardin, both of them older. How ironic that they were here now. He was probably more distant from her than he'd ever been, and she couldn't remind him of the past without also reminding him of every reason he'd rejected her.

She shrank from a knot of phone-fixated Americans, only to find herself on a collision course with a trio of French students talking animatedly about a *manif*—a protest. Her French comprehension was flooding back, though her speech was halting.

She didn't resist when Daniel took her arm and steered her through the gate onto a paved path of the Jardin. "It's been a while," she admitted. "I spent a year here studying with . . ."

"My father?" He met her eyes at last. "It's okay. We can talk about him."

As the golden-green light of the park closed over their heads, Eleanor snuck a glance over her shoulder. There was no sign of the boy in the white T-shirt.

"Have you called him?" she ventured, trying hard not to sound like a nag.

"You've been dying to ask that since Logan, haven't you?" But Daniel didn't sound angry, only a little amused. "I left a voice mail when we landed. He'll get back to me. He has an apartment in the Rue d'Ulm, and he never leaves Paris except in August when everyone does."

That was a relief. Even if they found the Book, Eleanor had no idea what to do about the anonymous demand to bring it to the library on Sunday. Allowing for time zones, that was tomorrow.

The Book belonged to the Library of Fates, and she was the librarian. Even if Will and his boss's thirst for donations hadn't been an issue, they couldn't hand the source of the library's power over to Marc, a scholar who believed Mariane's creation would allow him to become the author of the last book anyone would ever need. Either he was delusional, or the All-Things Book was possible—an apocalyptic scenario for all books and bookish people, much as Eleanor tried to dismiss it.

Theuthet could help them make sense of it all—and perhaps tell them how much danger Marc really posed.

Daniel had fallen silent. The intense light that came with their current northern latitude limned loose strands of his hair in gold.

"Your father's wife died a few years ago, didn't she?" Eleanor asked.

"Yeah." His long legs carried him a little ahead of her now, so she couldn't see his expression. "I wondered if Mom would come back here to live with him, but she seemed happy seeing him only once a year or so. Or maybe she was still worried about upsetting his precious daughters. When I was eight," he added after a moment, "I asked her if I could meet my half sisters. She said she'd promised him we would never disrupt his family."

Eleanor had already heard this anecdote from Daniel, but she was touched that he trusted her enough to tell her again. Maybe she hadn't alienated him with her requests to meet with Theuthet as much as she'd feared.

They strolled the allées of trees, some trimmed into boxy rows while others were allowed to wave their natural fronds over the heads of old men with tiny dogs and au pairs pushing strollers. A loamy smell rose from the leaf-strewn earth: the natural bouquet of an urban park, with a French twist of Gauloises ash.

"Maybe your mother just liked her space," Eleanor suggested. "She didn't want to leave her library."

Daniel paused as they reached the open area at the center of the Jardin, where an octagonal pool faced the sand-colored Luxembourg Palace, now the staid seat of the French Senate. He was looking at her, his focus disturbingly keen. "Like you?" he asked. "I mean, have you ever done anything else, Eleanor? Or has that library been your whole life?"

Eleanor's cheeks flared. Carlyle had called her a *loyal apprentice*, and Daniel must have picked up on that phrase—and its accusing tone.

Or maybe he was just curious. She reminded herself that she was more responsible for any tension between them than he was.

"Not my whole life, no," she said, gazing past him to the palace where the Duchess of Berry had once lived—and, according to the legend, Mariane had demonstrated the power of the Book in the library. The neoclassical façade looked cold and impersonal.

The Musée du Luxembourg was housed in a smaller brick building that had once been the ducal estate's orangery. As they headed down a wide avenue of yellow chestnut trees toward it, she told Daniel about the job she'd taken at another university and how she'd returned to Harvard just three years later, after getting that worrying call from Odile. As she'd noted earlier, Marc had shown up at the library one day and demanded the Book.

"Odile claimed Marc didn't pose any physical threat," she said. "But I stayed with Odile for a week after the incident, since it was my spring break, and she was different."

During that visit, Eleanor had registered for the first time that her mentor was getting on in years, despite Odile's fierce efforts to deny it. Odile had begun drinking too much wine with dinner and rising late and groggy in the mornings. She told Eleanor things she hadn't mentioned in their emails—for instance, that students were no longer eager to receive invitations to her seminar. The world had moved on from the theories of Julien Theuthet, and she felt as if her life's work had been in vain.

"So the next semester, I quit and came back," she said, feeling his dark eyes on her. "I put things in order, started doing the administrative tasks, took over some of the teaching." And eventually Will had recruited her to use the library's power on potential donors, which he claimed she did better even than Odile. She'd felt special and *needed* in a way she never had outside the library.

"It wasn't a sacrifice to leave your other job like that?" Daniel asked, shadows of the chestnut boughs playing over his face. "You didn't have, well . . . friends? Or someone more special?"

"No one that important." She said it bluntly, looking away from him into the shifting golden light of the trees, daring him to think less of her. "What about you?" He'd made it clear that he'd raised his daughter by himself, but surely he had plenty of company.

"Nothing long-term." Now it was his turn to be evasive. "I had my hands full learning to be a responsible adult with a kid."

They'd almost reached the end of the path, which led out onto the Rue de Vaugirard. Daniel turned to face her. "Do you think I should let my dad see Sandrine? I know my mom thought so."

The question surprised Eleanor—did her opinion actually matter to him? The open expectation on his face suggested it might. "If Sandrine is eighteen, then it's her decision now," she pointed out, leading the way to the stately brick-and-limestone façade of the museum. "You can choose to be part of it or not, but if she wants a grandfather . . ."

Daniel sighed. "I know."

As they stepped inside the museum, which housed temporary exhibitions of modern art, his mood seemed to darken another degree. "Having a daughter of university age, being back at Harvard, running into Carlyle—it's all made me think about our seminar and what happened to poor Drew. Did you hear about Genevra, by the way?"

Eleanor had been momentarily distracted by the giant abstract paintings in the stark, renovated gallery. But now she stopped short. Carlyle had said something strange about Genevra on Thursday. In the chaos of the break-in, she'd forgotten all about it. "Hear what?"

"Genevra's dead."

His voice echoed in the quiet, and Eleanor saw patrons glancing at them from the other end of the gallery. She was suddenly very aware of every breath she drew, of her tight jaw and newly clenched fist. "How?"

I need to talk to Odile, Genevra had said last year, dropping by the library on a trip to Boston from LA, where she had some fancy job in film marketing. She had on an expensive suit and too much eye makeup, and her words sounded slurry, as if she were overmedicated. *I can't take the nightmares anymore. I want to get rid of them.*

Daniel cleared his throat and spoke at a lower volume. "She died by suicide. In July. April told me when I talked to her yesterday. She said Genevra never dealt with the nightmares as well as the rest of us did."

Eleanor stared dully at a gigantic swoosh of crimson on the nearest canvas, reminding herself that Genevra had been unstable. All these years she'd been obsessed with her prediction, seeing it as foretelling her death. Odile always said some people lacked the knowledge and strength of character to handle a glimpse of their future. And they'd all confessed to the Book of their own free will.

But she came the library asking for help, and I . . .

She knew there was no cure for the nightmares, so instead, she'd ordered Genevra to ask her for a book. When

Genevra obeyed, Eleanor had used the power to find her old classmate the most soothing, enthralling book she could. It wouldn't banish Genevra's nightmares forever, but with any luck, it would give her some peace.

It had worked. Genevra walked out of the library with the book in her hands and a beatific smile on her face, having entirely forgotten her reason for seeking out her old professor.

She'd never bothered them again.

But I didn't really help her, did I? I just distracted her to make my own life easier.

In the office, an earnest-looking art student type offered them seats while they waited for the curator, but Eleanor was restless. She stalked around examining the prints on the walls, her own guilt slowly sinking in. She hadn't taken Genevra's problems seriously enough, and now it was too late.

Had Odile known Genevra was dead? Why hadn't she mentioned it?

Daniel came up behind her as she studied a triptych depicting women doing a wild, witchy dance, some of them carrying spindles from which long threads dangled.

He asked quietly, "Do you remember when Genevra was so upset about her prediction that she wouldn't come out of the Adams House swimming pool? Were you there that night?"

Of course I was. With you. Odile's note had said Eleanor should fill in the blanks in Daniel's memory, but what if she didn't want to tell him everything?

Before she could answer, they were interrupted by the curator, Lucie Delbarre, a small woman about their age with her hair in cornrows and a soft shawl that matched her eye makeup, the picture of a well-accessorized Parisienne. She cheek-kissed them both and then enfolded Daniel in a teary hug, telling him in French that his mother was an inspiration.

"And you say she wanted you to see the place where *The*

Book of Dark Nights was found?" The curator took a step back and gave them both a skeptical, sizing-up look. "Now, you do realize that's only a story? An urban legend, one might say. There's no proof of the Book's existence. That's what I told the young man Odile sent here last month."

Eleanor exchanged a glance with Daniel. "Young man?"

"Yes, a Harvard doctoral student doing research here. Odile asked me to show him the hole in the cellar wall, too, so he could snap photos for his monograph." Lucie led them out of the office into an older part of the building, with exposed beams and rough plaster walls. "It's just through here. I warned him there was nothing actually to see, but he'd read Juliette Aubry's book and was enthralled by tales of this supposed witch Mariane."

"I'm a fan of Professor Aubry's book, too," Eleanor said, shooting Daniel a significant glance. Odile could have used this student friend to plant a clue *where she hid the Book*, as her sticky note had specified.

They were in the right place.

"It's a beautiful story, but honestly more fiction than fact," Lucie said as they descended a staircase into the darkness of a cellar, cold air snaking around their ankles. "What do we really know about this Mariane? Nothing, and that encourages fanciful imaginings. Juliette was a friend of mine, too. Shortly before her death, she warned me that her work had spawned a loose sect of people eager to possess the Book—neo-pagans, antique dealers, and a few who wrote to her calling themselves *confessors*."

Confessors. People who had confessed to the Book. Eleanor wondered if Daniel was thinking what she was: that Marc Vasselin could have recruited other people like him, motivated by the same desire to wrest the Book away from Odile and write the All-Things Book.

As they reached the bottom of the stairs, she lost the thread of her thoughts. Damp chill rose thick around them, bringing scents of earth and stone that were disturbingly familiar.

My dream. The floor was concrete now, not earthen, and when Lucie touched a switch, LED bulbs illuminated the space, which appeared to extend all the way under the building. Eleanor had been here once before, years ago, with Juliette. But she was sure this was also where she'd stood in her dream, watching candlelight flicker on the walls.

"In the era of Voltaire and Mariane, this building was an orangery—a greenhouse, essentially." Lucie led them on a weaving path between looming crates and pallets. "This cellar was used to keep gardening equipment. If Mariane was indeed a servant in the palace, as Juliette believed, she would have had access. Today, we use it to store mounting equipment, stray canvases, works from past shows."

"And when the Book was found?" Daniel's voice was hushed; the atmosphere must be affecting him, too. "1968, wasn't it?"

"That was before my time, but yes, that's how the story goes. The whole Latin Quarter had erupted in student and worker protests that spring."

Eleanor recalled Odile telling her how she'd first met Theuthet amid the chaos of that historic uprising. Around the same time, according to the account Odile always gave in her seminars, Marc Vasselin had hidden from the police in this cellar, heard something scrabbling behind a wall, knocked down loose stones, and discovered the Book.

Lucie veered off from the central room into a passage where light fell short, leaving the far end in darkness. Eleanor made out an aged masonry wall with a jagged gap near the bottom, as if someone had taken a sledgehammer to it.

There. She froze as she took it all in. Everything was much older and more dilapidated than she recalled. But this was where she'd knelt in her dream and placed the Book inside the hole, never imagining that it would be found by a protestor centuries later, in a city transformed by countless upheavals.

Now the dream had merged into waking reality. Forgetting all about her companions, feeling as if she were in a trance, Eleanor walked straight up to the crumbling wall, kneeled beside it, and peered into the gap near the bottom.

Nearly three hundred years ago, Mariane created the Book, and then she changed her mind and stowed it here, where she thought no one would ever find it. Why would Mariane do such a thing after all the trouble she'd taken to craft *The Book of Dark Nights* for Voltaire, offering the philosopher a route to immortality through the All-Things Book?

In the distance, Eleanor heard Daniel and Lucie discussing Theuthet's close-knit circle of students and Marc's eventual divorce from Juliette.

She braced herself and reached into the dark hole in the wall, just as she had in her dream. Probably she should use her phone for light, to make sure she wasn't grabbing a rat or some other toothy thing. But it felt wrong to pollute this place with the blue glare of electronics.

So she let her fingers guide her. A few inches behind the wall, her touch met the clammy cold of a natural rock formation. Gingerly she felt around in the tight crevice, searching for anything that wouldn't normally be there. Wondering if Marc Vasselin had felt this way when he found the Book half a century ago.

Perhaps he'd sensed its power humming through the stones, and that was the real reason he'd knocked the wall down. If the Book were hidden here now, Eleanor was sure she'd be aware of it, too.

She could detect nothing alive in this dust of dead centuries, but her fingers encountered the sharp edge of a small, flat object.

Lucie's phone was buzzing in the background. "Sorry, I should answer this." She retreated a few steps into the main cellar.

One soundless stride brought Daniel within a few feet of Eleanor. "What's in there?" he hissed, bending to investigate.

"It feels like . . . a photograph?" Her hair had escaped from its bun and was hanging in her face, obscuring her vision. She pinched the object between two fingers and pried it out.

Sure enough, it was a Polaroid, but it was too dark to get a good look at the image. As she rose, she saw there was yet another sticky note attached to the photo, this one spring green. Odile's doing, all right.

Daniel had crouched where she'd been and was shining his phone's flashlight into the hole. "Nothing here," he said, sounding disappointed.

But their trip hadn't been in vain. They'd found another clue.

Halfway up the stairs, Eleanor turned for a last glance down into the cellar. Its cold wafted upward, sending shivers over her scalp and shoulders.

Then she looked down at the sticky note and made out Odile's handwriting:

> *You were both wrong about why your friend died. Find the book you used to mold him.*
> *Then find the Book.*

Him must mean Drew. Eleanor had to wait until the ambient light was stronger to make out the image in the Polaroid. But when she did, a breath snagged in her throat, and all she could do for a moment was stare.

Someone had snapped a photo of a page from *The Book of Dark Nights*. She recognized it instantly: the yellowed, irregular surface of the page. The printed words *Let me read you.*

Below was Drew Pollit's confession. And it was perfectly readable.

24

Then

April 6, 1995

Daniel was trapped in a dark place that smelled of mildew. All around him pressed a seething crowd of people, humming and swaying and moaning, the sounds echoing off a ceiling so high he couldn't see it. Mostly their noises reminded him of animals, full of senseless misery, yet sometimes he made out words: *Let us go.*

His mother was here—he could feel her. But when he tried to shove the people aside so he could find her, they forced him back like an inexorable tide. The air was thick with invisible dust, clogging his airways. He thought he glimpsed April's red hair, a momentary shimmer in the dark. Once he heard a whimper that sounded like Genevra. But the instant he noticed them, they were gone, too, leaving him alone in this . . . this . . .

Hell. The word was on his lips as he woke in his suite in Randolph Hall. *I dreamed I was in hell.*

Someone was knocking at his door. He'd stayed up late

walking with Eleanor last night and crashed right after the seminar. Now he was thoroughly disoriented on top of the clammy, sinister feeling the dream had given him, but he threw off the blankets and went to answer it.

He opened the door and took a panicked step backward as the exact same humming he'd heard in his dream swelled again in his ears.

"You have the Book," he said to Drew, who hulked in the doorway with his usual faint smell of weed and one hand behind his back.

"How'd you know?" Drew revealed his hand. There was the Book, the gold bands on its spine glinting through the gloom of the hallway. His grin faded, replaced by a surprisingly solemn expression as he said, "It's time for me to confess. And Will and Eleanor, if they want to."

The Book belongs in the library. Never remove it, or you remove the power as well. Over and over, Daniel's mother had reiterated that warning. And now, just like that, the Book was loose in the world. Seeing Drew display it so casually made Daniel's pulse race and his vision cloud, as if a wild animal had found its way into their suite.

"Give it to me," he croaked, advancing on his friend. "How'd you even get it?"

Drew backed away from Daniel, but he didn't give up the Book. There was a hard set to his jaw that Daniel had never seen before. "Watched you find the key. You told me the code is your birthday. Easy-peasy."

Daniel followed him into the common room, where Drew sat down on the futon with the Book clutched to his chest. "Your mom likes to keep a leash on this thing, doesn't she?" he said. "Funny, since it's not actually hers. She and her friends kept it secret, when historians and antique dealers would probably kill for it."

She'll kill me if it vanishes. Daniel's dismay must have shown on his face, because Drew released the Book and placed it on the table between them.

"Just pointin' it out," he said in a friendly way, raising one hand to stop Daniel from moving toward the Book. "Not trying to get you in trouble. Your mom asked you to make sure we wrote confessions, didn't she?"

Daniel's mouth went dry.

All this time he'd worried that Eleanor would figure it out, perceptive as she was, or cynical April. But his suitemate, who was always half stoned and chuckling over some warmed-over joke?

"I didn't know there'd be nightmares." He hated the defensive tone in his voice. "Once I started having them, I didn't want to get the Book out again, but the rest of you were so dead set on confessing."

It was true his mother had asked him to get confessions, but he hadn't done it just for her. He'd done it because he wanted to experience the thing she seemed to care about most in the world, and the Book was meant to be shared, and he hoped it would bring them self-knowledge, just as she promised. Do them good.

He hadn't meant to hurt anyone.

But the way Drew was gazing at him, with something approaching pity, it was like he was sizing Daniel up and seeing his limitations for the first time. *Judging* him. Drew had never done that before, beyond gently suggesting that Daniel should chill and go with the flow.

Daniel didn't want to make excuses for himself. He reached for the Book. "Look, I made a mistake, but it's time for us to stop—"

Drew got it first. "Nope," he said. "Not yet."

"Seriously, I'm *sorry*." Daniel was pleading now, and he

hated it, but he didn't want his mom to step into her library and find it cold and dead and powerless. That place was her whole life. He didn't want anyone else enduring the nightmares, either, but the Book couldn't just vanish. "Can't we just bring it back to the library?"

Drew kept looking at him with a serious expression that was utterly unlike Drew—not harsh, just way too observant, as if he could see past Daniel's façade to the frightened boy beneath, who *needed* to please his mother because she was all he had. "First I think we should call the others," he said levelly. "Get everybody over here, make it a party."

Daniel's worries must have been plain on his face, because Drew reassured him, "Nobody needs to know about your role."

He placed the Book on the table again, this time with a firm hand on top. "You want your mom to be happy, Daniel—I get that. And she'll get the Book back. But she doesn't own it, so I'm not sure why she should make all the rules."

The sense of being known and judged itched like an ant colony set loose on Daniel's skin. He was used to shaking off his mother's criticisms, but to be taken to task for his *loyalty* to her was new and unsettling. Maybe her influence ran deeper than he'd realized.

He didn't want to think about that, so he told himself they were only arguing because Drew wasn't acting like himself. Ever since Eleanor had given him that Dostoevsky book, he'd been different—spending hours reading, disappearing at night and refusing to say where, cutting back on his drinking and smoking and avoiding the harder stuff.

Maybe Drew was replacing his old habits with a new obsession, the way some people in recovery took up cigarettes. In his current volatile state, a dark prediction was the last thing he needed.

"You don't want the Book, Drew," Daniel assured his friend, keeping the tone light so he wouldn't sound like a buzzkill. "If you do confess, all you'll get for your trouble is a prediction that makes no sense and a bunch of creepy dreams."

Drew didn't blink. "It'll be back in the library tomorrow, Daniel," he said, as if that was all Daniel could possibly care about. "I just need to know something first that only it can tell me."

25

Now

September 28, 2019, 2:43 p.m.

Au Petit Suisse, just around the corner from the Musée du Luxembourg, was a bistro-café with wine-red woodwork that soaked up the light from globular lamps on tall brass stalks. It was Daniel's parents' favorite, so he hadn't been surprised when his father left a message suggesting they meet there at three.

Eleanor led the way past a gleaming pastry case full of golden-brown tartes aux poires, up the curve of the iron staircase to the loft, where they had a view of the main dining room, the street, and the edge of the park.

"Could you show me the clue now?" Daniel asked as they sat down, his voice hoarse with fatigue and more than a little irritation—at himself.

There were so many questions to ask his companion, and he didn't know how. After April's blanket warning not to trust Eleanor, he couldn't rely on her to be honest with him about the clues, the past, anything. He had tried to sound her out earlier by sharing the news of Genevra's death. She'd been clearly surprised, and her sadness seemed genuine, but he thought he'd caught a hint of guilt mingled with it.

A cold-eyed server in the traditional white tie arrived before Eleanor could show him the clue. Daniel ordered a double espresso and Pastis, while she asked for a pot of Odile's favorite Lapsang souchong tea.

When the server was gone, she placed a Polaroid on the table, beside another sticky note in his mom's handwriting:

> *You were both wrong about why your friend died. Find the book you used to mold him. Then find the Book.*

"This one's about Drew." Daniel frowned. The cause of Drew's death seemed unambiguous: a self-inflicted fall. Yet his memories of that time kept liquefying and shifting, making him unsure of anything.

While he was dozing on the plane, all kinds of images and sensations from junior year had trickled back, fresh and yet perplexingly familiar: snow running down Eleanor's cheeks like tears as they crossed the footbridge; new leaves rustling over the concrete bench as they sat there in the spring; the warm shape of her hand in his. All just as Eleanor's novel had described.

The visions unsettled him, like moments he'd seen in a movie and assimilated into his own memories. At one point he'd realized his head was lolling on Eleanor's shoulder and sat up with a start, telling himself to get a grip.

All he needed from Eleanor was help finding the Book. He didn't *need* to trust her. But he kept catching himself doing things like asking her whether he should let Sandrine meet his father—as if it were her business, as if her opinion should matter. As if they were closer than it made sense for them to be.

His mother's message had said Eleanor could help him remember, and now he knew he *did* need help. Every time he tried to focus harder on those new memories, he felt a vertiginous dread that reminded him of leaning over the balcony and gazing down four stories at Drew's body on the ground.

But how could Eleanor help him when she might have her own agenda?

"Who used a book to mold Drew?" he asked, mystified by that part of the clue. "What's that mean?"

Instead of answering, Eleanor touched the edge of the Polaroid. "This was his confession."

Foreboding tickled the back of Daniel's neck as he recognized a page from the Book, with its command to *Let me read you*. But the handwritten words following the prompt were easily decipherable:

I made A.C. fall in love with me, but will she keep on loving me the way I love her? Say yes. I'm not good with words, but I think I need her to get me through the next few months.

There was a space, followed by a quotation in the same handwriting, which Daniel supposed must be the Book's answer:

"What is truth? Where a woman is concerned, it's the story that's easiest to believe."

"What the fuck?" Daniel muttered, ignoring the server who'd returned with their order. "How can we even read this?"

Eleanor mixed water into his glass of sweet anise liqueur for him. "I told you Odile has methods of reading the Book."

A Polaroid camera had done the trick? But now the confession itself monopolized Daniel's attention. "*A.C.* Drew and *April* were in love?" he asked incredulously, gulping the espresso. "They were, like, polar opposites. A border collie and a golden retriever." April hadn't even hinted at this in their call—but then, he'd asked her about Eleanor, not Drew.

On the night he confessed, Drew had said he "just needed to know something" that only the Book could tell him. Daniel had assumed he planned to ask the Book whether his mother would survive her cancer. This love business was totally out of left field.

"Drew wasn't in love with anybody," he protested. "I would've known that. He was my closest friend. We lived together!"

But the Book had changed Drew, Daniel's memories told him. It had changed all the students—and not just in their seminar, if Carlyle's account could be trusted.

What was my mom thinking, giving that thing to students? She must have known about the nightmares.

Eleanor was peering down at the photo. "The message Odile left with her will said the underlined parts are important," she observed, tapping the underlined word *is* in the prediction. "In yours, it was the words *all things*, wasn't it?"

"Yeah." How would she even remember that? But Daniel supposed he should stop wondering how she remembered anything.

"And I'm not so surprised Drew confessed he was in love." Eleanor shifted her gaze to the window, then back to him. "Once, in the library, he told me he knew how it felt to be in that early stage of infatuation, where you're lightheaded all the time."

There was pink in her cheeks and something like a plea in her eyes, as if she expected him to know the conversation she referred to—or what had inspired it. Daniel was on the verge of asking the questions he hadn't dared to ask when the scratchy sound of a throat being cleared made him realize they were no longer alone.

An old man in an overcoat had paused beside the table and was peering down at them with surprisingly sharp dark eyes. He stank fiercely of cigarettes, and his voice quavered as he said in French, "Daniel. My son. It's been far too long."

I almost didn't recognize him. Julien was in his eighties now, and his proud profile and aquiline nose had thickened like melting candle wax. He walked haltingly with a bend in his back, no longer sailing through a room.

But he was still impeccably turned out, in his wool overcoat and Rolex, and his French was mellifluous and cultured. That was the man Daniel remembered from his childhood, the stranger whom his mother expected him to treat like a father, though they rarely met more than once a year.

Odile had always been part of those encounters, orchestrating everything, and now Daniel felt her absence like a wound. At the same time, the old rage surged inside him as he rose and allowed his father to embrace him clumsily, seizing hold of Daniel's hand as if it were an anchor. The man was trembling—with emotion or frailty, who knew?

Daniel didn't regret ending their meetings after Julien asked about Sandrine, who was eight at the time. He'd been furious with Odile for mentioning his daughter, and her refusal to understand why only made him more furious. He didn't want Sandrine to end up like him—a supplicant, having stiff and awkward dinners with a man who would never see them as good enough to be part of his family.

"Forgive me for not calling you as soon as I heard about your mother." The old man's breath hitched, and suddenly his whole body was shuddering violently, his free hand flat on the table to keep himself upright. "I know you choose to keep your distance, but I should have made the first move."

Daniel pulled out a chair that felt like a boulder. He'd never seen his father this weak or apologetic, but old age often made people seek amends, didn't it? It meant nothing. "I called because I need your help," he said, each word a painful lance through his pride.

"Anything in my power." Julien sat down, blinking rapidly, his eyes rheumy or perhaps full of tears. To Eleanor, he said in his courtly way, "If only we were meeting under better circumstances. What a loss this must be for you, too."

"It is," she answered in tentative French, with the winsome smile of someone meeting an old friend. "The whole university is in mourning."

"Ah, I wish I could return to the Library of Fates! Soon. For the memorial, perhaps." Julien plucked a linen handkerchief from his coat and dabbed at a rogue tear on his cheek. "But I don't travel well these days."

He's playing up to her. Julien always did that with women, Odile in particular. When he shifted his attention back to Daniel, though, the unconcealed pain in that gaze was startling. "I know it takes extraordinary circumstances to make you reach out to me. Tell me all, please, and what I can do."

Daniel couldn't help ducking his head. He suspected he was blushing like a child put on the spot.

Luckily, Eleanor came to his rescue. "*The Book of Dark Nights* has vanished," she said. "Odile left a message suggesting she hid it because she feared someone would steal it. We wonder if this someone could be your former student who recovered the Book—Marc Vasselin."

She launched into a rapid recap of the circumstances, from Odile's message to the ransacked house. She didn't mention the clues—because they were too personal? Daniel wondered—but she ended by saying that they'd found Mariane's letter and thought it might explain Marc's motive for wanting the Book.

Julien listened intently, a pained look coming and going on his face. "Ah, yes. We gave Odile the letter for safekeeping," he said when Eleanor was done. "Juliette found it among Voltaire's correspondence. After Marc made his remarkable find of the Book, we grasped that the letter contained instructions for its use." His eyes clouded nostalgically. "Such a thrilling discovery. For a hectic week or two, we almost believed in the idea of the All-Things Book—a book to end all books. A book whose author would tower even higher than Shakespeare."

"Don't you still believe in it?" Daniel sounded rude, even to himself. "I mean, you put it in your theory."

"He put it in his theory as a hypothetical," Eleanor said smoothly. "A useful impossibility, like the concept of infinity. But did Marc keep believing in the All-Things Book?" she continued, turning to Julien. "That's what we're wondering now."

Daniel was grateful she was here to steer the conversation, giving his father the same rapt respect that Odile always had. But in Eleanor's case, he suspected, it was more a tactic than genuine. She seemed to have a talent for saying the right words to make someone open up, like a reporter or detective.

They learned that Marc Vasselin lived with his son in Nancy. Julien hadn't seen him since his departure from Paris—twelve years ago, shortly after Marc had flown across the Atlantic to demand the Book from Odile. "I thought his mind might be going already, poor boy. Before he left, he came to my office rambling about how the Book was his lawful property, since he'd found it. I pointed out that if it belongs to anyone, that would be *la patrie*—the French republic—but Marc kept insisting that he would write the All-Things Book and seal his immortality. I do think he actually believed it."

Daniel could imagine the scene: the younger man ranting and raving while his professor listened condescendingly.

"And we can't go to the authorities," he said, "because the Book *isn't* ours, am I right?"

"Go to the authorities!" His father looked alarmed. "I certainly hope you won't report poor Marc. Whatever he believes, I can't imagine him breaking into your mother's house—the man's no criminal."

Eleanor nodded in the encouraging way she had. "Do you think Marc might have told any friends or students about *The Book of Dark Nights* and the All-Things Book? Any dealers in antiquities, for instance?"

Daniel remembered the young blond guy who he could swear had followed them from the train station. "There must be people who'd pay major coin for that, whether they believe in a book to end all books or not."

"Yes, I imagine Marc might have told people. Yes." Julien's gaze had begun to wander, as if he were losing interest. But when he looked up at Daniel, he seemed to click into focus again. "I know why Eleanor wants the Book back, of course. The Library of Fates has helped so many people find their paths. But why do *you* want it, Daniel?"

The question was gentle enough, but for Daniel it was the last straw. If his father didn't already know about the strange game his mother had played with her will, he wouldn't enlighten him. "Maybe I also care about the library," he snapped. "It was my mom's life's work. And whatever she may have told you, I did love her. After all, she was all I had."

He regretted the words instantly—they sounded bitter and childish. But it was also a relief to voice the resentment, something he had never dared do when he was younger.

When a quivering hand clasped his, he looked up in surprise. Julien had reached across the table, and his eyes were glassy with tears. "Of course you loved your mother," he said. "And she loved you, to her last breath. She told me what a good father you've been to your daughter . . . certainly a better one than you had yourself."

Daniel couldn't move. He'd never expected to hear his father acknowledge he'd been lacking. Now he didn't know whether to laugh or cry. "I did the best I could," he managed.

Can you even imagine how it feels to have a father who's a stranger? But he bit back the words. None of it could be changed, so why rehash it? *Water under the bridge*, his mother would probably say if she were here.

Julien continued to probe the wound, however. "It pains me how little I know you," he said, his earnest brown eyes putting weight behind the admission. "It's entirely my fault, yet I can't rest easy with it. And I understand why you don't want your daughter to know me at all."

So his father was going to broach that issue. "I made a choice," Daniel said through gritted teeth.

"And your choice hurt me. But I understand. Why should I deserve to know your daughter—or you, for that matter? These many years, I've treated you like strangers."

Daniel's chin wobbled, and he cursed the tears that blurred his vision. It was too late for his father to repair the effect of all those years of absence. Fiercely, he reminded himself Julien was only making this belated effort because his wife was dead and his "real" children were grown, freeing him to have a relationship with his illegitimate family if he chose.

Throughout his childhood, his mother had made excuses for his father. Sometimes she said that an absent parent was better than an abusive one, or that having one loving, attentive parent—herself—was better than having two parents who were disengaged. And sometimes she simply insisted that brilliant people like Julien couldn't live by the same rules as the rest of the world.

Now, for the first time, Daniel realized how much pain

those excuses must have hidden. His mother had *wanted* him to have a real relationship with his father, unlikely as that was.

"I guess I never knew what I was missing," he said in a thick voice. "But my mother—you hurt her when you treated me that way. And she adored you."

Julien's face crumpled. "Your mother was the love of my life," he said softly. "When I met her as a student, she shone like a flame. I regret every way I failed her—and you. I regret it very much."

Daniel's breath stuttered. He had to concentrate on counting the sugar cubes in the bowl to avoid letting the tears fall—an old trick he hadn't needed since he was a kid.

He was grateful when his father squeezed his hand and released it. "Now, let's see what we can do to assure her legacy. I don't suppose you have any hunches about where Odile might have hidden the Book?"

"We're pursuing some leads," Eleanor said—which was helpful, because Daniel wasn't capable of speaking right now. "But it would be good for us to know who else wants it—whether we're dealing with Marc again or someone more dangerous."

While Daniel recovered his composure, Julien assured Eleanor that he would get back to them after he'd made inquiries in the world of antique sellers, including some who dealt in objects of shady provenance. "I know a few friends with whom Marc might have been indiscreet. Anything I can do to help return the Book to the library, I will."

He folded his handkerchief and rose from the table, supporting himself with a shaky hand. "I'm glad you've changed your mind about the Book, Daniel. When you left school so abruptly, your mother told me you blamed the Book for your poor friend's death. She said you even asked her about destroying it."

Did I? Daniel didn't recall that, but with the benefit of hindsight, he thought his younger self had been on the right track. While the Book couldn't be directly blamed for Drew's or Genevra's deaths, it had certainly contributed.

"I want the Book back, yeah, but I don't think students should confess to it anymore." He didn't look at Eleanor as he spoke. She might disagree, because without the confessions, the power of the library would dwindle—so his mother had always said. But he had to take a stand on this. "I don't think it gives people real insight at all, just nightmares and self-fulfilling prophecies."

His father sighed. "*Every* book is a self-fulfilling prophecy, Daniel. It reads you as you read it, allowing you to watch your own possible fate play out on its pages."

Had the Book read him? Normally Daniel would have rejected this as academic foolishness, but now he wondered if Julien had a point. The idea of a personal literary canon was the only part of the theory of textual potential he'd ever liked. Since prying himself free of his mother's influence, he hadn't been a huge reader himself—at least not of classics—but he still loved hunkering down with a fat Stephen King paperback under the blazing Alpine stars, or with a book about a doomed Arctic exploration by the woodstove on a long winter's night.

The Book had given him a prediction suggesting he would turn away from his past, rejecting it as painful. "All things are taken from us, and become / Portions and parcels of the dreadful past." And he had turned away. He just hadn't realized he would *forget* some of that past, too.

Daniel rose to bid his father goodbye—a final farewell, for all either of them knew. "My daughter, Sandrine, is eighteen now," he said. "If you want, I'll give her your number and let her make the choice."

At the very least, he realized now, he should have done that earlier. His daughter had been old enough for a while to decide whether she wanted a grandfather. He'd allowed his personal resentments to become an obstacle on the pathway she was tracing through life.

Before he knew what was happening, Julien's arms closed around him. They brought a scent of the old-fashioned cologne that had reminded Daniel of cloves as a child, every time his father gave him the standard leave-taking of a kiss on each cheek.

He had always stood stiffly and barely endured those embraces, but now he hugged back.

Julien released him. "Thank you for allowing me to help," he said. "For trusting me when I've done little to deserve it. I hope to do my best to change that."

And, after giving Eleanor the double kiss, he shuffled away down the stairs.

Daniel sat down again heavily. The moment had wrung him out. It was a relief when Eleanor turned toward the window, giving him time to collect himself.

After several fortifying swallows of Pernod, followed by the espresso, he asked, "Where do we go next? If that clue is telling us, I'm not seeing it. We know now that Drew confessed he was in love with April, which doesn't make a lot of sense, from my point of view. But other than that . . ."

Eleanor emptied the dregs of the teapot into her cup. "The sticky note says we were both wrong about why Drew died. I'm not sure if that's true or why it matters. But I do know who used a book to *mold* him—me. I wanted to distract him from his worries, so I used the library to nudge him toward falling in love. It brought him *The Idiot* by Dostoevsky, and I think that was the beginning of the end."

26

THEN

April 6, 1995 (later)

Eleanor was in the Dunster House Library, reading about economic underdevelopment and listening to Carlyle's slow, sad rendition of *Moonlight Sonata*, when Daniel tapped her on the shoulder.

"It's Drew," he whispered. "He took the Book out of the library, and he wants to confess."

He took the Book out of the library? Eleanor was on her feet in a second, tugging on her coat.

As they hurried out of Dunster and through the dark streets, buttoning up against a scything wind, she tried to ignore the queasy knotting in her stomach. "Why would he do that? The Book isn't supposed to leave the library, ever."

"I told him that," Daniel said grimly. "But apparently he needs to know something that only the Book can tell him, whatever the hell that means."

Eleanor felt betrayed by Drew. She knew he hadn't meant

to hurt her, but nothing had ever made her feel special, extraordinary, *important* like being able to choose books for others in the Library of Fates. If the Book didn't return to the library, it would stop working, and then who would she be? A Meek little mouse again. Surely not the girl who'd caught Daniel's interest.

"He'll bring the Book back, right?" she asked anxiously as she followed Daniel through an archway into a grassy courtyard. "Or let us do it? Soon?"

"Tomorrow—I made him promise."

The four stories of Randolph Hall rose on all sides, topped with vertiginous slate roofs, chimneys, and gables with whimsical round windows. Eleanor still hadn't been inside Daniel's suite, but she'd admired how the building's standard Harvard red brick was twisted into gothic cornices and spires that the Puritan university founders surely wouldn't have condoned. Hip-hop beats drifted down from the upper floors, along with smoke from students getting their tobacco fixes on the iron balconies.

Inside, the stairwell seemed less Merchant Ivory and more like any dorm, with its dingy plaster and stink of wet socks. The suite was three flights up, built into the eaves.

The other four were already in the common room, drinking what smelled like beer from cracked mugs. April and Genevra huddled close together on a lumpy couch under a *Reservoir Dogs* poster, while a sulky-looking Will faced them across the room.

On the table in the room's center was the Book. The wrongness of it being here, plunked on the water-stained surface between a bag of Doritos and a glass bong, took Eleanor's breath away. "*Why*, Drew?" she demanded as Drew rose from where he'd sat cross-legged on the floor beside the table, as if guarding his prize.

Drew shrugged in a stubborn way, as if he'd already answered the same question from the others. "Professor Vernet doesn't own it. And the rest of us should get a chance to confess—you, me, and Will."

"I am *not* confessing," Will announced. "That thing creeps me out."

Daniel clasped Eleanor's hand for an instant, behind their backs where the others wouldn't see. She knew he was silently asking if she remembered her promise not to confess.

"I don't know if I'm ready," she demurred, then kneeled beside Drew, who'd sat down again. Something must have upset him to make him cast off his usual easygoing demeanor. "Everything okay?" she asked in a low voice. "Your mom . . . ?"

Drew dropped his eyes, and the hard expression melted. Underneath, he was still the same old Drew, with his good nature, premature smile lines, and unfocused eyes. "She's got a surgery date. No other news yet."

"It's scary. I'm sorry." That gave Eleanor an idea: Maybe he wanted to ask the Book about his mother's fate rather than his own. "But a prediction might not help," she added as Daniel went over to grab a beer. "When Professor Vernet said we needed self-knowledge, I think what she really meant is that our predictions won't mean anything to us until they've happened. Or if we can make any sense of them, we won't like it—think of Genevra's."

They both glanced over at the couch, where Genevra was guzzling from a mug and April was hovering over her.

"I'm not scared." When Drew raised his blue eyes to Eleanor's, she saw a surprisingly calm resolve in them. "Remember how I told you," he said, lowering his voice, "that when you first get really into somebody, you feel all tipsy and fragile? Like, you need to be sure they feel the same way, and not being sure could destroy you? Like when Prince Myshkin is going to marry Nastasya Filippovna, and she leaves him at the altar and runs away with someone she doesn't even love, someone who wants to hurt her. All because she's Self-Destructive, and life has already hurt her so badly."

It took Eleanor a moment to realize he was describing the plot of *The Idiot*. Then she thought she understood—Drew feared being abandoned, just like Prince Myshkin. When she'd tried to use the library to guide him away from morbid thoughts and toward love, had she succeeded, after all? "You want to ask the Book about . . . someone you love?"

Instead of answering, Drew abruptly got up and proclaimed they all needed "real drinks with liquor." Then he scooped up the Book and handed it to Eleanor. "You hold it for me," he said as if she were the only one he trusted. "Don't give it to Daniel. We'll bring it back to the library tomorrow. I already promised him, but he might not believe me."

While he went over to a makeshift bar, Eleanor settled on a beanbag chair under the large window that overlooked the balcony. The window draft made her shiver, but it felt good to have the Book humming quietly in her lap again—safe and secure. Drew was anxious on multiple fronts, she decided, and he'd made a rash move. But she would ensure the Book was back where it belonged as soon as possible.

She heard Daniel laughing, his voice mingling with April's as she described her spring break. He sounded already drunk—and relieved to discuss something that wasn't books, libraries, or magic.

I don't make him laugh enough, Eleanor thought. *I'm not fun*.

Handling the Book, she noticed something for the first time. The spine was slightly loose, bulging open at the top.

When she was a child, Eleanor had once written three wishes on a slip of paper and hidden them inside the loose spine of her favorite book. She wasn't sure why, but it had seemed like the right thing to do.

Now she slipped her finger into the gap between the Book's cover and its binding. Sure enough, something was stuck in there. Very gently, she tugged out a concoction of paper, flat wooden sticks, and cloth scraps, slightly shorter than her hand and featherlight on her palm.

After a moment, she realized she was looking at a folded fan. She held her breath as she opened it, half expecting the fragile accordion shape to disintegrate.

It didn't, perhaps because the paper was reinforced with cloth, giving the fan a fibrous texture similar to the pages of the Book. It was a paper made of threads, like the imaginary threads of their textual potential.

The sticks that formed the ribs of the fan weren't actually wood, she saw now, but something sharp-edged and yellowish. *Bone?*

The macabre thought made her cringe, but she didn't drop the fan. Words were written on it in faded amber ink: *Avec un mensonge, je meurs. With a lie, I die.*

She whispered the sentence to herself and remembered the warning from the frontispiece: *Lies are not tolerated.*

But who was this *I* who was dying? The person who was about to confess, or the Book itself? Was the Book threatening potential liars with death? Or was it only warning them that a dishonest confession would counteract its magic, killing their hopes of receiving a real prediction of the future?

With a lie, I die. Eleanor would never lie to the Book, though.

Daniel and April were still laughing, the sound grating on her ears. She knew their flirting meant nothing, but Daniel would probably flirt with girls this summer in Europe, too. She couldn't help resenting the promise he had forced on her.

Running her fingertips over the calfskin cover, feeling the evergreen thrill of the power trapped inside, she understood why Drew wanted to confess. He loved someone, and love craves certainty.

Could she ask the Book about Daniel, whether he cared enough to stay with her after college?

And would she be able to live with the answer?

***

Daniel had drunk three shots of whiskey way too fast. His head spun, and he felt like he might hurl. He tried to make his way over to Eleanor, but Will's chair was in the way. He caught her eye and gestured, silently asking her to bring him the Book.

Eleanor didn't move, just gazed back. Sitting there with the Book on her lap, she looked serene, as if she thought she had the whole situation under control.

Meanwhile, Genevra was busy warning Drew not to confess. She'd been describing her nightmares in vivid detail, while April looked alternately worried and bored.

"You have a wild imagination, kid," Will told Genevra. He twisted around to ask Daniel, "*You* don't have nightmares like that, do you?"

Daniel glanced at April. Should they tell the truth if it might dissuade Drew from his plan?

April only arched a brow and flipped her glossy hair over one shoulder, as if his scruples struck her as silly. "Nightmares? I dunno. They're weird dreams. Sometimes I'm in a kind of prison, and I feel Genevra and Daniel in there with me, but I can't talk to them."

"I feel both of you, too!" Genevra's eyes had gone enormous. "That's so creepy, like we're dreaming the same thing. Don't do it, Drew."

Daniel navigated around Will and reached over dizzily to snatch the Book from Eleanor's lap. But Drew got there first.

"I'm doing this," he announced, holding out his hand for the Book.

"I don't think you should," Daniel protested. But his head was swimming from the booze, and he didn't want Drew to tattle to the others that he'd helped his mother put them all in this position.

Odile had explained to him that the Book needed student confessions, ideally a few every year, to keep the library running. *They're more likely to confess if they think it's forbidden*, she'd added. *And their confessions will be honest. If the idea comes from me, it's an assignment. If you suggest it, it's a lark. A rare chance to disobey my rules.*

Now he appealed to Eleanor, who held the Book possessively clamped in both hands. "Maybe we should bring it back and leave the confessions for another day."

It's okay if you give it to me. This is better for Drew, he reassured her with his eyes, feeling glad she was on his side as he, too, reached out for the Book. Eleanor was naturally cautious. She must see how irrational Drew was being.

But when Eleanor looked at him, Daniel saw no warmth of mutual understanding, only a delicate furrow sketched between her brows. "You confessed, Daniel," she said. "You got a prediction. Why shouldn't he?"

She handed the Book over to Drew.

After that, the evening went blurry. *If he wants nightmares that badly, let him have them*, Daniel thought, throwing himself down on the couch.

He felt jaded and resigned—but more than that, he felt slighted. The sourness of whiskey mingled in his mouth with the bitterness of Eleanor saying no to him. Why couldn't she have trusted him on this? He knew his suitemate better than she did.

"Will, pen?" Drew asked.

Will tossed him one. Drew caught it handily and opened the Book with a glance around the room, as if daring the rest of them to interfere. Then he lowered his head and scowled at the page.

The Book was humming—a low-level but unmistakable sound of pleasure, as if it craved Drew's confession. When Daniel looked at Eleanor, he knew she heard it, too, and again he felt that pinch of disappointment that she hadn't listened to him.

Everyone had gone still—Genevra wide-eyed over her hunched knees, Will curious, Eleanor calm, April looking bored and a little sullen, but in a performative way. Everyone watching Drew.

Drew wrote for a few seconds and announced, "Done!" He closed the Book and held it out on his outstretched palms like an offering to the gods. "I have now fed you the truest of true confessions. Please tell me my future."

Will chuckled gamely, although Drew had sounded surprisingly earnest.

Daniel sipped his drink, trying to wash away the dread. He remembered his very first nightmare—the missing Book, the strange girl who ordered him to find it, and his terror. He wasn't sure which had seemed scarier in the dream, losing the Book or the Book itself. When he was younger, he'd thought of it as merely a treasure trove of secrets. But now that he'd confessed, he sensed unresolved sadness and fear and guilt in there, writhing and roiling and straining to escape the prison of the pages.

In his dream of earlier that evening, people had been crammed into a dark place together, just like the souls in Dante's *Inferno*. His own soul among them.

Drew opened the Book again. As his eyes flicked from

side to side, reading, his mouth twisted as if the words caused physical repulsion.

Then he said, "No," the word like a stone thrown into a still puddle. "No, that's not the answer. I don't accept that!"

His face was red, as if he'd drunk the whole bottle of Stoli in a gulp. He clutched the Book, knuckles whitening, and pulled the edge of his page sharply to tear it from the spine.

Daniel *felt* the rip of the paper more than he heard it—a wrenching, burning pain, as if his own hair or fingernails were being uprooted. "No!" he cried, on his feet in an instant.

Eleanor, who was closer, scrambled up from the beanbag chair and seized hold of the Book. But Drew wrested it away with an anguished groan, as if he felt the same pain Daniel did. The motion sent Eleanor stumbling backward.

"I'm getting rid of this fucking thing!" Drew shouted, fumbling the window latch open with his free hand and stepping onto the low sill.

Daniel dashed after his suitemate and caught his arm as Drew barged through the opening onto the wrought-iron balcony. Wind howled around their fourth-floor perch with a vengeance. Ignoring the frigid gusts, Daniel gripped Drew's sleeve fiercely with one hand and grabbed for the Book with the other.

For an instant, as he touched the calfskin, he could swear he also touched every person who'd ever written in the Book, some long dead and some still alive, their spirits pulsing around him in the raw wetness of the April night. With one touch, all those lives and emotions poured into his head.

Then, like a shockwave, the Book pushed him away. Scorching heat raced up his arm. He staggered backward, knees buckling. He was only dimly aware of his back hitting the bricks of the exterior wall and his body sliding down it.

Crumpled on the floor of the balcony, he watched helplessly as Drew straddled the railing, gripping it with his knees.

"No—wait!" Daniel scrabbled upright. "What are you doing?"

Balanced on the railing, Drew turned to him. His pupils were blown, his eyes like dark holes in the fabric of reality—and that was the part Daniel would never be able to forget: his friend's last, anguished gaze.

"Sorry," Drew croaked. "Not your fault."

He swung his other leg over the railing, and the momentum carried him over the edge. He was flailing limbs in the dark, and then he was gone.

Daniel didn't know how long it took him to move. The world had become a stop-motion film with missing frames, jostling him from moment to moment with no clue what happened in between. His back was against the wall. Then he was stepping forward to the railing. Feeling the cold of iron against his palms. Willing himself to peer over the edge.

He was aware of other people on the balcony now, but he couldn't look at them or understand their questions. He had eyes for only one thing: the Book.

Somehow, it sat balanced on the railing. Still open. When Daniel seized it, light spilling through the window showed him handwriting on the page, clearly Drew's yet illegible.

He'd expected the page to be torn at least halfway, if not entirely out of the Book. He could swear he'd seen the ancient paper come apart in Drew's hands.

But the page was intact. Not the slightest rip anywhere.

27

Now

September 28, 2019, 4:21 p.m.

"So *The Idiot* is the book we want," Eleanor said as they wandered down narrow Rue Racine toward the river. She wasn't eager to discuss how she'd *molded* Drew. Who knew how much she'd contributed to his death? Not just by handing him the Book that night, but by planting the need to confess in his mind, without even realizing she was doing so.

He'd wanted to *be sure* someone loved him, he'd said.

There was no accusation on Daniel's face, though, only curiosity. "You really think Dostoevsky made Drew fall in love with April?"

"I didn't know that at the time. But after seeing his confession, I think so. The librarian can exert a certain . . . persuasion." Daniel was furrowing his brow, clearly ready to ask more questions, so she changed the subject quickly. "I think we're getting close. 'Find the book you used to mold him. Then find the Book,' the clue said. The question is, which copy of *The Idiot*?"

"The one you gave him? Is it still in the Library of Fates?" Daniel seemed to be struggling to focus—understandably, after everything that had happened in the café. Seeing Julien embrace him had given Eleanor a lump in her throat, too, as she recalled the resentment that had shaped so much of his youth.

When Daniel ran off to Europe, she'd hoped he would let that part of his past go. Maybe now he was finally ready to forgive.

"I don't think *The Idiot* is in the library, no." She wasn't sure what had become of that book. "Did Drew still have it when . . . Daniel, do you remember that night?"

Daniel's gaze was trained straight ahead. "Of course," he said guardedly, as if he weren't entirely sure. "Drew was angry about the Book's prediction, so he tore the page—or tried to—and then he yelled something about getting rid of it. He was . . . distraught."

Eleanor's eyes passed over the beige stone façades without absorbing them. In her mind she was back in that stuffy suite in Randolph Hall, shivering in the cold wind from the window as Drew sprang out onto the balcony.

I handed him the Book. It's my fault he confessed. The old guilt seeped back through decades' worth of containment, like toxic waste into groundwater.

She'd been annoyed at Daniel for laughing with someone who wasn't her. For making her promise not to confess.

She could tell from Daniel's frown that he was remembering that night, too. But where was she in the scene? Had he censored her out of it? How could he remember Drew's death without her? "I always thought Drew died because he lied to the Book," she admitted.

"Lied? Why would he do that?" Daniel looked really confused—he *was* missing parts of that night, then. "I thought he asked about his mom, and the Book gave him a scary answer. Now I know what he actually confessed, though . . . maybe it *was* a lie, just a weird lie. I can't see him with April Carraway."

Based on what he'd said that night, Eleanor was sure Drew had been in love with someone. But Odile's clue said she and Daniel were *both* wrong about why Drew died. Maybe he *hadn't* lied.

I made A.C. fall in love with me, but will she keep on loving me the way I love her? Say yes. In his words, finally revealed to them, Eleanor heard an echo of her own nagging uncertainty about Daniel's feelings for her, her aching need to have them confirmed.

With its typical perversity, the Book had refused to give Drew the yes he needed. Instead, it had played with him, tossing his question back:

"What is truth? Where a woman is concerned, it's the story that's easiest to believe."

"The Book gave Drew a quote from *The House of Mirth*," Eleanor explained. "One of the books I gave April when the library was working through me. It's about two people who are in love and can't admit it. When she finally realizes she's meant to be with him, he rejects her because he believes malicious gossip about her. A tragedy of misunderstandings and missed connections."

Like ours, she added silently, though she feared that once Daniel remembered everything, he might not agree with that characterization.

They'd reached the intersection where boxed-in Rue Racine merged into the broader, tree-lined Boulevard Saint-Michel. The ruins of Roman baths on one side of the street confronted a Monoprix on the other. Daniel scowled at passersby, avoiding her eyes, as if he were working something out in his head.

"You were there that night," he said, and it didn't sound like a question.

"Yes." Eleanor gazed at the Roman archways and the crumbling ribbons of red-and-white bricks that had somehow endured for well over a millennium, and all the bitterness of that night welled back up inside her. "Yes, I was there, Daniel."

Are you remembering me? The question was so close to her lips. She was about to utter it when he cut her off.

"How can you give the Book to students, then?" He'd turned to face her at last. Fresh anger flashed under his beetling brows, mingled with confusion. "All this time I've been telling myself Drew was just in a bad place. Maybe it was his interpretation of the prediction that killed him—a self-fulfilling prophecy, like my dad was saying. But after hearing how Genevra died, I have to wonder. Was Carlyle right? *Is* the Book cursed?"

The Book doesn't hurt anyone. Some people just aren't ready for the knowledge it gives them. That was what Odile had always told Eleanor, and Eleanor in turn had assured Carlyle. Because she believed it, Eleanor had stood by and allowed Odile to use various ruses to coax students into confessing to the Book—failing to lock the office or the safe. And Odile seemed to be right—no one got hurt. There were the nightmares, of course, which bothered some students more than others, but no one else had ended up like Drew.

Until Genevra. It could be a coincidence, of course, but . . .

"I don't *give the Book to students*, Daniel. Your mother always handled that." Eleanor's voice was shaking, because she knew this was no excuse.

"Well, my mom's gone now. And you're the librarian, so it's up to you how to use the Book—or not." Daniel's eyes practically sparked with suspicion. "We both know that without new confessions, the library's power eventually wanes. And using the power, finding people the books they need—that matters to you, doesn't it? Being the librarian makes you feel special. Without confessions, there's no Library of Fates."

Eleanor felt battered by the words, as if they were a cold wind. It wasn't the first time he'd suggested she enjoyed wielding the library's power too much.

Caught up in the aftermath of Odile's death, pressured by Will's deadline for finding the Book, she hadn't had time for sober contemplation of what would happen after they did find it. She hadn't asked herself whether she really wanted to follow in Odile's footsteps.

"Maybe it is time to retire the Book," she admitted for the first time. "As long as people think they can use it to create the All-Things Book and make themselves immortal, someone will be after it." Especially now that there were only two blank pages left—a reminder that the magic couldn't last forever.

Daniel laughed harshly. "Are you sure you *could* retire the Book, Eleanor?"

They'd reached Boulevard Saint-Germain—the glittering expanse of designer boutiques dotted with famous old artists' cafés where servers gleefully mocked tourists' attempts to speak French. Sights like this had thrilled the younger Eleanor, who dreamed of being the woman in the café in the mural on the ceiling of the Library of Fates. But the fantasy had soured.

Daniel was right—the power mattered too much to her. Twenty-four years ago, it had drawn them together. After he left for Europe, the library had consoled her, filling the gaps in her life, giving her an identity no one could take away. She'd tried to leave once, but life outside the charmed sphere of the Book had seemed empty. And so she'd returned to the only place where she'd ever felt special, telling herself it was for Odile's sake.

Daniel kept right on talking. "When April called, she told me not to trust you. She said when Genevra came to you a year or so ago, asking for a cure for her nightmares, you used the library's power to distract her. You handed her a book that threw her off the trail. In fact, April accused you of brainwashing her."

Brainwashing. The old joke made Eleanor's chest constrict, because it hadn't always been just a joke.

"I shouldn't have done that," she said in a low voice. Perhaps when Genevra snapped out of her library-induced bliss, she'd found herself even more depressed than before, with no way out of the spiral. *Did I kill her?* she wondered, almost afraid to form the thought.

"So you *did* hypnotize Genevra?" Daniel asked mercilessly.

"No! I mean . . . I don't know." She wouldn't look at him now, and her voice sounded ragged with guilt even to her. She had spent way too long shifting blame to Odile. "The library sometimes does give me the power to influence people, but I've always tried to use it for their own good. When I gave Drew *The Idiot*, for instance, I was hoping to divert him from his morbid thoughts, to push him toward something more life-affirming. But it apparently backfired."

I tried to explain to you back then, but you wouldn't listen.

With his long strides, Daniel led her across the boulevard into Rue de la Harpe, a cobblestoned pedestrian route. "Yeah, but we're talking about what you did to Genevra. She wanted to ask my mom tough questions about how the Book was affecting her students, according to April. And you stopped her."

"I protected the library." Eleanor still wouldn't meet his gaze. Her shoulders had stiffened, a fist clenched at her side.

She was grateful for the bustle on the street, filled with busy cafés and food vendors as it slanted toward the Seine. When people jostled them apart, she had a few seconds to collect herself. But then Daniel was beside her again, too close, with his too-familiar gait and shoulder span and wool coat, saying, "You protected the *Book*, Eleanor. You've been protecting it all this time, haven't you? What if I said I think we should destroy it?"

"You can't do that!" The words burst from Eleanor before she could censor them. The thought of the Book going up in flames made her vision white out with terror. Juliette Aubry believed, based on her studies of eighteenth-century witchcraft, that the Book trapped its confessors' souls. And in some of Eleanor's dreams, she and Daniel and a crowd of other people did seem to be imprisoned in a mysterious space. All those confessions inside the Book, all those traces of people—where would they go?

They were both practically yelling. To avoid a public scene, she sidestepped the nearest knot of tourists and ducked into an alley between a storefront selling crêpes and another displaying multicolored Tunisian pastries. Daniel followed her, and they faced off across the weathered cobblestones.

"You can't destroy it," she repeated, this time almost in a croak. *The Book is us, all of us.* It would sound absurd and superstitious if she said it aloud, but a deep, intuitive part of her believed it.

"Eleanor." Daniel's hand reached across the space and grasped hers, warm and a little shaky, as if he were regretting his accusations. His voice had softened. "Why are you afraid of me? What did I do to hurt you?"

The change of tone made tears well in Eleanor's eyes, but she couldn't yield to them. "You're remembering."

"Just bits and pieces." His voice broke. "I saw the book

you wrote in my mom's study, and I . . . skimmed through it. At first I thought it was just fiction, but there were things that felt too familiar. Too real."

She couldn't look at him, but a shiver ran over her from head to toe as his grip on her hand tightened.

"I know I cared about you," he said. "Eleanor, what happened to us?"

28

——

THEN

April 6, 1995 (later)

Eleanor was the one who snatched the Book from the balcony railing where Drew had left it. The others were too busy thundering downstairs.

It had all happened too fast. One moment, she'd been trying to stop Drew from hurting the Book. The next, he was gone. The world had the oily texture of a nightmare as she threw on her coat, tucking the Book under it, and rushed after them.

They were huddled in a small group on the grass, gazing down at something. She elbowed her way in, looking for Drew. Daniel had said something about jumping off the balcony, but that couldn't be true. She must have missed Drew in the confusion.

I shouldn't have given him the Book. He got so upset. But she would calm Drew down now, and he would be fine, and . . .

Then she saw him.

He had landed on his back, one leg caught under the other at an ugly angle. His open eyes bulged from their sockets as if trying in vain to take in some enormous horror. His bloodless lips hung open.

The others were all talking at once, their mouths moving frantically, but Eleanor heard only the *thrum*, *thrum*, *thrum* of the Book under her coat, synchronizing itself to her heart. She stared down at Drew's broken body and told herself she was having a bad dream and any moment she would wake up.

It couldn't be real, because April was straddling Drew, trying to do chest compressions, and she was making sounds that Eleanor couldn't imagine coming out of April's mouth. Moaning, wailing, keening.

Words whispered in Eleanor's head: *With a lie, I die.* The message on the fan she'd found hidden in the book's spine.

Before, they'd seemed simply enigmatic. But now they echoed ominously, throbbing through the texture of the nightmare.

Strong arms wrapped around her from behind, and suddenly Daniel was breathing raggedly close to her ear. She rocked back into his embrace, grateful for him and yet not, because he felt too solid for a dream. *This is really happening.*

"I'm sorry I gave him the Book," she said for Daniel's ears alone. "I'm so sorry."

***

Gradually, poisonously, the reality of what had happened sank in. The House Master, in his bathrobe, made them all come inside and sit in the common room, draped in blankets. The campus officers asked questions.

As if they'd all agreed on it beforehand, no one mentioned the Book. Daniel said Drew had dashed out onto the balcony, yelling that he needed some air, and then jumped without warning. Genevra said they'd been playing truth or dare. Will said he had seen Drew pop "a few pills" earlier in the evening. April just shook her head and stared into space as if she could see to the other side of the world and nothing else interested her.

It wasn't until after four in the morning that Eleanor showed Daniel what she'd found in the Book.

The two of them were sitting side by side in plastic bucket chairs in the police station, where he needed to sign an official report on his suitemate's death. She unveiled the Book from her coat, where she'd been holding it close to her skin. Daniel flinched, as if he'd forgotten all about it. But she said, "You need to see this."

The homemade fan was still there. It felt wrong to expose it to the ugly glare of the fluorescent lights, but Daniel needed to know everything she did. Perhaps having a reason *why* his friend had died would bring him a little peace.

He stared at the fan. But instead of misting with tears, his eyes narrowed. "So what?"

"I think Mariane might have made this." Eleanor held the fan tenderly, because it felt almost as alive to her as the Book did. "She wanted to warn people not to lie to the Book, just like your mother warned us. Do you think . . . well, do you remember what Drew said? 'I have now fed you the truest of true confessions.'"

If you were going to confess the truth, why would you overemphasize it that way? It was almost as if Drew had wanted to test the Book, to see whether it could detect a lie.

She returned the fan to the Book's spine, waiting for Daniel to draw the same conclusion. She wouldn't rush him to it.

Daniel's chair grated on the linoleum, sliding away from her. The sallow light made his face masklike, the brows an angry ledge hooding his eyes.

"You're saying this was his *fault*?" he asked.

"Of course not!" How could this be Drew's fault? Odile herself had said she'd never actually seen the Book harm a liar. "I found the fan before it happened," Eleanor added, her voice squeaky with panic at his fury. "It's *my* fault. I should have told Drew."

Daniel raked his fingers through his hair and then rose in one movement, towering over her. She felt him vibrating like an engine running hot and rough, close to explosion.

"It *is* your fault," he said, not yelling but giving each word an emphasis that was somehow worse. "The Book didn't make Drew do anything, Eleanor. It did what it always does—creep people out with fucked-up predictions. He jumped because of what *you* did to him when you found those books for him in the library—*The Idiot* and the grief book. I know you didn't mean to hurt him—" his voice wobbled, then strengthened again "—but you changed him. You made him obsessed with death."

Eleanor was on her feet now, too, the Book cradled protectively in one arm. "I didn't! I . . . I tried to turn him *away* from death!"

"So you admit it?"

Eleanor opened her mouth to say she hadn't transformed Drew in any sinister way, only helped him see new sides of his own potential. That was all the library ever did—show readers the pathways that were open to them.

But the words wouldn't come out, because that wasn't the whole story. She *had* sent Drew in a new direction without knowing where the pathway would end, and she had relished having the power to do it. Power over him.

I can't be trusted with power. Hadn't she learned anything from what had happened to Renée? Eleanor had been the one in charge that day, the one responsible, and everything had gone so wrong.

Daniel's eyes were wide and damp, as if he were silently begging her to excuse herself. And she wanted to. But if she opened her mouth, she might lose control and scream and tear out her hair, so she stayed very still.

He swallowed hard. "I joked about you brainwashing Drew, but now I wonder if you really did. And last night you gave him the Book, even though I practically begged you not to."

I had a reason for that! But it was a selfish reason, Eleanor knew. Even in Drew's distress she'd seen only an echo of her own insecurities.

She stared speechlessly into Daniel's face and knew he was finally seeing her as she really was. *Selfish, bad, irresponsible. All my fault.*

"Daniel! My God, are you all right?" Odile's voice behind them, cracking from stress, broke the spell.

Daniel's cold gaze released Eleanor as he let his mother hug him.

Eleanor stood apart with the Book in her arms, watching Odile fuss over her son. She kept expecting to dissolve in tears. But nothing happened, as if a glass bubble had formed around her, insulating her from Daniel's feelings and her own alike.

He was ranting at his mother—something about the Book, something else about the library. She couldn't focus on it. Inside her bubble, she was safe from the shame.

When Odile eventually noticed her, Eleanor gave her the Book. "Here," she said breathlessly, almost shoving it into the professor's hands. "I guess I wasn't ready."

She didn't attempt any more pointless apologies. She just turned her back on both of them and rushed out of the waiting room and then out of the building, the world blurring to a watercolor around her as tears arrived, too late to do the slightest good.

She was sure Daniel Vernet would never speak to her again.

29

Now

September 28, 2019, 4:46 p.m.

"Eleanor," Daniel asked, "what happened to us?"

Clutching her hand in the alley off Rue de la Harpe, he regretted how harsh he'd been a moment ago. Who cared which book she'd given Genevra? Perhaps April blamed Eleanor for Genevra's death because she had simply never liked her.

Eleanor looked so miserable that he longed to tuck a dangling strand of shiny hair behind her ear, or to wrap an arm around her as he knew now he'd done in college. Just to reassure her that he didn't judge her for wanting to help people find their pathways through life.

I judged her before, though. Back then. Echoes of his own voice came back to him, hurling accusations. They were in a police station, pinned by the cruel glare of fluorescents. He'd been so devastated by his friend's death, so unwilling to believe it, that he'd lashed out at the one person who could have consoled him. You couldn't kill someone just by giving them the wrong books, and he should have known that.

"I think," he admitted, "I was a little envious of you. You could use the power, and I couldn't."

She nodded, just barely, but she didn't look up at him. "You were just a kid—we both were. You were upset and needed someone to blame. And I . . ."

Before she could finish, a man's voice barked behind them. "Hey! I need what you stole from the museum."

Daniel turned, dropping Eleanor's hand, to find the alley blocked by a stocky young man in a white T-shirt. The kid who'd followed them from the train station.

Then Eleanor gasped, and he saw the flash of a knife.

"I need what you stole," the boy repeated in an American accent, his tone too casual to match the threat in his stance. He peered around Daniel to address Eleanor. "From the hole in the wall."

How'd he know? Daniel had been mugged a few times in his travels. It had never seemed worth it to fight back. But he was brimming with chaotic feelings, itching for an outlet, and their attacker's attention was divided.

He sprang forward, grabbed the knife hand, and dug his nails into the boy's wrist, twisting the whole arm back toward his body.

The boy must not have expected a struggle. He kicked, but Daniel's grip was strong, and the knife clattered to the cobblestones. Releasing him, Daniel used the momentum to kick the weapon fiercely away.

Then he lunged. "Who sent you?"

The attacker turned on his heel and ran.

Daniel heard Eleanor protest—"Let him go!"—but he wasn't passing up a chance to get a lead on the person who'd trashed his dead mother's house. He took off, dodging wicker chairs and gawking tourists.

Frustration gave him wings. Adrenaline sharpened every reflex, narrowing his sensory awareness to his quarry weaving in and out of the crowd.

Even as he ran, he knew what he was actually chasing was distraction. He wanted relief from the memories buried in his head, because there were too many of them, and unearthing them like this hurt.

But it didn't work. Images flashed through his mind, transparent overlays on the crowded street in front of him. He was arguing with Eleanor on the pathway between Boylston Hall and Widener because she wanted to confess and he wouldn't let her. Swept up in the moment, he was using touches and kisses and his own sincere feelings for her to make her stop asking questions.

No, she hadn't invented their romance for her novel. He'd cared too much for her to let her go as easily as it nonetheless appeared he had. Had his stupid accusations after Drew's death been the end of their relationship, or was there more?

He forced himself to focus. With all the tourists in this area, the kid's white tee was the perfect camouflage. Daniel nearly lost him on Rue de la Huchette, then spotted the broad shoulders and towhead on the Place Saint-Michel. The boy was sprinting toward the river, probably trying to disappear in the traffic roaring off the bridge.

No one was going to get the Book—his resolution hardened as he ran. Not Marc Vasselin, not some rogue antique dealer or professor. Whether they hoped to sell it for millions or use it to create a book to end all books, they would just have to fuck off, because he would never let it mess with anyone else's head.

And he had a feeling Eleanor would back him on that. When he accused her of protecting the Book, he'd seen in her distraught face that she understood the dangers even better than he did, much as she wanted to deny them.

The boy bolted across the street against the light, and Daniel followed, careless of squealing brakes and honking horns. They were on the quais now, green-brown water crawling below them, beyond the tall stone parapet. He darted around two old men who were browsing a bookstall and barreled toward the would-be attacker.

"Leave us alone!" he shouted as the gap between them narrowed.

But the words had cost him a few strides. He was panting, losing focus and ground. And instead of running, the boy was straddling the parapet, swinging both legs over.

What the fuck? The drop was a good twenty feet or so straight down into filthy water. But then Daniel spied the bateau mouche slicing through the slick green waves a few yards from shore. In the same instant, he saw the boy leap.

The low sightseeing boat had an open deck, and the boy crashed directly into its railing. Daniel winced, expecting him to bounce or slide off, but somehow he grabbed a life preserver and clung. Water furled around his sneakers.

Then the kid was dragging himself up and over, onto the deck. The boat veered gently away from shore and chugged on toward the Île de la Cité and Notre-Dame—leaving Daniel halfway over the parapet and staring stupidly after it, knowing it was too late for him to execute the same maneuver.

"Hey!" The boy yelled across the water, his voice bouncing off the old stone walls of the quai. "Finders keepers! Sunday at five! Not without the Book!"

Rage swamped Daniel, but then a wave of exhaustion rose and washed it away. As he swung himself back over the parapet onto the pavement, his head spun. He shouldn't have chased the kid. Was he really up for heroics at his age?

He'd only been postponing the moment when he'd have to face Eleanor with all these new-old memories in his head.

"You're bleeding!" She was beside him already, cheeks pink and eyes wide with fright. She seized his hand and rolled up the cuff of his thrifted coat to reveal a gash on his wrist. "What were you thinking? Where'd he go?"

Daniel used his free hand to point at the river, where the boat was now disappearing. "Pulled a fucking action movie stunt. Must've nicked me as I came at him."

Blood trickled into his palm, but the wound was shallow. Eleanor pressed a tissue against it, then tugged off her scarf and wrapped it to create a makeshift bandage. Her movements were shaky but efficient. He felt sorry now that he'd frightened her.

"You didn't need to do that," she said, her tone grudgingly admiring. "If he's after the Polaroid, I doubt it would be much use to him. Odile designed the clues for *us*—to remind *us*."

Yes, she had. Daniel had regained enough memories now to know that each clue corresponded to a scene of their love story: the conversation about *The Red and the Black*, the bench, and that terrible night when Drew had written the confession. *Where love is shared*—his mother was a sneaky devil.

"The kid said 'finders keepers,' though." Daniel suddenly grasped the significance of the words. "Marc Vasselin found the Book. It *is* him."

"You're trembling. You need to sit for a minute." Eleanor led him across the street to the nearest café and found them a table. "I knew you were a risk-taker, but not like this."

Daniel tried to scoff as they sat down. "I've done aikido. Some of the hospitality jobs I've had, you have to break up fights between drunken tourists."

"I wouldn't want to meet you in a dark alley."

She said it lightly, but then her expression darkened, and he knew she was remembering everything that had been said in the alley before their attacker appeared.

"I understand why you don't want to destroy the Book," he said, trying to keep any hint of accusation out of his tone. "It feels alive. In some of my dreams, it's almost like I'm inside it, and you're there, too."

"Same with me." Eleanor took his hand again and unwound the scarf. "And I know there are good reasons to destroy it," she added softly, cleansing the gash with Vittel water, "but I don't want to take a match to it, Daniel. I don't have any proof, but something tells me that wouldn't be safe for any of us."

He understood—she meant all the people who had confessed. The others were in his dreams, too, though none of them as vividly as she was.

"Maybe we won't destroy it, then. Maybe we'll just bury it ten feet deep in the middle of nowhere." His mother had already hidden the Book, but presumably not safely or permanently enough, since she'd intended them to find it.

Make sure the last two pages stay blank, and keep the Book out of anyone else's hands. Your survival depends on it. Daniel wasn't sure they were any closer to understanding that part of her message. *Make sure the last two pages stay blank* might refer to someone creating the All-Things Book once *The Book of Dark Nights* was full. But how did their survival depend on that? A book to end all books was a disturbing idea, but he doubted it would kill him.

Or Eleanor. "When did you confess?" he asked, suddenly realizing he had no idea. "I made you promise not to."

Winding the scarf around his wrist again, she didn't raise her eyes to him. "I guess it didn't seem to matter so much after you left."

Maybe it was just the dregs of the adrenaline constricting his veins and making him think less clearly, or maybe it was her closeness, the flame-like delicacy of her, but Daniel yielded to an impulse. As she tied the scarf, he twisted his wrist to press his thumb to her palm.

She went still, but she didn't pull away. As their eyes met at last, hers still shy and furtive yet full of regrets, he felt anew how much he had cared for her. How foolish he'd been to throw it all away with one reckless, unfair accusation.

Why didn't I crawl back to her? Why didn't I apologize? Had his younger self been that proud or stubborn?

I'm sorry. The phrase was on the tip of his tongue, and he was about to release it when something caught his eye. A tourist couple was settling into the table behind Eleanor, surrounded by shopping bags, including one from the nearby English-language bookstore, Shakespeare and Company.

Odile's favorite store, where she'd been headed the last time he saw her alive. When Daniel first came over to Europe, wanting to travel light, he'd unloaded all his old college books on the proprietor for a measly sum.

Eleanor was staring at him—he'd released her hand without meaning to. But he'd just realized something, and he had to know if he was right.

"Shakespeare and Company," he said, rising from the table. "That's where I sold the copy of *The Idiot* that Drew was reading. The *book you used to mold him*."

***

The bookstore was a short walk down the quais. They didn't glance at each other, but now the distance felt more companionable than estranged to Eleanor. As if the bond between them, frayed by the years but never broken, were tentatively healing.

When Daniel touched her palm, sensory memories had

flooded her. The broad span of his shoulders between her hands, the faint dark stubble following the curve of his lower lip and the friction of it against her chin. Twenty-four years had passed, but perhaps for her body no time had passed at all.

Sunlight waxed orange on the western rose window of Notre-Dame. The used booksellers' stalls along the quai seemed to mock her—so many stories and no lasting answers in any of them. No All-Things Book that would magically tell the exact story its reader needed.

They turned into Rue Saint-Jacques, where the bookstore's bright green-and-yellow front faced the river. At the entrance, a sign begged patrons not to use cameras. Eleanor remembered it as a quiet refuge, frequented only by a few tourists in the know, but apparently social media had changed that.

"Mom loved this place," Daniel said as they stepped inside. "Her home away from home."

"You really think the book's still here? Didn't you sell it to them decades ago?"

"It was a nice edition," Daniel said. "When the owner saw it, with the stamp inside from the Library of Fates, he shook his head and called it *stolen goods.* Then he said he'd stash it in the library section of the store until my mom next visited. Maybe she decided he could keep it."

Odile had known Shakespeare and Company's founder, an eccentric lover of literature who had stuffed the seventeenth-century building with books until he died at the age of ninety-eight, leaving it in his daughter's secure hands.

They sped from room to room, breathing in the musty fragrance of a labyrinth of books. Shakespeare and Company was madcap and eclectic where the Library of Fates was serene, but Eleanor felt a similar spirit presiding here—not the power of the Book but simply the indelible personality of a well-curated collection. Every inch of wall space was crammed with volumes. Skylights and chandeliers hanging from the exposed rafters illuminated the warm reds and golds of old spines. Mismatched chairs and sofas tempted browsers to pause and read just a few more pages.

Normally, Eleanor would have gone off on a dozen tangents before finding what she was looking for. But now she headed to the small lending library on the second floor, Daniel beside her.

Each of the stairs' bright red risers bore a few words of a single line of poetry. They entered a room that held a small museum of the shop's history, complete with a vintage typewriter on a desk with a view of Notre-Dame.

"Look!" Daniel had removed a paperback from a shelf above her head.

It wasn't *The Idiot*, as she'd expected, but a copy of *Broken Thread*. Eleanor couldn't resist a thrill of pleasure as Daniel leafed through it—her scrap of a novel, her feeble attempt to tell her own story, sitting among classics of the Beat era and signed editions by now-famous visitors to the shop.

Had Odile been the one to donate her book to the tiny library? When they'd discussed Eleanor's novel last year, Odile had been so critical, almost scathing.

In her heart of hearts, Eleanor knew, she'd written her book as wish fulfillment, dreaming of a future with Daniel that could never be. Odile had seen it as sentimental and self-indulgent, and she wasn't wrong. But when Daniel skimmed through the book, as he'd admitted earlier today, he had begun to remember her. If nothing else, her writing was strong enough to revive the past for him.

Her heart swelled again at the memory of his touch, yet she shrank from her own hopes. *He doesn't remember* everything.

"Here we go!" Daniel seized another book from the shelf. *"The Idiot."*

Eleanor recognized the edition from the Library of Fates instantly, even after a quarter century. The dust cover was gone, if there'd ever been one, but the faded red binding was adorned with a stark silver cross. Elaborate gothic block lettering spelled out the title on the spine.

"I brought it overseas because it was my last memento of my friend," Daniel said, opening the book. "But then I guess I thought about what the library did to Drew, and I decided to ditch *The Idiot* after all. Bad vibes."

As he flipped through the book, Eleanor glimpsed a fancy two-color frontispiece and black-and-white woodcut illustrations. Timidly she said, "I meant to give him a book about love. Instead, I gave him this—a book about both love and death. You seemed to think reading it made him suicidal."

"I was a kid when I said that. I just needed a scapegoat." But before she could register the weight of those words—did they absolve her?—Daniel plucked a slip of paper from the pages. "Aha! Maybe this is the clue."

He unfolded the note and placed it on the open book.

"What does it say?" Eleanor asked as his thoughtful expression deepened to a frown.

Daniel didn't seem to hear her, his gaze faraway. He turned more pages and fished out a second note, which he placed on top of the first. Then he added a third to the pile.

Even all these years later, Eleanor recognized April's confident, swooshy handwriting.

I'm shelving down on Pusey 3 again tonight. Meet me there, same aisle. I know I'm being ridiculous, but I'm sappy about where we had our First Time. Indulge me. Mad for you, xoxo, Nastasya.

At first, the name threw her. Then she remembered that Nastasya Filippovna is the tragic heroine of *The Idiot*, the courtesan to whom Prince Myshkin has an ill-fated engagement.

"So it's true. *She* was the one Drew loved, the one he wanted to be sure of."

Eleanor remembered speaking with Drew in the library on a long-ago spring day. As he'd described the first tipsy stage of being in love, he'd gazed down into the Yard where April was talking to some guys. Wondering, perhaps, if she was flirting with them.

Drew's confession had been oddly worded: *I made A.C. fall in love with me, but will she keep on loving me the way I love her?* He'd been asking a question but also making an assertion: that April loved him in the first place. Maybe he'd wanted to test whether that assertion were true, whether he *had* made April fall in love with him. If April didn't love him, then he would be inadvertently lying to the Book.

Eleanor combed back over her other memories. When April brought them to see Genevra in the Adams House swimming pool, Drew had already been there. A week later, April had keened over Drew's corpse, desperately trying to revive him. She had been Drew's Lily Bart in *The House of Mirth*, his Nastasya Filippovna in *The Idiot*—flirty, vivacious, high-maintenance, potentially unfaithful. Despite all that, she *did* seem to have cared deeply for him.

The Book hadn't confirmed this for Drew, but maybe it had given him the answer he *needed*, even if he hadn't known it at the time. No one could assure him of April's love. If Eleanor had asked the same question about Daniel, it might have given her a likewise tricky answer.

She was old enough now to grasp that love exists in the moment-to-moment—the flash of eyes meeting, the warmth of hands clasping, the elusive understanding between two people. One can try to trap and imprison it, to forge an eternal bond, but there are no guarantees.

But if Drew hadn't lied, then what had killed him? Could they be sure the Book had harmed him at all?

And how did this tell them where the Book was?

"All three notes are similar." Daniel had a distant look, so Eleanor couldn't say if his thoughts were on the same track as hers. "Every time, they met in Pusey 3, part of the underground library connected to Widener. The same place where my mom died."

"Pusey." And just like that, things clicked into place. *A subterranean secret, / Where love is shared.*

"Daniel," she asked, her voice quavering, "could that be where she hid the Book?"

30

Then

April 10, 1995

The Monday after Drew's death, while his mother was out doing errands, Daniel made the long walk from home to campus. The sun was shining again, spring creeping back even as a brisk wind blew from the ocean. The simple act of putting one foot in front of the other steadied him. No one expected him to go back to class yet, but he'd been lounging on the couch too long.

On Saturday, once he'd had some time to think, he'd called Eleanor. On Sunday, again. She didn't pick up either time, and he didn't feel right leaving a message.

At the police station, he'd been unfair to her—he knew that. Angry and frightened, he'd lashed out. But once he'd stopped blaming her, he had only himself left to blame, and now he knew there was nothing romantic about Self-Destruction.

Yesterday, he'd broken down on the phone with Drew's mom, who wanted desperately to hear something, anything, that could help explain what had happened. It would be so easy to point to the drugs, but that would be a shitty cop-out. Despite what Will had told the cops, Daniel was pretty sure Drew hadn't been under the influence of anything but books.

Drew's words kept repeating in his head. *You want your mom to be happy, Daniel—I get that. And she'll get the Book back. But she doesn't own it, so I'm not sure why she should make all the rules.*

Now his mother had the Book back, all right. Was this Daniel's fault for following her rules? Doing her dirty work? Without him, no one in the class would have confessed to the Book in the first place.

Boylston's foyer felt deserted, everyone busy in classrooms or offices. He climbed the three flights of stairs and stepped into the library.

The curtains were wide open. A brilliant wedge of sunlight bisected the seminar table and continued through the *N*s. Daniel blinked as he crossed it, momentarily blinded, and went to retrieve the office key.

He wasn't sure what he was going to do, only that Drew was right. It was time to stop following his mother's rules, and the first step was to get his hands on the Book. There was just one problem, as he found when he knelt and tried to unlock the safe. The code had been changed.

He *felt* the Book in there, tugging at him like a magnetic field. Could he really just leave it be? What if his mother gave it to Eleanor, and she decided to confess? She might never want to see him again, but he couldn't abandon her when she might be in danger.

He was still sitting cross-legged, trying to figure out his next move, when familiar heels clicked across the oak boards outside.

Daniel didn't bother concealing his intentions. When his mother entered the office, he looked up at her from the floor and said, "We need to do something about it."

His mother just sighed. All weekend, she'd been making

him tea and bringing him blankets and fussing over him as if he were eight again, but they hadn't discussed the Book at all.

He understood why she wanted to keep things as they were. The library depended on the Book, and the library was her pride and joy. He'd never want to take that from her. But . . . "You didn't tell me about the nightmares," he said. "If you had, I would never have given it to anyone."

His mother fiddled with her scarf, twitching one tassel between two tapered fingers. "What defines a nightmare, Daniel?" she asked as if they were in class. "How is it different from any other ominous dream? Can you be sure that confessing to *The Book of Dark Nights* induces nightmares? Or could it be that students who take it into their heads to confess—despite being explicitly warned not to—tend to be unstable and nightmare-prone already?"

Daniel felt his cheeks flush with a new righteous anger. She was refusing to listen, as if she knew on some level she was in the wrong. Drew was right—she had no business manipulating her students into confessing.

"You know perfectly well you wanted them to," he said. "You *told* me to get them to confess."

"I'm not sure I ever told you in so many words. I only suggested." But his mother's tone had lost its classroom sharpness. "Please, let's not fight about this. Your friend is dead."

She held out her hand. Daniel accepted it and pulled himself to his feet, taller than her, yet feeling outmatched.

"Sweetheart." She touched the corner of his mouth, as if he were a child with dirt on his face. "I'm so sorry this happened. I should have explained everything to you, but I admit I feared you wouldn't understand."

"Understand what?" Daniel's voice was rough with irritation. "You *still* aren't explaining anything. Eleanor thinks Drew could've died because he lied to the Book." Even suggesting it felt like a betrayal of his friend. Why would Drew lie, especially after insisting he needed to know his future?

His mother patted his sweaty hand with her cool one. "Eleanor is a bright girl. I've offered her a scholarship, a future working by my side, and you could be part of that. The Book is my life's work, Daniel, and your inheritance. Our legacy."

When he was younger, Daniel had listened raptly when she talked like this, wanting to be part of the long history of the Book. Now he thought of Drew and snarled, "It's not any of that. It's a fucking *curse*. It gave Drew a prediction that upset him so much he tried to tear out the page and died."

But his anger was uselessly Self-Destructive. He knew that now, as his mother took his arm. "Daniel, come with me to the Phil stacks. I want to show you something."

Widener's philosophy collection was stored on the third level of underground Pusey Library, accessible only through the twilit bowels of the vast main building. His mother led him down staircase after staircase to the lowest of Widener's ten levels as if she were Virgil guiding Dante to the bottom of the Inferno. When she opened an inconspicuous door in one corner, the roar of a wind tunnel emerged. They stepped through, the door crashed shut behind them, and everything went dead still again.

"What's down here?" Daniel asked as they traversed a windowless concrete corridor lined with pipes and lit by flickering fluorescents—a tunnel, he realized with a shudder. They were underground.

It reminded him of his dream of a throng of people trapped in a great, dark room. Imagine being condemned to this place for eternity. Imagine if Drew's soul had ended up in a place like this.

What if, when you confessed, a sliver of your soul stayed in the Book? What if a piece of you was always stuck there, waiting? Perhaps those stifled souls were the source of the library's power, why his mother and Eleanor could use it to see into people's hearts.

Maybe he was being fanciful, but suddenly he wanted very badly to tell Eleanor about his dream.

His mother patted his arm. "You'll see. We're almost there."

At the end of the tunnel, they emerged into the Pusey stacks, from which they had to descend yet another flight of echoing stairs. When they stepped out again, they weren't in the underworld but on Pusey 3: rows on rows of massive mobile stacks, quiet as a tomb. Daniel couldn't stop himself from tiptoeing.

"How did you know to change the safe code?" he asked, as quietly as if something might be listening.

"Intuition," Odile said. "Mine is quite strong where *The Book of Dark Nights* is concerned. I consider it my duty to keep it safe, Daniel, and I hope what you're about to learn will make you feel the same way."

They stopped before a solid bank of stacks, where Odile pressed a button. Five shelves away, two gigantic units growled ominously and rolled backward on steel tracks to close an aisle. They had to wait until all the shelves to their left were stacked tight, with much whirring and clanking, before a new one opened in front of them.

A red light turned green. Odile stepped into the aisle, beckoning to Daniel, and pointed to the top shelf at the far end, well above her head. "You're tall enough. Fetch that metal box for me."

The box was an easy reach for Daniel. It felt light, with a catalog barcode and a top that lifted off, unsecured by any lock.

"No one comes down here, Daniel, except for a few scholars on obscure errands." Her voice was hushed. "Anything one hides on these shelves is like a needle in a haystack. It might as well not exist. Remember that—you may need a hiding place someday."

The box was large enough to contain a whole sheaf of documents, but all he found inside was a single folder. "Open it carefully."

Daniel quickly saw why. The one sheet of paper in the folder was so cracked and yellowed that he feared it would crumble in his hands. It bore the marks of a quill pen.

Monsieur de Voltaire . . .

When Daniel made out the signature, *La Sorcière Mariane*, his teeth began chattering in the cold of the underground library. "Mariane created the Book. Eleanor told me all about her." *And I dreamed of her.*

"Read it," his mother ordered.

Daniel did—and felt just as mystified as before. He didn't understand the business about the All-Things Book, and the humble tone of Mariane's letter made him uncomfortable. It reminded him of how his mother often spoke to his father, deferential and subtly arrogant at the same time, as if she were Ariel in *The Tempest* to his Prospero and not a lover and peer. Ariel did magic. Mariane apparently could, too.

His mother took the precious document from him and carefully returned it to the folder. "So you see," she said, "the Book does have a purpose beyond the library. When your friend lied to the Book—I don't know for sure, but I can only imagine he did—he tried to sabotage that purpose."

Daniel opened his mouth to protest that he still didn't believe Drew would have lied. He'd wanted so badly to know what the future held for him and his sick mother. But one look at Odile's face told Daniel she wouldn't listen.

"I'm so sorry about poor Drew," she said softly, ushering him out of the aisle. "He was a good friend to you, and he had real potential for Contemplation. But we have to look at the big picture, Daniel. This is the beginning of your real education. Let me explain . . ."

31

—

Now

September 29, 2019, 5:48 a.m.

"Daniel?" Already showered and dressed, Eleanor bent over the sofa bed in their Airbnb. Daniel lay under a blanket, his back to her. He had slept through the alarm, and soon it would be time to catch a cab to the airport for their return flight.

She herself hadn't slept well, alert to every unfamiliar noise. If Marc Vasselin had sent one person to steal the clues from them, he could easily send another.

They had left *The Idiot* in the bookstore's library, but April's notes to Drew were folded tightly in her coat pocket. Lying awake, she'd wondered if she should tear and flush them, given that they revealed the Book's hiding place—at least to her and Daniel.

Pusey, the underground library—Drew and April's favored meeting place. According to Daniel, it was also what Odile had meant when she wrote in her message *you know where I hide things*.

"How do you suddenly know that?" Eleanor had asked him in the cab he'd insisted on taking back to their lodging, hoping to foil any pedestrian followers.

He'd just shaken his head and looked vague. "Seeing those notes jogged something loose. Something I shouldn't have forgotten."

When Eleanor returned from the corner café with sandwiches for dinner, Daniel had been dead to the world, and she hadn't woken him. But now a whole night had passed, and it was time to go home. Time to reclaim the Book—and decide what to do with it.

She'd told him she was willing to destroy the Book or hide it more securely, whichever was the best way to keep it out of the hands of Marc Vasselin and others eager to use the power to their own ends. But to actually accept that the library would become merely a library? She was still trying to wrap her head around that.

Daniel hadn't stirred, breathing deeply and evenly. Eleanor sat down on the edge of the bed and gave his shoulder a slight shake. "You need to get up now, Daniel. We need to go."

To her relief, he mumbled and rolled over, seizing her hand as he did so. Heavy lids and dark lashes drooped, hiding his eyes from her. He clasped her hand warmly, as if she'd rescued him from something, and brought it to his cheek.

At first Eleanor froze, the way she initially had when he touched her in the café yesterday evening. But his closeness was so tantalizingly familiar that it tugged on something inside her, as if unknotting a long-snarled thread. And she found herself relaxing into the crook of his arm as he sat up and folded it around her.

"I loved you," she whispered before she could stop herself. Words she would never have dared to say twenty-four years ago. She hadn't forgotten the intoxication of their precious few nights together at Harvard, watching winter turn into spring. "I've missed you."

"Me too," he said in a voice still husky with sleep. "You were always there in my dreams. Don't know how I ever forgot you."

The world shuddered around Eleanor, her eyes suddenly hot and heavy. "It shouldn't have happened."

Did he know *why* he had forgotten her? Surely not, or he wouldn't be touching her so tenderly.

They sat very still, so she felt his breath on her hair and the slight tremble of his body against hers. She reached up and twitched a dark lock of hair off his forehead. And then both his arms were around her, and he was cupping her face, thumbs on the hinges of her jaw, and tipping it to meet his.

The kiss was hot and wet and hungry. Eleanor remembered how she had felt on that long-ago snowy night after their walk by the river: as if he had cracked open her brittle shell and let the sunlight flood in and warm her all the way to her bones. As if her real life started with that kiss.

They drew apart, slowly at first—and then quickly. Something seemed to change in his body, and he released her and withdrew to the far end of the sofa bed, his eyes wide and startled. "Oh, shit! I'm sorry. I was still half asleep. Did I . . . ? That was totally out of line."

Eleanor sprang up and straightened her clothes, wishing heat weren't rising to her cheeks. Daniel looked frightened and contrite, as if he feared he'd just committed some sort of violation.

But it was she who'd crossed a line, and he who hadn't been able to consent. She should have realized he wasn't fully awake, still submerged in some dream of their past.

"No worries," she said, walking briskly over to check the contents of her handbag so he wouldn't see the disarray on her face. She hoped he had no conscious recollection of most of what had just happened. "I was trying to wake you, and you were talking a little in your sleep, and then you grabbed my shoulder. You must have been deep under."

"I was. All this time-zone jumping is fucking up my sleep." Daniel reached for his phone. "Oh, shit, it's late. Give me just a sec."

While he brushed his teeth in the bathroom, Eleanor went to the window and twitched the lace curtain aside to let the sun shine in her eyes.

She could still taste him, could still hear him saying *You were always there in my dreams.*

But it wasn't real, and it never could be. Not after what she'd done.

***

After takeoff, Daniel promptly fell asleep again, and he didn't wake until they were about an hour away from Logan. It was the smell of coffee, wafting through the cabin, that snapped him out of his stupor. He sat up and rubbed his eyes, disoriented, hoping he hadn't done anything inappropriate this time.

Back in the Airbnb, he'd dreamed Eleanor was bending over him, touching him tenderly and asking if he remembered her. He was saying he'd never forgotten, and then, well . . . he'd snapped awake to find his arm really around her, and she'd only been innocently trying to wake him.

Fuck, that was awkward. But she seemed to have accepted his apology, and he couldn't help feeling subtly closer to her after everything that had happened in France. The mistrust that April had planted in his head two days ago was a distant memory.

As he became aware of the whine of the jet engine and the crick in his back, he also recalled how close they were to the end of their quest. Soon they would be on the ground, driving to Cambridge. Soon they would have the Book.

He wondered how he'd explain all this to Sandrine, who hadn't responded to any of his texts yesterday. Probably deep in the mountains, out of cell range.

What did you tell me, Mom? Daniel remembered descending with Odile into the underground philosophy stacks in 1995. He remembered reading the Mariane letter and learning about the All-Things Book. April's notes, with their mentions of Pusey Level 3, had cleared up those foggy spaces in his head.

But his mother had also promised she'd explain everything. And when he tried to recall her explanation, he landed headfirst in the fog bank again.

Two flight attendants were wheeling the beverage cart down the aisle. He peered over Eleanor's shoulder and saw she was scribbling words on a napkin: *All things (Daniel) lie (April) mort (dead/death; Genevra) is (Drew) and (Eleanor).*

"What's that?" he asked, taking a coffee and handing her one. He still felt awkward.

She didn't make eye contact as she accepted the coffee, but he saw no wariness of him in her body language. "Each of us received predictions from the Book with underlined words in them. Your mother said the underlined parts are important, and I'm wondering why."

A few years ago, Daniel had googled his prediction, which turned out to be from Tennyson's "The Lotos-Eaters." Appropriately, a poem about forgetting.

"*All things* makes me think of the All-Things Book," he said. *The book to end all other books. The book to secure your immortality.* "I wonder if there's a connection?"

"I was thinking the same thing." Eleanor's pen tapped the napkin. "Daniel, if the Book is really on Pusey 3, where

Odile had her heart attack . . . do you think maybe she was hiding it when she died?"

"Maybe, yeah." For the first time, Daniel realized the location might not be a coincidence. "Or maybe she'd already hidden it, and she went to Pusey to check on it or move it. Either way, it might still be there—right in the aisle where she had her accident."

Unless Odile's death hadn't been an accident. Someone else had been there to close the aisle on her, deliberately or not. But if that person was after the Book, wouldn't they have it already? Why were they still demanding it from him? Had they not guessed that the spot where they'd ambushed Odile was precisely where she'd hidden it?

"Mom showed me Mariane's letter down there," he said. "After Drew died, after you didn't want to see me anymore. She had the original hidden in the Phil stacks. I don't know why I forgot that."

It felt strange to talk about Mariane's letter when you were soaring through the clouds, surrounded by the civilized clinking of bottles and the glow of devices that would have seemed to Mariane and even skeptical Voltaire like magic.

"Odile showed *you* that?" Eleanor's eyes had widened, and he thought he glimpsed regret in them. "She knew I was fascinated by Mariane, but all these years, she never told me she had the letter or what it said. I wonder why not."

"She could be so secretive," Daniel said apologetically—though he had to wonder, too. Why would his mother trust him with that information and not Eleanor, especially when he was the one who'd talked about getting rid of the Book?

Maybe it would help if he had a better understanding of the letter's implications. "So Mariane wants to help her favorite philosopher write the book to end all books, and she weaves this weird spell that involves filling an empty book with true confessions. But then somehow the Book ends up bricked up behind a wall for about two hundred fifty years—why, do you think?"

"This is going to sound a little woo-woo." Eleanor dropped her eyes. "But I've seen someone in my dreams who I believe is Mariane—her ghost, her psychic remnant, whatever. You have, too, haven't you?"

Images from Daniel's nightmares flitted through his head. In the ones where he'd lost the Book, a strangely clad girl always urged him to find it. In the ones where he was trapped in the dark, he could sense the presence of Eleanor, Drew, Genevra, April, even his mother. Now he wondered if the dreams connected everyone who'd confessed to the Book—including its creator.

"Anyway," Eleanor continued, "in the dream I had on the flight here, *I* was Mariane. And I was hiding the Book behind the wall because I'd made a mistake. Maybe she'd confessed to the Book herself, and she was having the nightmares and wanted to spare other people from them."

"Or she came to her senses and decided that Voltaire was just another philosopher with a swollen head and not worthy of writing the book to end all books," Daniel suggested. "Let's give Mariane some credit."

"Either way," Eleanor said, "she hid *The Book of Dark Nights*, so the conditions for the All-Things Book were never fulfilled. Fast-forward a quarter millennium, Marc Vasselin found it by chance and gave it to his professor—your father—who gave it to your mother. According to its legend, the Book was designed to be used in a library, so one might assume its purpose ends there. A librarian feeds the Book confessions, and the Book gives the librarian the power to choose books. Maybe only a few people have ever known that its true function is to create the All-Things Book. Your mother clearly did, because she had the letter." The way her narrowed eyes caught the light made Daniel uneasy.

"What?"

"A book to end all books is the last thing I'd want. I can't imagine what that would mean in modern-day, real-life terms, but I'd guess . . . the end of bookstores and libraries in general. The same thing that some people say will happen once computers learn how to write full-length novels with a few key strokes. Stories tailor-made to each individual reader's needs, where that reader is the hero." Eleanor took a gulp of coffee as if she needed fortification against the prospect. "I love books—the whole universe of books written by human beings to communicate their individual truths to other human beings. And I know Odile wanted what I wanted—to use the Book's power to show students pathways through that universe. If I have to guess, I'd say the All-Things Book goes directly against her vision."

All this speculation was too abstract for Daniel to get excited about. "I think you're right," he conceded. "My mom couldn't possibly have wanted to make all libraries redundant."

But hadn't she told him all those years ago that the Book's *purpose beyond the library* was the real reason she was protecting it? Daniel pushed that thought away. "Maybe that's why she decided to hide the Book now, when there are only two pages left." According to Mariane, the first person to read the full *Book of Dark Nights* would harvest the power to write the All-Things Book. "Before it's full."

As he spoke, he let his fingertips brush Eleanor's on the tray table. He could tell she needed to believe she and his mother had been on the same page, even if Odile had kept secrets from her. She wanted to know she'd helped people with her work in the library. And however Daniel felt about the Book now, he wanted that for her, too.

Eleanor didn't withdraw her hand. "When I was letting Odile give the Book to students, I told myself it was for her sake, so her life would have meaning. But all that time, it was for my sake, too." She raised her eyes, and in them he saw her reluctant acceptance of what they had to do. "I knew there was a price, and I accepted it . . . for far too long."

Tentatively, not wanting to repeat his mistake of this morning, Daniel took hold of her hand.

When he left Harvard, he'd told himself a story about becoming someone new, leaving the dark memories of Drew's death behind. For a while, it had worked. But why on earth had he blocked out every memory of her?

"I don't blame you now," he said, "and I didn't blame you back then, either—or not for long. I tried to apologize." Now he was struggling with foggy memories again. "I swear I did."

32

Then

April 10, 1995 (later)

After the trip with his mother down to Pusey Level 3, Daniel went in search of Eleanor. This time he didn't bother leaving a phone message. He hurried to Dunster to knock on the door of her suite, where her roommate advised him to check the Library of Fates.

Daniel rushed back to Boylston and took the stairs at a run. He knew Eleanor didn't want to see him, but what he'd just learned from his mother changed everything.

For the first time in his life, his mom had spoken to him as one adult to another, telling him her secrets and trusting him to understand. She didn't seem to grasp that with every word she spoke, she pushed Daniel further away.

The true purpose of the Book was to create the All-Things Book. That in itself he might have shrugged off as meaningless, but certain things his mother had said—*Our souls will be immortalized, all of us characters in the book to end all books*—

made him wonder if she was losing her mind. She'd practically glowed with pride at the idea.

It all weighed on his heart, an impossible burden that only Eleanor could lighten. More importantly, Eleanor deserved to know the truth about his mother's intentions before she applied for that scholarship and built her own life around the Library of Fates. Once she knew, they could figure out what to do together.

He burst into the library, out of breath. Eleanor must have heard his hectic footsteps on the stairs, because he found her standing by the door, a book open in her hand.

When she saw him, her face fell. She tried to turn away.

Daniel seized her by the arm and pulled her to him. Sunlight brought out the copper in her hair. He saw hostility in the set of her mouth and in the tension of her shoulders. But in the tremor that ran over her at his touch, he also sensed the connection neither of them could deny.

"I'm so glad I found you," he said, kissing her on the forehead. "And I'm so sorry. I was upset, and I was unfair to you." How could he tell her his mother wasn't fit to be her idol? If he described the conversation he'd just had with Odile, she might think he was making things up—it was all so bizarre. "But I'm also concerned about you," he added, trying to ease into it.

Eleanor had gone limp in his grasp. Her head drooped, so he couldn't see her eyes. "Why would you be concerned?"

Because I love you. But he had to focus on finding a way to warn her. "My mom's trying to make you into the next librarian, and—"

"What if I *want* to be the next librarian?" Though the words seemed defiant, her tone was meek and almost childlike. Maybe she would listen to him. Maybe he could persuade her.

"You care too much about using the power, and you don't even know what she's doing it all *for*. You're playing with things you don't understand. We need to talk. We need . . ."

But before he could explain, Eleanor raised her head.

"Daniel," she said, looking steadily into his eyes, "ask me for a book."

33

——

Now

September 29, 2019, 3:53 p.m.

For the second time in his life, Daniel was descending to the lowest circle of the Harvard University Libraries.

The journey began in Widener—vast, echoing marble stairways and foyers and antechambers, like a museum. From the golden-brown elegance of the circulation room, you reached a bottleneck, scanned an ID, and ventured into the dim immensity of the stacks, which encompassed eight stories aboveground and two below. They felt like a giant metal cage, he thought, that vibrated quietly under the impact of hundreds of feet at a time. A shadow world for people who had chosen to live their lives through books instead of climbing mountains in the sunlight.

Here the ceilings were low, the stairways short. As they hurried down flight after flight, approaching the last of the subterranean levels, Eleanor said, "I asked Will to put extra security on the Library of Fates at five, when we're supposed to meet whoever delivered that ultimatum to your mom's house. With any luck, the guards can get an ID. But we won't be going to that rendezvous ourselves, agreed?"

"Agreed," Daniel said firmly as he followed Eleanor through the labyrinth of Level D, skirting the towering shelves. No one else was getting their hands on the Book.

Still, he couldn't help wondering if the wording of Odile's will might allow him to stow the Book in the library office on the day of the memorial—as she had stipulated—and then remove it later for better safekeeping.

Eleanor headed toward a door in a far corner, so inconspicuous that Daniel would have missed it. "As long as we have the Book, they could be after us," she said. "We won't be able to let down our guard. It wouldn't even be enough to destroy it—we'd have to prove it to them."

Her voice was tight with anxiety. Daniel touched her shoulder, wishing they had a face to put to that creepily impersonal *they*. "If that kid with the knife is the best muscle some antique dealers can muster, I'm not scared. *He's* the one who ran from *me*, remember?"

Underneath the reassuring words, though, he feared she was right. There were bound to be people who placed way too much value on the fantasy of creating a book that granted its author everlasting fame. And some of those people probably had the means to make their lives very uncomfortable.

With an inward shudder, he thought of the photo of Sandrine that had been paired with the note they'd found in Odile's ransacked house. *They know who I care about.*

In Daniel's memory, the door to the Pusey stacks opened on a wind tunnel. He thought he might have imagined or misremembered. But no, here was the roar of trapped air, slamming straight into them.

They stepped through the noise into a windowless concrete

passage that slanted subtly to the right, giving Daniel an unsettling sense of not knowing where they were going. The door they'd entered through shut with a bang, and they were in dead stillness.

"These levels don't get much traffic, Mom told me," Daniel said as they walked, each footfall crashing in the silence. "Nothing but dusty, forgotten stuff—the perfect hiding place."

When she brought him here, his mother had said it was time to start his "real education." She'd ranted about how their souls would be immortalized in the All-Things Book, which had disturbed him so much he'd run to find Eleanor . . . and then? Why hadn't he told her everything? Trying to bridge the gap between that moment and the much clearer memories of dropping out of school and packing for Europe, he encountered yawning blank spaces that still refused to be filled.

Their journey down the tunnel felt like purgatory, the exposed pipes on the wall evoking a factory or the belly of an ocean liner. Daniel considered taking Eleanor's hand, but it still felt a little too presumptuous. "I don't understand why I didn't tell you about Mariane's letter as soon as I found out," he said. "It changes the whole meaning of the Book—and of the library. You should have known." *My mom should have told you, too.*

Eleanor had crossed her arms over her chest, clearly feeling the tunnel's chill. "You were probably still blaming me for Drew's death when you left."

"I wasn't! I could *swear* I went to talk to you."

But the memories turned to vapor when he tried to hold them fast.

The tunnel took a sharp turn to the left, and suddenly they were at a door. Eleanor pushed it open and led him into a long, carpeted room full of books, where signs directed them to yet another staircase. "If you'd told me the purpose of the confessions was to create the All-Things Book, I wouldn't have forgotten."

"Would you have changed your mind about studying to be the next librarian?" Drew's death, followed by his mother's revelations, had convinced Daniel he needed to find his own pathway through life. He'd done a lot of floundering, but he didn't regret it.

"Then I wouldn't be here with you now, would I? I might have a family. A whole life elsewhere." She was smiling dreamily, a little ruefully. "Or maybe not. Maybe I was fated to land here. At that age, I just needed a place to belong, a way to feel useful, a story that would offer meaning. Your mother and her library gave me all those things. So . . . no. Knowing might not have changed much for me then. But now that I'm old enough to feel a little more at home in the world, it changes everything."

Was it partly his fault she'd felt so adrift back in college? Had they parted in bitterness? Daniel didn't dare ask that yet, so he switched to a lighter tone. "You're stuck with me this time, huh? Just the two of us against the would-be Book thieves?"

As they took the last flight of stairs, each footfall a loud clip-clop, Eleanor said, "I don't feel stuck at all."

Her smile was so tentative and yet so encouraging, like the earliest green shoots of spring, that it flustered Daniel. To cover his embarrassment, he indicated a camera above the door at the bottom. "The campus cops said they had no footage of whoever closed the aisle on my mom, but this place looks covered."

"Maybe they couldn't make an ID from the cam footage," Eleanor said.

She opened the door into pitch darkness.

Summoned by their motion, strips of light leaped to life

on the ceiling, illuminating floor-to-ceiling banks of bone-white shelving that made Daniel think of drawers in a morgue. Oppressively white fluorescents and an antiseptic tiled floor completed the resemblance. Only the books, visible at the open end of the mobile stacks, contributed warmth and color.

They walked the central aisle between two long cabinets of rolling shelves, locked tight together and marked with catalog numbers. Daniel had expected to locate the hiding place again easily, but Odile was right—it was like a needle in a haystack.

Then Eleanor pointed, her voice tight. "You see?"

Daniel spotted a shred of caution tape, a yellow stain on the pristine whiteness, and his throat convulsed. His mother's body had been found in that aisle.

The closed shelves blocked it from sight, cold and impersonal as a mausoleum. She'd drawn her last breaths here, her struggle to live muffled by the silence of centuries' worth of seldom-read pages.

And now he had to wonder if she'd really been alone, or if someone else had witnessed those final moments.

"Is this the aisle where she brought you?" Eleanor asked quietly, and he could tell she was affected, too. "Her hiding place?"

Daniel checked the catalog numbers—they were in the *Phil* section. "It could be."

Eleanor pressed a square button beside the caution tape. He held his breath, waiting for the shelves to part and reveal his mother's death scene, but nothing happened. The light stayed red.

Eleanor shook her head sternly—at him or at the shelves, Daniel wasn't sure. "They must have cut the power to this block to test it for malfunctions. I'll ask my friend Lindsay at the circ desk to turn it on."

"No, never mind that." If they'd come this far, they were

going to find that damn Book. The edges of the shelving cabinets were flush with the ceiling, blocking access from the aisle, but if Daniel could just bypass them . . .

He hurried back toward the entrance, where the last cabinet in the row was open to expose the books. Something skittered under his running shoe; he kicked it away. "Tell me when I get to the aisle where we just were. I won't be able to see much from up there."

"Up *where*?" Eleanor bent and retrieved the object he'd kicked—a clip from a disposable pen.

Daniel gauged the gap between books and ceiling and took two long strides back. "There!"

A running start launched him halfway up the side of the cabinet. He heard her gasp behind him, but it was an easy climb. Nudging the heavy books aside, he grabbed the top edge of the cabinet and hauled himself up until he was flat on his belly, atop the books and just barely skirting the light fixtures. Now all he had to do was crawl and slither his way to the right shelf.

That part was trickier. The hard edges of book spines jabbed him in all kinds of sensitive places, and he had to navigate around protruding volumes and the metal-tube architecture of the shelves. Kicking out to propel himself forward, he winced as a book crashed downward through a narrow crack. The fluorescents kept blinding him, their ominous hiss so loud he could swear he felt their heat on his face.

But he was making clumsy, swimming progress. One shelf, two, three. The high edges of the metal cabinets hid Eleanor from him, intensifying the sensation of being trapped. "Hey!" he called. "Bang on the side where I'm heading?"

A knock sounded ahead to his right. He floundered toward it, then swiveled his head, searching for the metal box his mother had hidden at the far end of the aisle, against the wall.

"You're there!"

Instead of one box, there was a row of them, each probably full of fragile or unbound materials. Daniel swore under his breath as he realized he had no wiggle room to remove each box and examine the contents. The barcode labels told him nothing.

Then he felt it.

The second box from the left wasn't like the others. The air around it vibrated with that living sensation he remembered all too well from his memories of holding the Book.

He knew what he was hearing was just the hum of the fluorescents. Yet that continuous sound seemed to weave itself into a cacophony of distant voices. He could almost make out words: *We're here! We're trapped! Help us!*

Confessions. Pieces of people's lives caught in the Book, pieces of *his* life included.

Daniel grasped the box and tugged it out. It felt hot and cold at once. Maneuvering it back to his entry point would be tricky, but he would manage. The Book wanted out.

Once he'd gotten himself turned around, he shoved the box ahead of him, nudging it with his forehead and lifting it over the many obstacles. It was a huge relief to reach the far edge of the cabinet. "Catch it so I can climb down, okay?"

Eleanor's anxious face appeared below him. "Please be careful—not just of the books. Of you."

Daniel tipped the box over the edge. Standing on her toes, Eleanor caught it easily but staggered backward. Maybe she also felt the hum of the Book inside.

He swung his legs over the edge and found footholds again, aware that he was sweating and panting. He was getting too old for stunts like this.

It felt good to hit the floor. "Right box?" he asked Eleanor, knowing it was.

Kneeling, Eleanor held out the Book in both hands—as if she were offering it to him, or as if she didn't want it close to her. "Yes," she said.

When Daniel took the Book, the prickle of life inside it gave him a shock that ran up his fingers and wrists to his arms, and from there straight to his heart. Touching it felt disturbingly like coming home to a part of himself he'd abandoned long ago.

The Book itself wasn't what he wanted. It hadn't been for a very long time. But in its gentle humming, he felt his mother's enduring presence—her tireless energy, her determination. Her love for him, which he'd too often pushed aside over the years because it came with expectations. Her desire to leave him a legacy.

If there were only two pages left, then she could have written the All-Things Book herself. But instead, she'd hidden the Book, preventing anyone else from doing so. *Keep the Book out of anyone else's hands*, she had written. But also *Trust your instincts.*

Daniel's instincts told him that any conventional way of destroying the Book was too risky. When Drew had tried to tear out a page, the Book had somehow remained intact while Drew had thrown himself off the balcony.

"What do we do, then?" he wondered aloud. "Bury it as deep as we can?"

"Wait!" Eleanor snatched up a sheet of thick paper that had floated to the floor. "I think Odile left us one last message."

***

The letter that had fluttered from the Book was written in Odile's handwriting on Odile's monogrammed stationery. Eleanor willed herself to hold it steady so they could read it together, sitting side by side on the floor:

My dear son,

When I first told you about your legacy, you ran. Now the days of my life are running out, as are the blank pages in this Book—there are just two left. With any luck, I'll explain everything to you in person. But I'm leaving you this letter in case I fail in the purpose of my upcoming trip abroad. If you're reading this, I may no longer exist except on the page that bears my own confession. And it's time for you to stop running.

Several months ago, while I was handling the Book, I accidentally tore the corner of a page. When I examined the Book later, it appeared to have healed itself. I thought little of this until I learned that poor Genevra had died, seemingly by suicide, on the very day when the page was torn. (I remembered because it was your father's birthday.)

I had always assumed your friend Drew must have died because he lied to the Book. The frontispiece of the Book says Lies are not tolerated, while Mariane's letter to Voltaire says Warn them not to lie, for the Book is like God and sees into their hearts.

But now a dark new suspicion took root in my mind. You had told me that Drew was so unhappy with his prediction that he tried to rip out his page. Perhaps he actually died because his page was torn, just as Genevra died because I tore hers.

As I write this, I'm about to travel to France to talk to your father about changing our plans. I now believe Mariane hid the Book centuries ago because she realized she had made a terrible mistake in its creation.

To craft The Book of Dark Nights, Mariane must have drawn on magic far older and more powerful than she could comprehend. I suspect she failed to master it thoroughly, and she made a crucial error. Like so many mad scientists after her, she didn't grasp the consequences of her own creation until it was too late.

To fulfill the Book's purpose, according to her first letter, you must tear out every page. In her letter, Mariane speaks of "harvesting" the confessions-reaping them like stalks of grain. What that letter does not say, what Mariane herself perhaps did not know yet, but what I now believe in the wake of Genevra's death, is that harvesting the confessions also means harvesting the confessors.

We are our pages. When someone tears out a page, the person who confessed on that page dies.

Given that, I wouldn't risk attempting to destroy the Book in any way that would physically injure the pages. Do you understand what I'm saying, Daniel? The Book must be kept absolutely secure, unless you find some way to undo the spell. The All-Things Book must never be created. Your life depends on it-as does mine, and Eleanor's, and those of all the other confessors who are still living.

Had I known this earlier, I would never have risked so many lives. But love is a powerful thing, and power is all too tempting. Ask Eleanor about that. Ask her about your memory.

I love you and I trust you. O.

"Shit," Daniel whispered. "When your page is torn out . . ."

"You die." The words of the letter blurred with Eleanor's full-body trembling.

For an instant, they stared at each other—and then their eyes turned to the Book, sitting innocently on the tiled floor. The pounding of Eleanor's blood rose in her ears, as if she'd just run a marathon.

That's why Odile said our survival depends on it.

"It's still just a theory," she said in a small voice, trying not to let dread overcome her as she thought of the fragility of those old pages. "A guess, like the thing about lies. We don't know all the Book's rules."

"Yeah, but it's another reason to stow it safely." Daniel jumped to his feet and gave Eleanor a hand up. "For all we know, they've been watching us this whole time. Let's get the Book out of here—off campus, somewhere remote. Ideas?"

Eleanor had to brace herself before she could pick up the Book and tuck it into her handbag with the letter. As she followed Daniel back the way they'd come, the urgent need to secure the Book narrowed her focus. The chilly spookiness of the tunnel barely registered over the booming of her pulse.

Ascending stairway after stairway back to Widener's entrance, they discussed and dismissed possible hiding places.

"There's a wrecked barn out by my mom's old place," Eleanor was saying as they stepped through the main entrance and gazed down into the Yard.

Instead of answering, Daniel dug into his jacket for a buzzing phone. "Just a sec. It's Sandrine—she only calls in emergencies." He lifted the phone to his ear, and his eyes widened as he spoke in French to his daughter. "Wait, wait, slow down. *Where* are you? No, stay on the phone, *please*. Oh, shit."

He jabbed the screen viciously, trying to reconnect, then raised his eyes to Eleanor. His bloodless grimace was a jarring throwback to the night Drew had died—the most frightened she'd ever seen him.

"We're going to that rendezvous in the library," he said. "Sandrine's there. She says if I don't bring her the Book, I'll never see her again."

34

——

Now

September 29, 2019, 4:58 p.m.

As the crow flies, the distance from the steps of Widener Library to the top floor of Boylston Hall was a wing flap or two. To Daniel, it was endless. He was barely aware of Eleanor beside him as they hurried down Widener's endless front steps, Sandrine's unbelievable words ringing in his ears.

The Book of Dark Nights *is my legacy. Were you really going to keep it from me? Bring it to the library at five if you ever want to see me again.*

He'd never once mentioned the Book to his daughter, and now she was demanding it as if she were the one who'd ransacked her grandmother's house and sent the knife-wielding goon. Daniel might have thought she was reciting the words under duress, but he recognized the steely tone she'd inherited from Odile. Sandrine meant what she was saying.

Should they have brought the Book at all? Maybe Eleanor should backtrack alone and return it to the bowels of Pusey for safekeeping. Climbing the steps of Boylston, he was about to suggest this when the door swung open, and Will Cheltenham nearly barged into them.

"Eleanor! I got the extra security you asked for!" Will looked excited, at least for a university administrator, and a little harried. He held the door open and ushered them inside. "But I thought you didn't want to be here in person. Did you find *it*?" He dropped his volume on the last word, clearly referring to the Book.

"We're still on the trail," Eleanor answered with a cool that Daniel admired.

Two burly men loitered in the foyer, neither uniformed but at least one looking to an untrained eye like he might be packing. Deciding it didn't matter—he just had to get to Sandrine, *now*—Daniel plowed straight past them to the stairs.

One of the men barked, "Where're you going?" But neither attempted to stop him as he took the stairs two at a time. Behind him, he heard Eleanor saying something to Will about a possible hostage situation in the library and the necessity of assessing everything before taking action.

"A hostage situation?" Will sounded horrified. "But I was there just a few minutes ago!"

Daniel reached the third floor, panting so hard he had to pause to catch his breath and rest his elbows on the newel post. *Let me not be too late. Let her still be here. Let there be a good explanation for everything.*

He was so primed to barge straight into the Library of Fates that it was a shock to find only the shiny oak surface of a closed door. He twisted the handle wildly, but it was locked.

"Where's your key?" he demanded of Eleanor.

She'd just reached the top step, sweat sheening her brow, Will and the two security guards thundering in her wake.

Instead of answering, she stood dead still, staring past Daniel at the door to the library.

He turned back to find it open this time.

Sandrine stood framed in it, wearing a full-skirted floral dress he'd never seen before and stylish sandals, black hair in a messy ponytail. Daniel's breath caught. That harsh tone on the phone had chilled him—it was her and yet not her. But this was very much the daughter he knew, a teenager excited about her first major trip abroad.

"You're here!" She extended her hand to him, smiling in the radiant way that always lifted his mood. "And so is Grandfather. Three generations of us. Please, please, come in."

***

Will came up behind Eleanor just as Daniel and Sandrine disappeared into the library. He was worrying one of his Uniball pens again, thumb stuck through the clip. "Everything okay, then?" he stage-whispered. "False alarm? Can I tell these guys to go? Because they're on overtime pay."

"Maybe just ask them to stay a minute." Eleanor hadn't loosened her death grip on her shoulder bag, which held *The Book of Dark Nights.*

So is Grandfather, Sandrine had said. Had Julien Theuthet flown over for tomorrow's memorial after all, despite saying he didn't travel well?

Whatever's going on, the Book stays with me. She drew a deep breath and deliberately let the bag swing free on her shoulder, so it wouldn't be obvious what she was carrying, as she stepped into the Library of Fates.

Daniel had rushed to join his daughter at one end of the seminar table and was speaking rapidly in French. He must be asking her the obvious questions, because Sandrine was glaring at him. With her strapping height, expressive dark eyes, and black brows, she was stunning and very like her father.

Facing them sat Julien Theuthet, wearing a spotless cream-colored double-breasted suit, perhaps the same one he'd worn on the cover of *Unlock Your Textual Potential.* He smiled and nodded at Eleanor in his gentlemanly way. "How nice to see you again so soon. Have you met my granddaughter?"

The door of the library closed with a loud thunk, making Eleanor start. But it was only Will, stepping inside and throwing the dead bolt. "For privacy," he said with an apologetic smile.

Sandrine left her father and came to shake Eleanor's hand. Her gait was self-possessed, almost strutting, but a hint of nerves in her eyes suggested it was for show. "How nice to meet you," she said in careful English, smiling as if she meant it. "Grand-mère told me all about you and how you find the books here. I would like very much to see this *Book of Dark Nights.*"

How much does she know? Eleanor's heart rate had finally settled down after the mad dash over from Widener, but she was still acutely aware of the Book against her side. "How nice to meet you, too. I'd love to show you the library," she said, pointedly ignoring the implied question about the Book.

Sandrine crossed her arms, one jutting eyebrow indicating that she felt patronized. "Do you have it?" she demanded.

Daniel jumped in. "The Book's dangerous, Sandrine. Before she died, your grandmother hid it, and she wanted it to stay hidden—but I suppose you know all about that." His gaze swept from her to Theuthet. "What exactly the hell is going on here?"

"I *do* know all about the Book, and I wish you'd been the one to tell me." Sandrine's scowl resembled her father's, and there was something more substantial than petulance behind it. "All this time we had a priceless asset, an inheritance, and you kept it from me? I know you're proud, but that's simply unfair. We're supposed to be a team, running the inn. I keep the books for you—I know how thin our margins are."

"She has a point, Daniel," Julien said in his patient way.

"This isn't about *money*!" Daniel stabbed an accusing finger at his father, his voice rising. "And you weren't even supposed to see my daughter. Now you're filling her head with lies and conspiring behind my back? Did you have Odile's house searched, too?"

"No one's filling my head with lies." Sandrine spoke evenly. "Grand-mère hid the Book because she wasn't in her right mind before she died." She cocked her head at her grandfather. "I told him I wanted to attend my grandmother's memorial, and I thought you and I should have our fair share of profit from the Book. So he bought me the ticket and arranged everything."

"Odile *was* in her right mind." Eleanor curled one arm protectively around the shoulder bag, trying to be subtle about it. She couldn't blame Sandrine for being fascinated with the Book and the library, just as she had been in her youth. But the girl had clearly been misled. "I saw your grandmother the very morning of the day she died. Believe me, she knew exactly what she was doing when she hid the Book."

"It's not an asset or a family legacy, Sandrine. It's a curse!" Daniel wheeled on his father again. "You told her that lie about Odile, didn't you? Why?"

"Because he's right—Odile wasn't in her right mind!"

To Eleanor's surprise, this outburst came from Will. He stalked down the table to flank Theuthet, facing them. "You know what *The Book of Dark Nights* means to the university," he told Eleanor, his voice full of accusation. "Your whole life is based on this library. I thought we agreed that the Book belongs here."

Eleanor couldn't blame Will for being surprised. When they spoke here on Thursday, they'd been on the same page. But now she knew the Book's true purpose—and that bringing it to fruition could be deadly.

Something was still nagging at the back of her mind: *all things, lie, dead, is, and.* The underlined words in their predictions, the ones she'd written on the napkin.

As if someone had been sending their class a message in code. Was Mariane writing the Book's predictions from beyond the grave?

"Do you remember what happened to Drew, Will?" she asked, hoping to make him understand why she was defending Daniel. "He tried to tear his own page out of the Book, and he died. And Genevra . . . you must know about her?"

Her voice came out thin and shaky, but somehow it silenced the others. Will frowned. "Genevra was depressed. A suicide."

"Was she really?" Eleanor's brain kept reordering that nonsensical sequence of words. *Lie is all things and dead. Dead is all things and lie.*

"Of course she was!" Will said testily. "Are you suggesting the Book killed Genevra? She was nowhere near it!"

Daniel rounded on Will. "You don't know anything about the Book, so stay out of this. You never even confessed to it, did you?"

"Not my thing," Will snapped. "Look, let's get down to business. Have you found the Book or haven't you?"

They were looking daggers at each other when Theuthet's dry voice cut across the silence. "Eleanor, bring me the book I need."

Now that *The Book of Dark Nights* was back in the library, his command brought the power surging from every direction, like a stream after its dam breaks. Eleanor stood immobile, submerged against her will.

This deep, thrumming vibration had given her life meaning for so long. For the sake of the power to choose the perfect book, she had accepted too much that was unacceptable. Drew's death, the nightmares, Odile's manipulation of vulnerable students.

Now she tried to resist and redirect the flow of power, the way she had when she'd chosen *The Idiot* for Drew. But there were no crosscurrents, no alternate possibilities, no subconscious doubts. The force of the old man's need was a torrent she couldn't resist.

The world turned gray and fluid around her. The book spines blurred into a single mass. But this time no one book suddenly stood out in vivid color, because the book Theuthet wanted, the book he believed he was fated to have, was not on the shelves.

It was in her bag.

Eleanor still strove to fight the power, but it was inside her, an extension of herself. All she could do was watch, carried along by the flood, as her fingers undid the clasp of her bag and drew out the Book.

The cover practically sizzled in her hands, teeming with all the emotions that had been bound inside. Her nightmares suggested the confessors' souls were trapped on these pages, desperate for release. But tearing out the pages wouldn't release them.

She walked to the head of the table and held out the Book to Theuthet. "This is the Book you're looking for."

If Odile was right, ripping out the pages would destroy their mortal bodies, as it had those of Drew and Genevra.

If someone ripped out every page, trying to create the All-Things Book? That would kill each one of them. Perhaps it would even doom their souls to an eternity of being mere characters in someone else's story to end all stories.

Lie and all things is dead.

"No!" Daniel sped to Eleanor and plucked the Book from her hands. "Don't let him have it."

Eleanor felt as if she'd just surfaced from a deep plunge underwater. The compulsion to give Theuthet the book he craved still worked on her, woven into the fabric of the library itself. But now she could breathe.

"She has no choice." Theuthet didn't try to take the Book from Daniel, only flicked an index finger in Will's direction. "William? It's time."

35

——

Now

September 29, 2019, 5:16 p.m.

Everything happened so fast that Eleanor, still woozy from the power, struggled to register the whole train of events. She scuttled back a step as a tall form rose from the armchair that faced the window—a large young man with butter-colored hair and a square face.

The boy who'd pulled a knife on them in the Latin Quarter.

She saw Will nod and use his Uniball to gesture crisply to the boy. She saw the boy cross the library in four strides and yank Sandrine up and out of her chair, clasping her firmly against his body with one long arm.

The next moment he was yelping, because Sandrine had kicked him in the shins. But he didn't loosen his hold. "Let her go!" Daniel cried.

He slipped the Book to Eleanor and launched himself at the young man—then stopped dead. The boy was holding a gleaming, long-barreled pistol to Sandrine's temple.

The energy in the room changed instantly. To Eleanor it was as if flames were racing over the shelves and smoke rising from the singed pages. A shooter in the library, where she had always felt safe.

She fluttered backward a few steps without meaning to, as if the books could somehow suck her in and hide her. Time seemed to have stopped—she was dissociating, losing focus, her mind adrift in Mariane's word scramble.

Lie and all things is dead.

Where had she heard something similar?

The message on the homemade fan. Knowing she would be able to hold on to the Book for only a moment longer, she dug her fingers inside the gap in the spine, found it, and fished it out.

With a lie, I die.

Not a second too soon. Time was moving again, and Will had shoved his way between her and Daniel. "We need this, thanks," he said, yanking the Book from her hands.

Eleanor kept the fan hidden in her palm. She didn't know if the object had any power of its own—if it was part of Mariane's spell or simply a warning not to lie to the Book. But she knew now that there was another way to interpret *With a lie, I die.*

When she found the fan in college, she had wondered who was supposed to die—the confessor or the Book? The message formed by the underlined words of their confessions suggested the latter.

Lie and all things is dead. Meaning, *a lie kills the All-Things Book.*

Lie to The Book of Dark Nights *and it dies, so that the All-Things Book can never be written.*

Daniel had raised his hands in surrender. Will gave the Book to Theuthet, who said, "Would you please tell him to be gentler?" He jerked his head toward the gunman. "I asked for no violence. My granddaughter isn't our enemy."

Sandrine stood stone-faced in the boy's arms. "No, I'm not," she said, but her pallor made it clear she hadn't expected this development.

"Your daughter is much more sensible than you are, Daniel." The old man opened the Book. "You understand," he added almost casually, "I just can't wait anymore. Your mother took nearly four decades to fill the Book. It was lucky Will and I connected when he started working in the dean's office. He kept an eye on Odile for me."

Odile's words flashed through Eleanor's head. In the message she'd left with her will, she had begged Daniel to forgive her mistakes—mistakes she had learned about too late, much like Mariane. *Keep the Book out of anyone else's hands. Your survival depends on it. We allowed it to read us. We are all captives to its pages.*

"Odile was doing it all for *you*." Eleanor felt lightheaded as she confronted the brilliant architect of the theory behind the library, the one who'd made it all possible, and finally understood *why* he'd set Odile up as the Librarian of Fates. "So *you* could write the All-Things Book."

Theuthet confirmed it with a shrug. "And then when there were only two pages left, she called me and said there'd been a change of plans."

"That's why she had a ticket for Paris when she died—she must've planned to explain to you in person." Eleanor tried to meet Daniel's eyes, but his attention was on Sandrine and the gunman. "Odile realized something that changed everything," she said breathlessly. "If you follow Mariane's recipe for the All-Things Book, you could kill us. Daniel, me, and anyone else who's confessed. Tear out our pages and we die."

Odile had devoted her life to helping her lover create the All-Things Book. She had changed her mind too late—after realizing that by encouraging her own son to confess to the Book, she might have condemned him to death, along with herself and so many others.

"Even you!" Eleanor said frantically, trying to appeal to Theuthet's sense of self-preservation. "You did confess, didn't you?"

The old man glanced at her and away, as if she were a child who'd blurted out something embarrassing. "The business about tearing out pages was only Odile's paranoid fantasy. She was succumbing to dementia—a sad thing to see."

So Odile had already told him what she'd discovered. Perhaps she'd hoped that by flying to see him in person, invoking their decades of love, she could change his mind.

Tears clouded Eleanor's vision as she grasped the depth of the old man's betrayal. She watched him press his palm to the Book's cover, closing his eyes as if inhaling a rare perfume. She hoped he really believed Odile had been wrong, because the alternative was that he just didn't care.

"If you tear out the pages," she said, trying to put all the conviction of the Ruthless in her voice, "your son will die, just like his friends Drew and Genevra. Even if you *didn't* confess, even if you survive it, what will you get in return? A book that every person on Earth wants to read? Fame greater than Voltaire's? Will that truly make you happy?"

Theuthet didn't meet her eyes, and Eleanor knew with a sudden, chilling certainty that in fact it would. He didn't *want* to kill Daniel, but his theory's popularity had waned considerably since the '60s, and he didn't want to be a footnote in literary history, either. For the possibility of immortal fame, he would risk his own son's life and perhaps even his own.

Will chuckled with a covetous eagerness that unnerved Eleanor. "A book that every person on earth wants to read should sell a few copies. It'll make your dad rich, Daniel, and he'll share the wealth with you. With all of us."

"You actually believe in this All-Things Book?" Daniel asked incredulously, and she knew he was trying to appeal to Will's pragmatism. "You're willing to risk hurting people for a legend about the book to end all books?"

"*You're* the one who thinks it's going to kill people. I think that's bullshit. Maybe the rest of the legend is, too, but what do we have to lose by trying?" Will turned to Eleanor, and she was startled by the contempt in his gaze.

He slipped his thumb from under the pen clip, and its click sounded loudly in the silence. "Eleanor, you need to start thinking outside the box if you ever want to be more than a librarian. If this All-Things Book is one-thousandth what he hopes it is—" he indicated Theuthet "—and he can actually write it, well, we have a written agreement. He'll give Harvard University Press the exclusive English rights. If I can make my employer the publisher of the only book in the world anyone wants to read, that would be beyond a coup for me."

Eleanor could only stare at him, numb with the realization of who he'd been all this time. She'd thought of him as a little cynical but basically decent. Now he sounded like one of those tech industry "disruptors," high on the single-minded determination of the Ruthless to win, win, win and not caring what might get lost in the process.

Or who might die.

"You knew Odile had hidden the Book before I did, didn't you?" she said to Will, recalling their conversation here on Thursday. He had asked her to use the library's power so he could make her admit the Book was gone. "Theuthet said you were *keeping an eye on* Odile for him. Did that mean breaking into the safe?"

"I've been doing it every semester for the past fifteen years or so." Will shrugged defensively, like a student caught cheating. "Odile was stingy with her secrets, so when I was in France on a business trip, I went to the source." He indicated Theuthet, his tone suggesting that Odile's mistrust had injured his pride. "He was kind enough to tell me everything Odile wouldn't, and I agreed to monitor how close the Book was to being full."

Again he clicked the pen, and Eleanor remembered the pen clip. She could see it as clear as day, a glint of silver on the drab tiles of the level of Pusey where Odile had died. Will had a nervous habit of worrying at those clips until they snapped clean off.

"And then you decided to confront her and demand the Book," she said. "You ambushed her on Pusey 3."

Odile had hidden the Book to save her son—and herself, and Eleanor, and every other confessor. And she had died hiding it. Heat pressed behind Eleanor's eyes as she saw it all clearly for the first time. Odile had been severe and demanding, far too careless about giving her students nightmares. But once she figured out that Drew and Genevra had died because of the Book, she had tried to set things right. She had warned her son.

"Odile wasn't supposed to hide the Book from us." Will's voice was a whipcrack. "I tried to reason with her once I found out, believe me. I gave her a chance to cooperate."

"You tried to reason with her, yes." Eleanor couldn't stop the terrible story from unfolding in her mind. She could see Odile's eyes wide with fear and outrage at Will's betrayal. "You cornered her in an aisle of the mobile stacks, and she climbed up on a shelf, trying to get away from you."

Or had Odile climbed the shelf to put the Book there, and then been surprised by Will? Either way, the result was the same. "You closed the aisle on her because she wouldn't tell you where the Book was." Will would have known the aisle couldn't actually crush Odile, because the sensors on the floor would stop it from closing on anything that was resting there, but he'd wanted to get her attention. "You never guessed that you were already in its hiding place, because you assumed she would put the Book under lock and key."

"It was actually *there*? On Pusey 3? Shit." Will's expression was crestfallen now, but not especially guilty. "I never meant to hurt Odile, just scare her," he added, throwing the glib words in Theuthet's direction.

"You killed my grandmother?" Sandrine sounded horrified.

"Accident!" Will looked even more uncomfortable. "Odile was totally on board with the plan to create the All-Things Book, for *decades*," he added. "She's the one who tipped me off that we could use the library's power to get those big donations. She used me to keep the library on the dean's good side, Eleanor, just like she used you."

"I *let* her use me." Eleanor knew she should have left the Library of Fates long ago, but there was no point in imagining all the different paths fate could have taken. Like Renée, her mentor was dead, and all she could do was pick up her own story from here and keep writing it.

Odile's letter suggested she'd hoped Daniel and Eleanor could finally "undo the spell" of *The Book of Dark Nights*—destroy it. And doing so might be their only chance of survival.

She shot Daniel a glance. *Trust me. I think I know what to do.*

"Please, let's not squabble." Theuthet seemed really unhappy as he looked at his granddaughter. Judging by her murderous glare as she stood in the gunman's grip, she wasn't buying Will's justifications. "What happened to Odile was a freak accident for which she bears partial responsibility. I regret it deeply, because I loved her."

You knew. Eleanor saw the realization register on Daniel. His face crumbled as they both grasped that the caring father who'd embraced him yesterday in Paris was also the mastermind who'd known all along his ally was responsible for Odile's death.

"For better or worse, however, her death brings together three generations to fulfill the promise of the Book." The old man turned to Will. "Could you please ask your rather intimidating friend to let my granddaughter go? There's no need for violence now that we're all on the same page, so to speak."

"I hope we *are* on the same page." Will signaled to the young man, who released Sandrine and plunked her down in the armchair. The barrel of his gun remained pointed at her temple, Eleanor noted.

"The same page?" Daniel looked sick, and not at all reassured. "If you tear out our pages in the Book, we'll die. How many times do I have to say it?"

Theuthet opened the Book to the penultimate page—an empty one, Eleanor saw from across the table—and laid it down flat.

"Two blank pages remain," he said. "Now, who is going to confess?"

Sandrine glared. Will shook his head.

Daniel asked his father, "If you're so sure that tearing out the pages won't hurt the confessors, why don't *you* do it? You never did confess, did you? I assumed you did, but Mom never actually said so."

Theuthet said nothing, but Eleanor could sense from his lofty silence that Daniel was right. Theuthet had known about the nightmares, possibly even about the risks of tearing out a page. He hadn't taken any chances—even as he'd convinced Odile and his other students to confess, then used Odile to obtain more confessions.

Only his lover would have devoted herself so fully to the cause.

But Odile had suspected there was a way to break the spell, and maybe she was right. *Lie and all things is dead.*

Eleanor stepped forward, knowing they might have one last chance to unknot the dark thread that Mariane had unwittingly spun. "Daniel and I will confess. We've already done it once. One more time can't hurt."

She held out her hand for the Book. Theuthet slid it down the table to her, still open, and she felt the thrum of power close by.

One last time.

"No!" Daniel tried to intercept the Book. "What are you doing, Eleanor?"

Will was on Daniel in an instant, yanking him backward. "Do you want your kid to get hurt?"

"You would not dare," Sandrine said from the armchair, but Eleanor heard the undercurrent of fear in her voice. Learning that her grandfather knew what Will had done to Odile had shaken her.

The Book seemed to ripple with electric tension under Eleanor's hands as she gazed down at the page.

Pressing her fingertips to the yellowed paper, she felt the turbulence of all those confessions, straining to get out—her own among them. *Let me read you*, the print taunted her, and she could swear she felt Mariane nearby, as she had in her dream on the plane. *With a lie, I die.*

She felt an urge to unburden herself, to let her true feelings flow onto the paper. There was something she hadn't found the courage to say to Daniel, something he needed to know. Telling the Book might be easier than telling him directly.

But this time she also needed to lie.

Mariane had fashioned the Book's paper from the garments of the condemned, suffused with their despair. On top of these pages already full of painfully sincere, unresolved emotions, each person who wrote in the Book added a confession without absolution, feelings without closure. Such would become the raw materials of the All-Things Book. But if one person lied to the Book, perhaps that sincerity would be compromised, corrupting the whole endeavor.

Eleanor shot Daniel a significant glance, trying to tip him off to what she was doing.

To attempt to break the spell, she would lie. But she would also confess truly, in case this was her last chance to be honest with him. He deserved to know why he had forgotten her.

Will tried to hand her a pen, but she found her own in her shoulder bag. When she touched it to the paper, she could almost feel the ancient material cringe under the onslaught of modern, industrially produced ink. As if the paper were whispering, *Not another*—but there had to be another. Just two more.

She wrote several sentences, then set down her pen and shut the Book, suddenly aware of her heart booming as if she were a vessel on the verge of shattering.

"Open it again," Theuthet commanded. "Read your prediction aloud."

Eleanor opened the Book again. "I'll read my confession first," she said, but she had to swallow before she could get the words out. "'I used the power of this Book to make Daniel Vernet forget me. I took his will and choices away from him.'" That was the true part.

The second part was harder to read aloud. "'And I never regretted it. I never once missed him.'"

That was the lie.

36

THEN

April 10, 1995

Eleanor had come to the Library of Fates because it was a safe place to lick her wounds. Because while she was there, she would never have to hear the phone ring and wonder if it was Daniel, offering her forgiveness and hope.

I'm a bad person. If not for me, my sister and Drew might be alive. She didn't want to look into Daniel's eyes and see the image of her recklessness and irresponsibility reflected back at her. As long as he remembered what she'd done to his friend—*brainwashed,* he'd called it—then she would have to burn with the shame of it. The pain of knowing she had let down someone who had loved her.

Now he had invaded her refuge. His arms were around her, his warmth enveloping her, his voice vibrating through both of them. "I'm so glad I found you. And I'm so sorry. I was upset and I was unfair to you."

Eleanor's heart leaped, and before she knew it, she was

melting into him the way she had that first night of the snowstorm. The kiss he placed on her forehead was a reminder of so many kisses past. She yearned to kiss him back, to assure him there was nothing to be sorry for. All the fault was hers.

Then he said, “But I’m also concerned about you.”

Her body stayed limp, but something inside her froze. *Concerned*—it was such a cold word. Not a word you used for someone you loved.

“Why would you be concerned?” she asked tonelessly.

“My mom’s trying to make you into the next librarian, and—”

“What if I *want* to be the next librarian?”

Her senses were still responding to his touch, but now alarms were ringing in her mind. With this patronizing *concerned* talk, he wanted her to think he still cared about her. But what he was really going to say was that she should give up the power and the possibility of being the librarian—for her own good. Because if she kept the power, she might hurt someone else.

He’s pretending to forgive me, but only to control me.

She knew she was right when he said, “You care too much about using the power, and you don’t even know what she’s doing it all for. You’re playing with things you don’t understand.”

He doesn’t respect me anymore. Doesn’t trust me. So how can he love me? Soon Daniel would forget everything he’d loved about her, while the memory of what he believed she’d done to Drew would endure.

Meanwhile, Odile would still need Eleanor’s support—and her loyalty. She would offer Eleanor a scholarship to study in France, then perhaps a graduate fellowship here at Harvard. A career in the library she loved. A home.

Power. I have the power to show people their paths through life.

If he thinks I'll give that up and be Meek just to get him back, he's wrong. Here, I matter.

Eleanor made herself meet Daniel's eyes without really seeing him, shutting her senses to the arch of his brows, the distraught tone of his voice, the familiar musk of his body. He was not a person anymore, only a collection of personality traits that she could sum up in one A-worthy essay. He was vain Dorian Gray, self-hating Raskolnikov, social-climbing Julien Sorel.

As if from a great distance, she heard him begging her to talk to him. But maybe they'd already talked enough, and every word hurt her.

In Juliette Aubry's book, Mariane had used the Book's power to make a man forget all about his faithless sweetheart, purging him of pain and memory at the same time. If only Eleanor could wipe Daniel from her memory, she would do it in an instant. But she couldn't use the library's power on herself—it didn't work that way.

If she made him forget *her*, though, then the sting of his disapproval and disappointment might fade more quickly. And wouldn't she actually be doing him a favor, freeing him from any lingering feelings he had for her?

She raised her head. "Daniel, ask me for a book."

He protested. "I don't want a book, Eleanor! Why aren't you listening to me?"

His closeness nearly undid her resolve. But if she yielded to the warmth of his lips and his hot breath, she might be sorry in the end.

"Ask me. I need to know you still care about me," she lied, knowing it didn't matter whether he cared for her, because he could never care *enough*. But she needed an excuse to make him summon the power. "Or," she asked, her tone hardening, "are you afraid I'll *brainwash* you, too?"

"Of course not!" Daniel hung his head. "I'm sorry I ever used that word."

"If you trust me," she said, emphasizing each word, "then ask me for a book."

She saw his internal struggle in the hunch of his shoulders, the clenched fists at his sides. Empathy flared up in her—*How can I do this to him?* But she told herself he was only reluctant because he *didn't* trust her. He knew that by asking her for a book, he was letting her into some intimate place he'd withheld until now. Giving her power over him that she might abuse.

Then the struggle ended, and he looked straight into her eyes and said, "Find me the book I need, Eleanor."

The power surged up between them, around them. The library throbbed with that deep, drumlike vibration. Daniel's face, the windows, the table, the books—everything blurred into one indistinct mass, as if the world were a piece of celluloid film catching fire and melting.

Eleanor stepped away from Daniel, into the center of the library. The booming grew louder, like an overstrained heart, and she pressed her hands over her ears, trembling with the effort of giving him the *right* pathway.

A future without her, because he deserved his freedom, and that meant escaping far from his mother's domain to travel and figure out what he really wanted in life. And a future for her without him, because she couldn't endure knowing he'd seen the worst side of her.

This was the last chance to change her mind, and a traitorous part of her still wanted to. But she had to be strong. She closed her eyes and opened them.

Please let him forget me. Everything about me. For both our sakes.

And now she spotted the book she needed, sitting serenely in the *T*s: *Collected Poems of Alfred, Lord Tennyson.*

Of course. Mariane had used *The Odyssey.* A passage from Homer's epic had inspired one of Tennyson's best-known poems, a poem about forgetting.

Slowly, so as not to hasten what she knew was coming, Eleanor went to the shelf and pulled out the book. Her fingers went instinctively to the right page, and the large volume fell open at "The Lotos-Eaters."

Around her, the library returned to normal. The booming subsided into silence. But she knew there was still no turning back as she brought the open book over to Daniel, carrying it as solemnly as a priest might present the Bible.

"This is the book you need," she said, placing it in his hands.

Daniel glanced at her, but only for a second. Then his new fate sucked him in. Cradling the book in both arms, he gazed down at the designated page and began reading the poem aloud.

Eleanor stood very still, listening to Tennyson's lush reimagining of Homer's story. War-weary sailors come ashore in a beautiful land where the inhabitants greet them with sweet fruits that make them forget their former lives. The narcotic lotus steals away their memories of home, their fear and angst and uncertainty, leaving them with only a blissful now. No incentive can make them desert their new lives of lazy, mellow forgetfulness.

"'Death is the end of life; ah, why
Should life all labor be?
Let us alone. Time driveth onward fast,
And in a little while our lips are dumb.
Let us alone. What is it that will last?
All things are taken from us, and become
Portions and parcels of the dreadful past.'"

Here Daniel smiled, as if enjoying a private joke. With a start, Eleanor realized that the lines he'd just read were the prediction the Book had given him back at the beginning of the seminar, when he was the first to confess.

She had chosen correctly, then, she told herself. Forgetting the *dreadful past* was his fate. She had simply aided the process.

All things are taken from us—memories, regrets. If the magic worked for her as it had for Mariane, the act of reading this poem should make him forget her.

Daniel continued reading to the end of the stanza, and then to the end of the poem: "'O, rest ye, brother mariners, we will not wander more.'" Then he shut the book and looked up at Eleanor, who held her breath. Tears swam in her eyes, because in her heart of hearts, this wasn't the fate she'd wanted.

It was safer, though. It would stop her from being hurt again.

When her vision cleared, she saw that Daniel's own gaze was vague and polite, as if he couldn't place her features. "Uh." He glanced down at the book, which also appeared to confuse him, and back up at her. "You're my mom's assistant, right? I'm not sure how I . . ."

"That's me." Eleanor relieved him of the heavy volume of Tennyson. Clearly and slowly, she said, "You're looking for your mother, but she's not here. She's at home in Porter Square. You have a room in Adams House. This summer you're going to Europe. Remember?"

Daniel's face brightened. "Yeah, I'm psyched for that."

The library's magic hadn't taken *all* his memories, then—good. Eleanor hoped it had taken enough of them.

"I think," she said, leading him to the door, "you shouldn't come back to your mother's seminar. A tragedy just happened—your roommate died—and no one will expect you to finish your work for the semester. You need to go away and see new things and forget."

"Forget. Yeah. Totally agree," Daniel said.

In the doorway, he paused for an instant, as if trying again to place her. "I hope you have a great summer. It was really nice getting to know you, uh . . ."

"Eleanor." And she pushed him out the door into the stairwell. "Goodbye, Daniel."

37

Now

September 29, 2019, 5:38 p.m.

"You fucked with his memory? That's *cold*," Will said, sounding impressed, but Eleanor ignored him.

Did Daniel understand that the last part of her confession, that she hadn't regretted what she'd done to him, had been a deliberate lie? Something shifted in his face, his mouth hardening and his eyes squinting as if against a cold wind.

Of course she had missed him all these years. Every time she passed their familiar haunts or saw the spire of Dunster above the trees, every time Odile mentioned him, every time she read a love scene in a novel, every time she touched the Book or felt his presence in her dreams. By making him forget her, she'd hoped to forget him, too, but it hadn't worked at all.

In the Book before her, the prediction appeared beneath her confession in its eerily exact facsimile of her own handwriting. She read the quote aloud, her heart swelling with joy and apprehension. *"'Sache que je t'ai toujours aimée, que je n'ai aimé que toi.'"*

"'Know that I have always loved you, that I have never loved anyone but you.'" It was a quote from the end of *The Red and the Black.*

When Eleanor met Daniel's eyes again, tears blurred his image as she yielded to the feelings she couldn't speak aloud. The quote spoke more eloquently than she could: She *had* always loved him and only him, though she'd sometimes tried to deny it. *The Book knows the truth of my heart.*

She thought she saw him nod as he took the Book from her and turned to the last page.

"Go on, Daniel." A beneficent smile bloomed on Theuthet's lips, but otherwise he hadn't reacted to Eleanor's confession or prediction, as if she were a child whose play was beneath his notice. "Just one more confession, and the Book will finally fulfill its purpose. Once every page is full, it should finally allow me to read all the confessions, absorbing the emotions that inspired them into my own brain. And your gift of human experience will enable me to write the book that Mariane and Voltaire dreamed of."

First you'll have to tear out all the pages. But Eleanor knew Theuthet was omitting that bit of Mariane's instructions on purpose, because deep down he feared she and Daniel were right about the consequences.

Daniel scribbled something in the Book, his mouth twisting with concentration. Then he closed it, opened it, and read his confession: "'Erasing my memory was an unspeakable violation that took away a piece of me. I will never forgive the person who did it for her own selfish reasons.'"

Will's eyes popped. "Fair enough!"

But Eleanor's attention was on Daniel. When he looked

up, she saw the warm brown of his eyes and the reassurance in them.

He lied, too.

Did that mean he *could* forgive her, even after what she'd confessed? Her mind was so full of that possibility that she barely heard as Daniel read his prediction: "'*Les vices de l'esprit peuvent se corriger; / Quand le coeur est mauvais, rien ne peut changer.* The vices of the head can be corrected, but when the heart is bad, nothing can change it.'"

Head versus heart. They had both made mistakes of intellect and vanity, but she wanted to believe that both her heart and Daniel's had always been in the right place.

"Voltaire. Fitting," Theuthet said. When Eleanor looked up, his gaze was on his son, more solemn than triumphant, as if he were finally grasping the enormity of what he planned to do. "Well, give it here."

Eleanor glanced at Daniel once more before she gave the Book to his father. He nodded almost imperceptibly.

One lie should be enough. But two lies couldn't hurt.

"If I were you," Eleanor said to Theuthet, hoping he hadn't noticed what had just passed between them, "I would think twice. Voltaire left a towering legacy without writing the All-Things Book. So could you."

Theuthet sighed. "Don't patronize me. You think my works are out of date. Besides, Voltaire didn't have to compete with the virtual world." He slid his fingertips over the Book's cover. "At least mine will be a work of the human imagination."

"But not just *your* imagination." If he succeeded, all those voices in *The Book of Dark Nights*, all those confessions, would be digested and spat out in the form of whatever abomination he produced. "You can call yourself the author of the All-Things Book, but it will never be truly yours."

"I know. And this I accept." Each motion deliberate, almost

reverent, Theuthet opened the Book to the frontispiece and then to the first page. As he lowered his eyes to the writing there, Eleanor wondered if he would actually be able to read it.

But his eyes were flitting left to right, left to right. He *was* reading.

Eleanor saw her own anxiety reflected on Daniel's face. *Did our lies do anything at all?*

She tightened her grip on Mariane's fan, still concealed in her palm. Could they be sure they'd saved themselves?

The first page made a tender smile appear on the old man's face. After the second, he frowned and shook his head. When he read the third, his eyes opened wide as if he'd seen a ghost.

And he was seeing ghosts, she knew. Every confession was the specter of an emotion, some three centuries old and some more recent, starting in the '60s with the confessions of Odile and his other students. All those past bits of the living and dead were cramming themselves into his brain and making themselves at home there. Meek, Ruthless, Contemplative, Self-Destructive, and all the subtle shades of humanity in between—these were the makings of the All-Things Book.

After the fifth or sixth page, the reading sped up. Pages flickered. Emotions flitted over Theuthet's face too swiftly for Eleanor to register anything concrete. A quirked brow, a mocking smile, the glint of a tear—so many people's hopes, fears, regrets, shames, desires. How could one mind hold all that?

Daniel reached for her hand. She grasped his and knew that if they did die, they would die together.

"What's happening to him?" Sandrine cried suddenly.

"I don't know!" Will edged over to Theuthet, as if he expected the Book to blow up in his face.

Theuthet was flipping pages faster and faster, his gaze whipping left to right over the lines with inhuman speed. As if he weren't even reading the confessions, Eleanor thought, but devouring them.

As he turned another page, sparks soared from his fingers and struck Will's cheek, making Will wince. "Is this supposed to happen?"

Eleanor had flinched, too, biting the inside of her cheek. "Who knows?" she whispered in awe. "No one's ever tried this before."

Will reached for the Book but recoiled immediately, as if it had given him a strong electric shock. "What the fuck! Professor, talk to me. What's happening?"

Theuthet's face was turning the color of a ripe plum. His eyes bulged sickly from their sockets, even as they continued to read.

Will wheeled from Daniel to Eleanor and back, his movements loose with panic. "He said everything would change once the Book was full!"

"Everything is changing," Daniel said, and she heard the dread in his voice.

Theuthet's chair scraped across the floor. He stood up abruptly, like a puppet on strings, and paced the library with a mechanical stride, still holding the Book. His face was swollen, his eyes distended and riddled with red veins—yet he kept moving. Kept reading.

Daniel shook his head, tears glittering in his eyes, and she knew that even after everything, it was still painful for him to see his father this way.

Will waved frantically at the gunman. "Get up, you idiot! Take the Book away from him!"

The boy balked. When Will nodded impatiently, he hauled himself to his feet, pistol still in hand, and tried to wrest the Book away from the old man.

But one touch seemed to send a current surging up his arm. He yelped and retreated.

Theuthet was marching in tight little circles, turning pages with the regularity of a metronome and muttering under his breath. *Reading aloud*, Eleanor thought, as if the Book were speaking through him. He was its instrument now, not the other way around.

And the process was putting a terrible strain on his already frail body. She heard it in the breathless cracking of his voice, saw it in his grimace. The library vibrated madly, uncontrollably, as if mimicking his irregular heartbeat.

The gunman succeeded in grabbing Theuthet around the shoulders and forcing him back down in his chair. But he didn't try to touch the Book again, just stood staring down at the old man who appeared to be reading himself to death. The weapon dangled forgotten from his hand.

Sandrine crept over to her father. Her face was white, and she couldn't seem to remove her eyes from Theuthet.

Theuthet's head was still bent low over the Book, his hand turning pages at lightning speed. He must be close to the end now. With a guttural cry, the old man wrenched his gaze from the Book and threw back his head as if to contemplate the vibrant colors of the ceiling mural. A low, hideous rattle came from his throat. His eyes rolled up to show only the whites, his mouth twisted in agony. On the table before him, the Book lay open to the last page—Eleanor recognized Daniel's handwriting.

Lie and all things is dead. Both of them had lied. Now what?

Daniel seized a chance to advance on the gunman. Eleanor gasped as he snatched the boy's wrist, wrenched it hard, and grabbed the gun by the barrel, just as he'd done with the knife in the Paris alley.

The boy cried out in pain. But one good jerk and Daniel

had the pistol. He racked the slide to chamber a round and aimed it straight at Will.

Will didn't seem to notice. The old man had toppled face down onto the table, his forehead resting on one edge of the still-open Book.

"Check his pulse, Trent," Will hissed.

The younger man shook his large blond head, his cheeks bloodless. "Let's get the fuck out of here."

Daniel cleared his throat. "Will?"

When Will noticed the gun trained on him, he seemed to forget all about Theuthet. Eyes wide with terror, hands in the air, he inched toward the door. "What the fuck do you think you're doing?"

"Sorting this out." Daniel's voice was sharp with nerves, but he looked at home handling the firearm. "Maybe stay still?"

The boy disobeyed this command and dived for the door. Footsteps echoed as he pounded down the stairs. As if in a chain reaction, Will grabbed his chance and dashed after him, but Daniel blocked the way. "You're gonna tell the authorities how my mom really died. She deserves justice."

She did. For all the mistakes Odile had made, Eleanor missed her mentor intensely in that moment. She wished she'd been able to say a real goodbye.

At the table, Theuthet lay on top of the Book, unmoving.

While Will faced Daniel in the doorway, hands raised and eyes wild, Sandrine ghosted to her grandfather's side and placed two fingers on his pulse point. "He's still breathing," she whispered to Eleanor.

"Sandrine, Eleanor, stay up here," Daniel called to them, then turned his attention to the cowering Will again. "Look, asshole, if you try to weasel out of this—"

But Will had taken advantage of Daniel's instant of distraction and plunged through the door and down the stairs.

"Let him go!" Eleanor hurried to the door, where she could hear Daniel's footsteps thudding in hot pursuit. "You shouldn't be the one who gets caught with the gun!"

She was about to run after Daniel when a flicker of movement in the library made her whip around. Sandrine had taken hold of the edge of *The Book of Dark Nights* and was sliding it out of her grandfather's grip.

As the Book lost contact with the old man's body, the gilt edges of the pages wavered and flickered like a reflection of unbearably bright sunlight on water, momentarily blinding Eleanor.

When her vision cleared, there were no pages. She blinked, confused—and then realized the pages had crumbled, leaving the Book's binding holding only a few handfuls of ashy brown dust.

Our confessions! She clutched her arms to her chest reflexively, half expecting her body to begin crumbling, too. But she was still there. Solid, breathing.

And all around her and Sandrine, the power resounded, stronger than ever, throbbing like a distant organ. A storm of dust rose from the Book's empty shell and filled the library, clouding the air and catching the light to glint gold and silver.

The dust blotted out Sandrine's frightened face, obscuring windows and bookshelves. With it came the same electric shiver of magic Eleanor had always felt when she touched the Book. She could feel tiny remnants of pages entering her mouth and nostrils, her very pores, yet they didn't make her cough or squint. Her body absorbed them easily.

Touching the Book, she had often felt as if it were a prison full of spirits desperate for escape. Now those spirits were free, her own among them, and they no longer roiled with anguish. They simply caught the air currents and settled on the library, on her and Sandrine, rediscovering the world outside the pages.

As I have, Eleanor decided. *As I will keep doing.*

Out of the corner of her eye, Eleanor thought she saw the dust thickening into dozens of ghostly human forms. But they disappeared when she tried to look directly at them—until suddenly she recognized one. A pair of sharp eyes behind glasses, shoulders with a firm set to them, a scarf.

Odile! She reached out to the phantom of her mentor, knowing she wouldn't endure yet needing desperately to make one last contact.

"Thank you," Eleanor whispered to the air. "We stopped him. I wish you could have told me everything."

She was lightheaded from the magic dust, no longer sure if anything she was seeing were real. Another form seemed to rear up beside Odile's and overlap with it, this one familiar from her dreams.

Mariane. Like Odile, the witch had devoted her life to the glorification of an ambitious man. Now, at last, she was free from the dark consequences.

Eleanor felt the dust tingle on her palms, her eyelids. "Thank you," she said softly, addressing both Odile and Mariane, to the extent they existed briefly in the library with her. "Your power gave me a pathway, a life I loved . . . for a while. Thank you." *But now I'm ready to move on.*

By giving people the stories they craved, the stories that healed them, she'd done her best to console herself for her own unfinished story. But she couldn't let her own thread drop, any more than she could erase Daniel's memory permanently.

The phantoms were fading. Perhaps they had only ever been her imagination. The dust that had been the pages of *The Book of Dark Nights* was falling to earth, vanishing. The throb of the power was dissolving back into the rhythms of the everyday world.

"What *was* that?" Sandrine asked in an awed whisper. Meeting Eleanor's eyes, she suddenly looked like the child she'd so recently been. "My grandmother . . . I thought I saw her."

Her eyes filled with tears. "I never imagined Julien would do anything to hurt her."

"He never intended to." But gazing down at the old man's limp body, Eleanor knew he'd been willing to hurt them, even if he hadn't wanted to.

Sandrine stared flatly at her grandfather with those dark eyes so like Daniel's. Her cheeks were tear-streaked, and her hair had escaped from its clip and haloed her face. Edging close to him, touching his wrist, she said, "I think he's gone now."

Eleanor nodded solemnly. Theuthet's body was already weak, and he had *absorbed* the confessions, as he'd put it. Perhaps death was the punishment for an unsuccessful attempt to create the All-Things Book—*With a lie, I die*—or perhaps he had simply lacked the strength to endure the shock. She knew only that as the Book's pages crumbled, his life force must have crumbled with them.

She opened her hand and found that scraps of paper and fabric were all that was left of Mariane's fan. Had she crushed it without thinking, or had it crumbled spontaneously, too?

Sandrine glanced around the library, from the mural to the tall shelves to the shadows gathering in the corners. Her lip trembled. "I've always wanted to come here. My grandmother told me about the power, and how you and she could choose the perfect book for anyone. That's gone now, isn't it?"

"I think so," Eleanor admitted, feeling her voice quaver. Sandrine would never be able to experience the library as she had. "I'm sorry you couldn't have come here earlier. Maybe you could have used the power, too."

"I would have liked that. But what really matters to me is saving the inn." Sandrine's voice had taken on a brisker, less wistful note. "I can go away to university, but Dad's business is all he has."

"I know." Eleanor took a careful step toward the girl. "I'm sorry. I want to believe Julien loved you both and meant to provide for you."

Looking at the empty binding of the Book, she wondered if there were still a way to meet the conditions of Odile's will. After all, *she* was the one who was supposed to attest that the Book was securely in the safe.

In the distance, sirens keened. Someone had called an ambulance.

"Oh, I'm not worried about that." Sandrine's face brightened, something canny and very Odile-like in her eyes. "Before we left France, I made my grandfather add a provision for me to his *testament*—his will. He was good with stocks, did you know?" She gazed ruefully at the corpse draped over the table. "It's not a fortune, but it's enough."

Below them, a door banged. Footsteps pattered up the stairs, cutting through the wail of the sirens a few blocks off.

Hoping that was Daniel returning, Eleanor stepped toward the bank of windows on the Yard side. One was slightly open, and perhaps some of the dust of their confessions had escaped to swirl and dance among the golden trees.

Dramatic swooshes of quill pen, earnest curlicues of ballpoint, fragments of her own past self and so many others'—all mingled in the strange new life of debris on the wind. Perhaps they would glitter in the last rays of the sunset, and some student would see that ethereal dust and be inspired to write a poem as powerful as Shelley's, or a text or email that changed their life. You never knew.

The footsteps arrived—brash and confident on the stairs, then more hesitant as Daniel entered the library.

Knowing he had no reason to forgive her, knowing he had anyway, Eleanor turned and went to meet him.

38

—

Then

April 10, 1995

Alone in the library, Eleanor listened to Daniel's steps fade into the distance. Then she found the spare office key and unlocked Odile's sanctum.

The need to confess throbbed through her every fiber, like a starving person's hunger, because she finally had something to confess now. Not her sister's death, an act of fate for which she'd chosen to blame herself as a naïve child. No, this was something she had done of her own free will as an adult.

Nightmares? She welcomed them as the punishment for everything she'd done. She deserved them.

Hadn't April and Genevra said that in their nightmares, they felt the presence of the other people who'd confessed? In hers, she hoped, she would feel close to Daniel again. Almost close enough to touch.

The safe code had been changed, of course, but Eleanor

knew which dates were important to Odile. She tapped in 051468—the first day after the general strike in that turbulent year of protests. The first meeting of her mentor and Julien Theuthet in the Jardin du Luxembourg. The beginning of Daniel, of the library, of everything.

The door opened.

When she touched the Book, it tingled in her hands, sending pins and needles up her arm, but it wasn't an unpleasant sensation. Despite what had happened to Drew, she couldn't bring herself to be afraid of it. After all, this volume had become the beginning of her own chosen pathway, the foundation of her new life.

Cross-legged on the floor, she opened to the first blank page and wrote:

I used the power of this Book to make Daniel Vernet forget me. I stole pieces of his memory from him so he wouldn't be able to tear my heart from me. I think he'll be happier now, living in the present like the Lotos-Eaters. But what I did was wrong, even if only I remember it.

She closed the Book, held her breath for a few seconds, and opened it again.

Beneath her confession, words in her handwriting had appeared:

And yet for all her hate, each parting glance would tell
A stronger passion breathed, burned, in this last farewell.

Unconquered in my soul the Tyrant rules me still;
Life bows to my control, but Love I cannot kill!

Love *I cannot kill!* The words of the Emily Brontë poem were still ringing in Eleanor's head as she encountered Odile on the stairs.

"Hello, professor," she said.

Odile stopped her with a hand on her arm. "I ran into Daniel coming out of the building. Tell me, what did you do to him?"

"Do to him?" Eleanor was surprised at how easily the wide-eyed innocent look came to her.

But when Odile fixed her with one of those piercing gazes, she knew the professor wasn't fooled. Perhaps she never had been. "Please don't insult my intelligence," Odile said. "I know quite well you've been using the power of *my* library."

Should she be Meek this time, or should she hold her head high? Eleanor made a split-second decision. "The power worked for me," she said, "so maybe it's *my* library, too."

Odile's stare was so cold that for a second, Eleanor thought she'd ruined everything. But then the professor smiled in her ironic way and said, "Maybe. I do have you to thank for making sure the Book returned to the library after poor Drew decided to steal it."

Eleanor sensed they'd stepped over a boundary; from now on, she would be not a student but an apprentice, someone who was allowed to know things. "The confessions feed the library, don't they?" she said. "You pretended you didn't want us to write in the Book, but then you used Daniel to make sure we did."

Odile sighed. Close up, Eleanor could see lines at the corners of her mouth, a mole on her right cheek, circles under her eyes. The professor wasn't all-powerful. She was already in midlife, and someday she would die.

"The Book must have confessions, raw bits of volatile energy and human weakness, or it will stop guiding us in the Library. The best ones come from young people—*students*," Odile said. "But I didn't expect what happened to poor Drew."

"That won't happen again." Eleanor didn't want to think about Drew. If she dwelled on the Book's darker possibilities, she would end up like Daniel, seeing it as a curse instead of a tool.

All you had to do was follow the Book's rules.

"I hope not." Odile gave her a canny expression. "Did you really think I wouldn't notice that you altered Daniel's memory? He doesn't seem to remember you—or *anything* that happened today."

At the reminder, Eleanor's newfound confidence faltered. Her cheeks warmed, and she bowed her head, waiting for Odile to tell her that she was a terrible person.

But Odile only played with her scarf. "I have to say, I'm impressed. I know Mariane did such things, but I've never pushed the power that far myself."

"I wasn't sure it would work." Eleanor's voice had fallen to a whisper.

"You did that without his consent." Odile's tone was stern, but it lightened a moment later. "Perhaps it was for the best, though. Daniel was reeling from his friend's death, and I may have made the mistake of giving him more information than he could handle. You seem to have clouded his memories, convincing him it was all just some trauma-induced hallucination."

She doesn't blame me? She's actually glad? "I think Daniel's happier living in the present," Eleanor ventured, trying to persuade both of them.

"Hmm. Yes. He tells me he means to drop out of school." Odile's expression darkened a shade. "His father won't be pleased. But Daniel never had the aptitude to be the next librarian anyway. You, on the other hand . . ."

She leaned toward Eleanor, eyes narrowed in a way that was almost sinister. "You're very good at showing people their pathways of textual potential—and even pushing them onto a path you choose. How would you feel about giving the Book to other students, just as innocent and unsuspecting as you once were?"

The words sent a faint shudder through Eleanor, but she held the gaze. It felt too late to turn back now. "I wouldn't like to trick people."

"You might need to someday. If you want to keep using the power, you'll need to harvest the confessions."

Harvest. The word had a bloody tinge, but it was only a figure of speech. "You never exactly lied to us, Odile," Eleanor said. "You told us the risks of using the Book, and you let us make our own decisions. And you've confessed to the Book yourself, haven't you?"

Odile just barely nodded. "As have you."

When the library was very quiet like this, Eleanor could sense the hum of the Book inside the safe, like a witness to their conversation. Perhaps she was sealing her own fate as she said, "I want to stay here in the library, with you. This is my pathway."

Daniel had tried to discourage her from becoming the next librarian. But Daniel was gone.

She had so many questions to ask Odile. "If confessions in the Book give the library its power, then what happens when the Book runs out of pages?"

Odile opened her mouth as if to answer. Then a wary look washed over her face, and she said, "This is something we will need to find out together when it happens. Wouldn't you say?"

Together. The three syllables thrummed warmly in Eleanor's head like the Book's power. Until this moment, she hadn't realized how much it meant to have someone include her in a *together* and a *we*.

The library and the Book were so much larger than she was, and she was part of them now. She was needed.

"Yes," she said, "we'll find out together."

39

Now

June 15, 2021, 3 p.m.

Eleanor was nearly finished shelving the nonfiction section when someone came up behind her and asked, "Can you find me a book?"

"We're not open yet." Had she left the door unlocked when she went upstairs for coffee?

But then she turned and found Sandrine, dressed in shorts and a tee and a face mask printed with marigolds. "Oh, hi!" She reached for her own mask. "What kind of book? And what do you think? I've got almost everything shelved now, but I want to add some comfy chairs. Rugs, too, so it doesn't look so much like a basement."

Sandrine glanced around the shop. Through the younger woman's eyes, Eleanor saw a rugged room with unfinished stone walls, now fitted out with tall shelves of glossy yellow pine. Somehow she had managed to cram most of the collection of the Library of Fates into the basement of a whitewashed gastropub on one of the less fashionable streets of Annecy.

It wasn't fancy, and there would be only a colorful sign pointing downward to alert tourists, skiers, and attendees of the big animation festival to the presence of the Librairie des Sorts. But as sunlight lanced through the narrow windows and pooled on the familiar book spines, illuminating dust motes on the way, she felt the books were at home here. In winter, the space would be cozy. Perhaps Daniel could install a gas fireplace in that empty spot. It wasn't Shakespeare and Company, but as a bookstore with an eclectic, passionately curated inventory, it would do.

"I know where to get some nice old rugs," Sandrine said, clearly assessing the place with an innkeeper's eye. "I'm excited to start hiring staff." And then, as if she were a little embarrassed, "But I wish you weren't leaving Annecy so soon. This place is yours, even if my dad's name is on the lease."

"I wish I weren't leaving on Friday, too. But I only have a tourist visa, and I'm teaching a summer school class." Eleanor didn't mention that she would love to return in the autumn and stay—if Daniel suggested it. To change the subject, she asked, "What kind of book did you want?"

She treasured the tinge of approval she'd just heard in Sandrine's voice. Over the long months of pandemic lockdown, Eleanor and Daniel had talked every few weeks, with various degrees of awkwardness. She'd tried several times to broach the issue of what she had done to his memory, but he always defused the tension with a wry comment and changed the subject, as if he wanted her to think it didn't matter.

Whenever he expanded their video chats to include Sandrine, the girl had seemed polite but a little sullen. She was still grieving her grandparents, the larger family she'd hoped to have, and Eleanor knew from Daniel that Sandrine was angry Will hadn't been punished for his role in Odile's death.

In Eleanor's mind, it was enough that Will had taken mental health leave and then resigned his post, cutting short his ambition to occupy the dean's office. He deserved worse, no doubt, but that day in the library seemed to have changed him for good.

With Eleanor's attestation that the Book—or the husk of it, anyway—was in the library on the day of Odile's memorial, they had managed to fulfill the conditions of Odile's will. But Will's withdrawal had left the library without administrative support. With the campus near-empty during the lockdown, certain university officials had finally seized their opportunity to "repurpose" the precious space occupied by the Library of Fates into departmental offices. This precipitated a handful of angry letters from alums and an editorial in the *Crimson*. But in the end, just like the Adams House swimming pool and the Freshman Union with its butter-pat-covered ceiling, the Library of Fates had passed into Harvard history.

The collection now belonged to Eleanor, the empty binding of *The Book of Dark Nights* included.

The bookstore had been Daniel's idea. In May, once all the books had shipped, she'd flown over to set it up, staying in an airy room of Daniel's inn. After more than a year of huddling in seclusion, it felt good to walk the sunlit streets of this beautiful mountain town and see the tourists trickling back into the cafés.

Sandrine said, "Now that I'm finally going to start at Harvard, really living on campus, I'd like a book about that. Going to Harvard and figuring out who I am."

Eleanor's breath caught. She still braced herself whenever someone asked her for a book, as if the Librarian of Fates part of her were a phantom limb.

She would always miss the power a little, she knew, as she turned to scan the shelves of her own volition. The books were just books now, and she felt no mysterious thread tugging her to choose a particular one.

But they were books she knew intimately, cover to cover, and she loved to share them. She went to the fiction section and pulled out Elif Batuman's *The Idiot*, very different from the book of the same title she'd given Drew long ago.

"Thank you." Sandrine examined the book. She was never effusive, but when she was willing to give you the time of day, it meant something. "Dad asked me to invite you to join him at seven on the terrace for a glass of wine," she added, not meeting Eleanor's eyes. "He wants to show you some of the local cheeses."

"Thank you." Eleanor felt touched by the gesture, knowing Daniel could have just texted her. "I'll be there."

***

Daniel had laid out an elaborate spread of cheeses, starting with his neighbor Marthe's Emmental, because food gave them something safe to talk about. Wine, cheese, the Alps and their flora and fauna, occasionally books—all these were subjects that helped them postpone bringing up the past.

When Eleanor joined him on the terrace, a rainstorm had just swept through the mountains, leaving clear skies and cooler air in its wake. He waved her into a padded wicker chair under the umbrella and handed her a glass of Viognier, then went to finish slicing a baguette.

They still had barely discussed what she'd done to his memories. The sterility of virtual conversations had made it seem impossible. Even now they were face-to-face, he wasn't sure how to lay her worries to rest—or to tell her how much he'd enjoyed her company over the past month.

But he needed to find a way, because she had a ticket to fly back in just three days.

"I wish your mother could have been here to see everything you've built," Eleanor was saying. "This beautiful inn in a beautiful place."

"So do I." Daniel sighed. It *was* a beautiful place, and he was happy with his life. But now he had to live with the unsettling knowledge that he hadn't fully or freely chosen this pathway. When Eleanor made him forget her, she had cut off another possibility.

If she hadn't abused the power, how much in his life would have been different? Would they have stayed together? Had their own children?

When he brought the tray over, Eleanor was gazing off across the pastures that rose like stairsteps into the blue haze of the mountains. "I think Sandrine is warming up to me, though it's hard to tell with her."

"That's good to hear." He could feel her prodding and probing, trying to nudge him toward the subjects that were less safe. If he let her leave without really talking, without asking her to come again and consider staying, this might be the end of their conjoined thread.

Eleanor picked up her wineglass and gazed into it. "I think Sandrine loves you very much," she said, "and she wants to understand you. Not just who you are now, but who you were when you were her age."

I'd like to understand who I was, too. Every time Daniel thought all his memories were restored, something new popped up to jump-scare him.

He reminded himself that Eleanor had been very young, around Sandrine's age, when she had made the decision to alter his memory. She'd been sad and directionless, and Odile had given her a home, an identity, a thread to follow. What had he offered her? Only the excitement of first love, which so quickly fades.

"You know," he said, pouring wine for himself, "when you made me forget parts of my college years, it was like a second chance. I spent a while just running away, living in the now, and then I made a new life as a better person—I hope, anyway." His voice faltered on the last words. "But when I read your book and those scenes between us, I knew they'd really happened. I could feel it. Why did you do it? Why did you erase us?"

Eleanor raised her eyes to him, burning with an emotion he couldn't name.

"The first time we really talked in college, I told you I didn't believe in love," she said, "but actually I didn't think I deserved it. The way I felt when you smiled at me . . . I knew it couldn't last. After I confessed to the Book what I'd done to you, it gave me a quote from Emily Brontë about a love that can't die. I thought it was mocking me."

Daniel set his glass on the table and sat down opposite her. "In your book, you brought us together again years later."

Now she wouldn't look at him, one of those stray strands of hair wavering on her cheek. "Fantasy of closure. It's a trick that inferior authors use, according to your mother, to avoid confronting life's realities."

"You aren't my mother's apprentice anymore." Very carefully, Daniel took her hand, holding it lightly with his thumb against her palm. The long-delayed touch startled him with its potency, making shivers surge from his feet to his fingertips, his pulse racing against hers.

"I know that." Eleanor was almost whispering now. "Odile gave me something to hold on to when I needed it."

"Then maybe she shouldn't have been so critical of your book. In it, I told you that you were afraid to chase happiness." He closed his other hand over hers. "Is that one of 'life's realities'?"

When she finally did look at him, under the shadow of the umbrella, her eyes were dark pools hiding golden glints of misgiving. "I used to think you never would have noticed me if I hadn't been able to use the library's power. Well, now the power's gone. And a Meek person isn't the best match for a Self-Destructive one."

"You're not fucking Meek, and I'm not Self-Destructive. Maybe in college, but not anymore." Instead of releasing her hand, Daniel drew her imperceptibly closer. "What did you have me saying in the book? 'You don't have to be this version of you, and I don't have to be this version of me.'"

Eleanor's cheeks flushed as he quoted her words back to her, and her skin warmed against his. "Maybe we're not who we were in college, but we can't just transform into new people. I'll never be able to forget what I did to you. To us. I'll always be sorry."

"I know." *And I forgive you*—but Daniel didn't have to say it aloud, because she knew what he'd written in the Book was the opposite of what he felt. "Maybe I like this pathway," he said instead, interlacing his fingers with hers and bending almost close enough to allow their lips to meet. "Maybe I want to go on from here. You?"

She nodded, her breath hitching softly against his cheek. "The only thing I ever miss about my nightmares is that in them, I felt closer to you."

They shared a shiver that reminded Daniel of the Book's energy, though perhaps it was only the thrill of being close after so long apart.

Then he drew back and raised his glass. "To us—and to my mom, wherever she is now. Reading, I hope."

"To us and to Odile."

As the glasses clinked, their eyes met, too, and Daniel knew he would ask her to return and run the store. He suspected she would say yes.

Their fates would never be completely under their own control, woven into the vast tapestry to which every living person contributes a thread. But right here, right now, they were the only versions of themselves that mattered, and today was their story to write.

★★★★★

Acknowledgments

This book came together quickly thanks to the efforts of a generous and efficient team. My agent, Jessica Sinsheimer, offered steadfast and invaluable support. Thanks also to the rest of the Context Literary Agency team, especially Monica Rodriguez. Melanie Fried gave me a new appreciation for the subtle magic of story structure through her tireless and insightful edits. Heartfelt thanks to Sara Rodgers for guiding the book through the home stretch and to the rest of the Graydon House team, including Andrew Davis and Tara Scarcello for the gorgeous cover, Stephanie Choo, Ashley MacDonald, and Leah Morse. Thanks to Jennifer Stimson and Erin Pinksen for your careful eyes on the manuscript.

Once upon a time, I studied and taught comparative literature. The PhD didn't get me a job, but it opened a wonderful world of stories and history to me. I want to thank all the professors at Harvard and the University of California,

Berkeley, who introduced me to works like the ones I reference in this book, with special recognition for the memory of Dorrit Cohn (1924–2012), my much warmer and kinder equivalent of Odile Vernet. Thanks also to the folks at r/Harvard for research assistance, particularly u/haltheincandescent, who contributed a video of the descent to Pusey Library.

Rachel Carter and Dayna Lorentz offered vital early input. I wouldn't be writing this without author friends like Lisa Kusel, Aimee Picchi, Nicole Lesperance, Grace Shim, and Elizabeth Bonesteel. Thank you to my bookish parents, who taught me well—Harvey Sollberger, perhaps Iowa's most avid reader; and Sophie Quest, who was so eager for the story of an evil book. Eva Sollberger, thank you for making waffles, talking about books, and patiently commiserating, week after week.

Librarians are unsung heroes, especially when the freedom to read is under threat. I want to thank the many, many who've touched my life.